POISON FOR THE PRINCE

POISON FOR THE PRINCE

ELIZABETH EYRE

HARCOURT BRACE & COMPANY

NEW YORK   SAN DIEGO   LONDON

Requests for permission to make copies
of any part of the work should be mailed to:
Permissions Department, Harcourt Brace & Company,
6277 Sea Harbor Drive, Orlando, Florida 32887-6777.

Library of Congress Cataloging-in-Publication Data
Eyre, Elizabeth.
Poison for the Prince/Elizabeth Eyre.—1st ed.
p. cm.
ISBN 0-15-172540-3
1. Renaissance—Italy—Fiction.
PR6009.Y74P65   1994
823'.914—dc20   94-7333

The text was set in Times Roman
Designed by Camilla Filancia
Printed in the United States of America
First edition   A B C D E

CONTENTS

Contents

THE PEOPLE IN THE STORY

SCIPIONE, *Prince of Viverra*
PRINCESS ISOTTA, *his wife*
PRINCE FRANCESCO, *his son*
PRINCESS ELENA, *Prince Scipione's mother*

DONATO LANDUCCI, *a hostage*
RIDOLFO RIDOLFI, *called Gatta, a condottiere at present in the pay of Prince Scipione*
DOCTOR VIRGILIO, *an alchemist*
LEONE LECONTI, *an artist*
GINEVRA MATARAZZA, *a court lady*
THE PRINCE'S PHYSICIAN
BISHOP UGOLINO
THE VENETIAN AMBASSADOR, *Signor Loredano*

MICHELOTTO DELLA CASA, *Gatta's captain*
CATERINA RIDOLFI, *Gatta's daughter*
COUNT ANTONIO CARLOTTI, LORD OF MASCIA, *a rebel*
SCALA, *a condottiere in his pay*
COUNT LANDUCCI, *a defeated rebel, father of Donato*
LADY LANDUCCI, *his wife*

The People in the Story

BROTHER AMBROGIO, *a Franciscan friar, a travelling preacher*
BROTHER COLUMBA, *his assistant*

MASTER BUSELLI, *an apothecary*
ROSARIA, *an innkeeper*
A WITCH
A BARBER
CITIZENS, SOLDIERY, LABORATORY WORKERS, PAGES, LADIES,
    COUNCILLORS, VILLAGERS
ALDO   ]
FRACASSA] *cousins on a mission*
PIO   ]
SIGISMONDO, *a soldier of fortune*
BENNO, *his servant*
BIONDELLO, *a dog*

POISON FOR THE PRINCE

1. "THEY WANTED YOU DEAD."

'Have you come from the grave?'

She had crossed the big, crowded room, at a run in spite of her bulk, to embrace him. Her hug reassured her of his reality, and she looked up into the face shadowed by the hood, at the dark eyes, strong nose, smiling mouth, and she reproached him: 'I heard you'd been killed in France.'

She had not managed to get her arms round him, and to make up for it she laid her head on his chest. 'Two years since you came this way. I thought you never would again.'

'France did offer me a grave, but I refused.'

She laughed, her whole body heaving joyously, and let him go, to stand back for another look. 'But you're a generous man! I'll bet you offered it to someone else.'

She had to speak loudly to be heard above the clatter of pots, the talk, the sound of dice and dishes, and a drunken song from a corner, and now she raised her voice to a shriek. '*Wine here!*' She took his hand affectionately. 'You have this on the house, lover. Rosaria never forgets a favour.'

He was found a place in the corner opposite the singers. They had reached a verse of which none could remember the words, and were making up for lost words by hitting their table in a rhythm more erratic than they were aware of. Rosaria, pouring a cup for herself as well as for her long-lost friend, cast them an indulgent glance.

'Foreigners. I asked them where they came from, and they don't even know: one of them thought up a place and the others contradicted him. Your health, lover.' She raised her cup. 'Keep avoiding that grave.'

They drank, and he looked round the big, dim-lit room. 'That gets less easy. You heard I was dead in France, I heard you were dying in Italy. How near is the plague?'

She crossed herself. 'Not yet in Viverra, but we've heard of it over to the east. They say there are villages where no one's left to bury the dead.' A wild roar from the table in the corner drowned her next words. She repeated, 'They say we can expect it here as a punishment for our Prince.'

'They say. What do you say?'

She studied him. She had knowledgeable black eyes set slanting above wide, padded cheekbones. For all her size, which was more breadth than height, she was pretty, with confidence and humour in her face. Her cap, with the long lappets falling to her shoulders, was of fresh linen, and though her apron was stained and splashed, the gown it protected was good blue wool, and clean.

'What do I say? I say, a man has a right to his hobbies. A prince can pay for his pleasures, let him have them.' She wiped the table, and slapped the cloth back across her shoulder. 'You pay; you take your choice.'

He glanced round, smiling. 'You've plenty here doing that.'

A party of travellers had appeared in the doorway and was calling for service, stamping mud off their boots, shedding cloaks and hats. The harassed girl who was serving broke free from one of the drunken chorus and hurried towards the door. Rosaria herself rose with authority and went to find them a place.

The man from France, left alone, poured himself wine and waited. The delay in the arrival of his servant meant trouble with the horses, which had come a long way today and would need care. He was perfectly ready to pass the time watching the human landscape.

The big room of the inn was nearly full, patchily lit by a few wall torches, an iron candlestick or two, and a big iron ring hung above the long table, on which little hills of grease supported candles. Smoke hung in the roof almost as far down as the gallery. The long table, patterned by the rings of a thousand winecups and furrowed with cuts made by men slicing their bread and meat, was crowded with drinkers and dice players. Most were talking. It was safer to travel in a group, and the inn was the place to pick up information from the locals about the next city on your way.

The three singers in the corner had reached the quarrelsome stage. Two argued over the words of their refrain, with increasing heat. The third, who from his manic anxious bearing seemed afraid of some terrible event about to happen which he could not locate or even identify, was trying to calm them.

They would have none of it.

'Pio: *your mother was a whore.*' The blond might have been handsome if his hair had been less greasy and his face less often contorted by grimaces. He clearly felt that settling his friend's parentage also settled the matter of the song.

Pio, his hair cropped, his face expressionless as though he had never discovered how to work his features, stared back. He too had his solution to the musical question, which he enunciated with a certain care.

'Fracassa: *Your* mother was a whore *and your father was a goat.*'

Fracassa's reaction to this insult was so extreme that it might have been true: sputtering, he reached with both hands behind his head for the hilt of his sword, a two-handed monster whose scabbard's tip rested on the floor. Pio ignored this movement. He upended a flagon over his cup and then over his mouth. The third man wrenched the flagon from him and, as Pio's head was jolted forward, knocked both their heads together. As they sat, stunned, he spoke to them both urgently, his glance flicking round the room to see if they had attracted attention.

3

The man from France saw that Rosaria was watching from across the room, and at her side a usefully large man had come out from some lurking-place and waited for her signal to intervene.

However, the trouble came not from the three but from the long table. The dice had been rattling, cries of triumph and rage had risen above the general noise. Now the shouts came with blows. There was a grapple, wine was flung, someone brandished a stool, knives flashed out.

It spread like fire. Partisans joined in, then the affronted victims of flailing arms, hurled cups and trampling feet. Rosaria's useful man was at once in the thick of it, forcing two men apart, throwing another out of the door. Rosaria had got a heavy stick and was guarding the entrance to the wine store, dealing out crippling blows to anyone who even stumbled near.

It boiled outward. A hefty lad ran along the table and launched himself at the useful man, who staggered and went down. The man from France stood up.

A boy with wild eyes and a knife as long as his forearm was up on the table and feinting at the fighters on either side, glorying in his potential for destruction. He lunged at one, found his wrist caught in a grip that numbed his hand, and was picked up and tossed into the gallery where he broke his fall, and his wrist, on a bench. A small bearded shabby man, who had come up the outside stairs from the stable, stepped over the writhing body and peered cautiously down into the mêlée. At shin level, a little dog stuck its head through the gallery rail.

The man from France fended off a toppling scrum, caught a flying stool and cracked it down on a shoulder here, a forearm there. Someone grabbed his hood and jerked it back with intent to throttle him, but its neck fastening gave way and the attacker fell back with it. The man from France was shown to possess a head bare and brown, totally shaven.

The three in the corner had, surprisingly, not been drawn

into the fight, but sat alertly watching as if some opportunity might arise. Then one of them caught sight of the shaven head.

'Michelotto!' The yell rose above the noise of blows and shouts and won the attention of the man from France. As he looked, the three shrank into themselves, one peering into his cup, Fracassa's greasy hair veiling his face, Pio stooping to pull at his boot.

Someone tried to take the man from France by surprise, and as he ducked to let this assailant hurtle over his back and crash into a man with an iron candlestick who had been creeping up on him, the three emerged from their corner.

Pio, a suddenly activated machine, pulled out a knife with a wicked curve to its blade and stuck it into a passing man as though he had to find somewhere for it to go. The man fell without any sound that could make itself heard and Pio trod over the body as he advanced. Fracassa followed, treading on the body in his turn, then came the peacemaker, an unnaturally tall, stringy man with a knife not up to his height, stepping high over the fallen man. The target of all three was the man from France.

'MICHELOTTO!' It was a war cry this time. Fracassa drew his sword in one splendid movement of force, the blade swinging in a great arc towards the shaven head. The man from France turned at the same moment as the blade lodged with a vibrating thud deep in the low beam of the gallery. He dropped on one knee and with an iron candlestick he had just acquired he scythed at Fracassa who, gripping the hilt of his sword, jerked up his legs in frantic recoil and hung like a spider over the hurly-burly below. The man from France moved on, to help Rosaria's guard to throw out an immense black-bearded brawler, one who had felled two men with a single blow of a fist that was a club in itself.

Fracassa, making desperate efforts to free his sword, found a splinter group of the battle around him. A dreadful little grandfather with a bludgeon was swinging it near ground level and brought a swathe of wrestlers down. Fracassa saw him coming, got a tight grip of his sword hilt and picked up his feet again. The club swung harmlessly under him and he improved on his success by kicking out at the dangerous little grey head. The impetus freed the sword and projected Fracassa forward over the grandfather to land supine on one end of the table. This, being on trestles, tilted, hit the iron ring of candles, and shot cups, pottery jugs, candle-ends, lumps of grease, bread, dice, three apples, fifteen olive stones, six radishes and a ladle on to Fracassa on the floor.

His tall friend came to the rescue, but Pio was seizing his chance. He did not trouble to attack from the rear and he omitted to yell 'Michelotto', but his intention was the same. His problem was to get the wicked knife past the guard of the iron candlestick which seemed to be the only weapon the man from France was deigning to use.

The small bearded man in the gallery had been monitoring the scene and now crouched and reached out through the gallery rails with cudgel poised. The man from France grinned and, with sweeps of the candlestick, drove Pio back and watched the cudgel come down.

The brawl was faltering. Rosaria had just flung a bucket of water over one battling pair. Her man was propelling others out into the night in fast succession and the man from France thrust several towards him, one bellicose, two groggy, one very wet and already sneezing. The tall thin man had got Fracassa to his feet, collected his sword and helped him to stagger towards the door, where he was ejected. He himself came back to search for Pio, whom the useful man hauled up and loaded on to his friend's shoulder. Rosaria stopped them on the way to the door, and relieved Pio of his purse.

'The fight's on the house, stranger, but you pay for the drinks and the damage.' She gave a strong push to the laden friend, and he vanished protesting into the night at an ungainly run.

The man from France restored the candlestick to the reinstated table. Some survivors were picking themselves up or venturing from corners.

'What did you do to those three, lover? They wanted you dead, that's for sure. Why did they call you Michelotto?'

A man had come into the inn now that people were no longer being hurled out of it, and he stood there observing the scene. His reaction to the shaven head was as sudden as Fracassa's had been. He stepped forward and asked with a voice of hope.

'Sigismondo?'

2. "I NEED A VICTORY."

'I am Sigismondo.'

'The man who helped the Duke of Rocca find his Duchess's murderer?'

The shaven head bent to acknowledge this. Rosaria had come to hang on her friend's arm, and the stranger indicated her.

'When I was here some months ago, she swore she had never heard of you.'

Rosaria tossed her head, the lappets of her cap bouncing like a spaniel's ears on her shoulders. 'I didn't know why you wanted him. Nor does *he* know yet. There's been three men trying to kill him tonight. How is anyone to know you don't want to slip a knife into him too?'

Sigismondo patted her hand, then lifted it to his lips, disengaging his arm. 'I'll fight my own battles, sweetheart, and ask my own questions now that I'm here. You were looking for me some months ago, sir? You've found me.'

The stranger looked at Rosaria, who tossed her head again, beamed unexpectedly at Sigismondo and went off to supervise the sweeping up. She called back, 'Go with God, lover, and make that man pay you the fortune that you're worth.'

'You'll be paid, Master Sigismondo, as generously as you could desire. That, I am authorised to offer. But I am not authorised to answer questions. Someone else will do that if you'll come with me.'

'Where do you want to take me?'

'Into the city.'

Sigismondo, putting on his hood, smiled. 'Hey, that answers another question.' He turned to the small, bearded man who was gaping at them from a respectful distance. 'Is that my cloak you've got, Benno? Wait here. Rosaria will find you a bed.'

The stranger, leading the way out, did not spend time in wondering why a man of Sigismondo's reputation employed a halfwit for servant. He failed to notice the little woolly dog regarding him from its refuge inside the halfwit's sagging jerkin.

Outside, past the penitent flock of travellers waiting to be allowed back into the inn for the night, the stranger called up his servant leading a big black horse, which he courteously offered. 'It is not far to the city.' He took what was evidently the servant's horse, and the man walked alongside. It was dark now, beyond the inn's flambeau, and they rode among cottages more sensed than seen, and past locals making their way home from the inn. The wind drove the clouds from the moon and showed the rutted road that led out of the village towards the city. The clouds had drifted away by the time they reached the walls, and the moon gave a silver edge to the dark crenellations towering above. Here Sigismondo's comment about having his unspoken question answered was justified. The stranger had only to show a seal at the postern and they were at once let in, proving, as Sigismondo had known, that whoever wanted to speak to him was well able to pay him his worth.

They rode down a narrow street which followed the line of the city wall. The sound of their horses' hooves on the stones was thrown back by the tall housefronts. Few people were about; a horse and servant waited outside one door, music and song came from an upper floor, but street windows were dark behind their iron bars.

They rode across a paved street, and paused at a gatehouse in a long wall. Again the seal had them admitted and here the stranger left horses and servant and led the way on foot. They crossed a garden. To the left, the city wall circled away from them. To the right, beyond a spread of formal parterre, fountains, and a series of terraces, the lighted palace glowed. Ahead, the path led across a quarter-mile or so of rough ground, among cypresses, to an apparent great ruin.

They came to the mouth of a huge doorway in the half-demolished wall. To one side a broken tower rose like an eroded cliff. At this angle, the moon shone brilliantly on the iron studs in the oak door. A series of sharp knocks from Sigismondo's escort, and the door opened enough for them to be inspected. It swung wide.

Sigismondo followed along a vaulted stone passage down which a draught blew keenly, like a giant's breath, carrying a metallic taint. Sigismondo raised his head and sniffed. There were stairs worn shallow by centuries of passing feet. At the top they came to a leather-curtained doorway where the smell cut at the lungs like acid, and where a little man like a gnome had to be stirred awake to go in and deliver a message. A curious loud gasping came from within, as if the giant struggled to breathe.

The room they entered strongly resembled Hell. Furnaces and fires glowed here and there, stronger than the lamps. Sharper reflections gleamed in the core of glass vessels like demons' eyes. The giant's gasp came from both a huge bellows worked by a sweating boy with his foot, and the little furnace that roared white-hot at each blast. A man strained at the iron arm of a press that squealed as it produced, from a basin under the screw, a green liquid that dribbled into a bowl placed under its lip. Thuds, dull and regular, resounded from a pestle wielded by a grimy man in a leather apron. Round everything, above all, wreathed heavy smoke, violet, bluish or grey, and the pungent, eye-watering smell.

'Master Sigismondo! You are found at last. I have had

11

men seeking you throughout Italy. I have heard you were dead, become a monk, gone to Tartary.'

The man had appeared from the shadows. He was shorter than Sigismondo by a head, and wore a stained canvas robe, but Sigismondo did not hesitate to bow low. The man smiled, which transformed his pale face. He had a slightly crooked mouth, and an anxiously furrowed brow from which the light brown hair had receded. Pulling off a glove he extended his hand for Sigismondo to kiss. Its forefinger carried a heavy gold ring with an intaglio emerald, and Sigismondo had no need to study the engraved civet cat to know to whom he was speaking.

'How may I serve your Highness?'

Behind the Prince a man, who had held his head at an angle as if straining to listen above the noise, turned to snatch a glance at Sigismondo; he had a deeply lined face with keen dark eyes that caught Sigismondo's glance and were at once turned away. A glass vessel beside them bubbled suddenly and threw up a jet of steam, and the Prince swung towards it with interest but then resolutely turned back.

'Come. This is no place to talk.' He took off the other glove and cast the pair on a book full of diagrams and symbols, open among glass phials of coloured liquids and powders. Assistants ducked their heads as he passed, but no one stopped working. The gnome outside the curtain must have been on the lookout, for the curtain was raised the moment the Prince reached it. Sigismondo followed down the worn steps and along another vaulted stone corridor. The Prince opened double doors set in the rough masonry. A lobby, with rush matting and a carpeted bench, seemed to remind the Prince that he still wore the canvas robe, and he shed it as he went. It was caught by a page who had appeared from nowhere and who darted ahead to open the far doors.

Inside the large room beyond, the chemical smell was faint. Any lingering odour was superseded by the scents from a majolica bowl of cloves, thyme and rosemary on the dais of a studio, a room within the room, a cedarwood construction that protected the scholar from draughts, and which held all his books and papers on its partitioned shelves, and his chair and desk. Pens, compasses, ruler hung to hand. An oil lamp on a hinged arm was adjusted to illuminate the slope of the desk; a clock on the wall ticked gravely at the pull of its weights, and a small grey cat rose from a shelf, stretched, and picked its way among the papers to the Prince, who scratched it under the chin.

'Sit, sir. Sit.' Sigismondo took his seat on a chest-cupboard beside the desk, while the Prince swivelled a big lectern out of his way; both its sides held a huge book, open as if he had been reading them alternately.

The Prince looked at Sigismondo with close attention for a little without speaking. His gown of black velvet banded with cloth of gold made his face seem even paler than before.

Finally he spoke. 'I have heard a good deal about you, and although half of it may well be invention, as it has a sound of embellishment, the rest gives me confidence. You know what state Viverra is in, sir?'

Sigismondo shrugged. 'I know the plague is not far away, Highness.'

The Prince's mouth twitched impatiently. '*That* is all in God's hands. I mean that my enemies ring me round. My vassal Carlotti has claimed my city of Mascia for his own, while His Holiness waits the moment to declare a successor to my title if he thinks me too weak to hold Viverra as a Papal state.'

'I heard, Highness, that you have Ridolfo Rodolfi fighting for you.

The Prince's mouth twitched again. '*Gatta*. Yes, I have Gatta on my side, which is why I still hold Viverra.'

'I heard also that he defeated the Count of Landucci for you and that he's besieging Mascia as he besieged the cities taken from you by Landucci.'

The Prince poked fretfully at the papers before him. 'He has been before Mascia's walls for a month. He is *dozing* at Mascia.'

Sigismondo put out a hand to the little grey cat, which had come to investigate the stranger. 'You think he's not doing what he could, Highness?'

The Prince sighed, and dabbed at his nose with a piece of linen he took from his sleeve. 'I mean that I need a victory. Condottieri have been known to change sides.' Both men were silent. A condottiere sold himself to the highest bidder, naturally, and the most successful were sure to put their price up. It was not tactful to ask if the Prince was able to continue paying what Ridolfi chose to demand.

The Prince spoke again, in irritation, 'One day I shall have uncounted gold to give him . . . but, at the present time . . .'

Sigismondo had seen enough to understand: the Prince hoped with his experiments in alchemy to find the secret, pursued by so many, of making gold. Meanwhile, the experiments cost the gold he so needed.

The little cat, pleased with Sigismondo's caresses, climbed on his thigh and lay there, purring and contracting its claws. The Prince pointed. 'You see. They call Ridolfi the Cat, and what's more fickle than a cat? They only seek their pleasure.' His face darkened as though at an unwelcome thought. 'Master Sigismondo. I want you to find out if he intends to betray me.'

'Your Highness wishes me to go to Mascia.' The deep voice was smooth, with no hint as to how the thought of being a spy was received.

The Prince dabbed his nose again, and pulled a scroll towards him. Taking a pair of spectacles from a nail, he pulled the lenses apart on their hinge and perched them on his nose. 'See here.'

Sigismondo brought the cat against his shoulder as he came to look. The scroll, flattened out and weighted with an hourglass at one end and a round wooden comfit box at the other, showed an architect's plan of a city, a polygon of walls with circles that were towers at the angles. The Prince's finger, indicating the plan with a sweeping arc, was reddened and scarred. Evidently he was apt to forget his gloves when he worked in the laboratory.

'Mascia. I discovered this plan only last night. My grandfather lived in this wing. His room is being cleared for Doctor Virgilio, who needs to store chemicals, and these, his papers, were brought to me. It was he who last fortified Mascia. Look, here, and here, are the wells. And you see these lines here?' His finger followed dotted lines that cut across streets from one tower to another, from other towers almost to the centre of the city. 'Supply passages. To rush men or ammunition without using the streets. Gatta would give his eye teeth . . . His sappers have been trying to find these passages for weeks.' He paused, and added, 'Or so he tells me,' pushing a letter, its scrawled signature just visible, out of the way. He looked up at Sigismondo. 'You could take it to him? Use it in any way that you can?'

Sigismondo nodded. He studied the cursive writing on the plan, the architect's gloss written nearly a hundred years ago.

'Gatta is not a cat like the one you're holding,' said the Prince. 'For my soul's sake I would not send you without a warning: he is a leopard or a tiger, and quick to spring.'

Great cats are suspicious of strangers. Captains use spies, but any found in their own camp, they will kill.

3. "WE'VE GOT THEM."

Benno had not supposed, on their return from France where Sigismondo had engaged in some hair-raising events, that his master would be taking a holiday. As he rode along behind him, Biondello asleep inside his cloak, he drowsily reflected that his master perhaps remained so calm by making sure that he had no hair to raise. Why Sigismondo shaved his head was one more mystery presented by his master, and Benno was proud that other people were as baffled as he was by what Sigismondo did. For instance, he had no idea why they were riding to Mascia, which Rosaria had said last night was being besieged. He did not really expect the gates of Mascia to open by magic when Sigismondo rode up. His master might equally well be bringing help to the city as organising its surrender.

As they rode, there were signs that war had come that way. Benno, reared in Rocca, whose dukes were successful in keeping the peace, had never seen any landscape like this. At the sight of smoke rising beyond a hill ahead, Benno had thought of cooking, and hoped they might stop to buy something hot to eat. The smell as they got nearer was not of food, and when they breasted the hill they could see a village itself cooking.

It had never been a very ambitious village; those that existed there probably only hoped to scrape a living out of their patches of ground; at best, to survive. Now, those who had survived wandered aimlessly among the smoking rafters and burning straw of what had been their homes. An old man sat, head in hands, in front of still-smouldering rubble. He did not look up as these strangers' horses picked their way down the path between the ruins. A girl, half naked, sprawled on her back staring at a sky she couldn't see. A child's foot stuck out from under her hip. Benno, shuddering, caught up with Sigismondo and demanded, 'Who *did* this? Why?'

'It's war. Who did it and why doesn't count. Probably Gatta's men, belonging to the captain we're going to see. Perhaps one of the dead here refused them bread or swore at them.'

'But aren't these people on the same side?'

'It's war. Don't ask for logic. It's done to frighten. Other villages will hear.' An old woman, almost automatically, held out her hands as they passed, and Sigismondo reached in his saddlebag and threw her a flat loaf of bread. 'We're on our way to try to stop more of this.'

'To stop *Gatta*?' Benno had heard of Gatta at Rosaria's and now he had seen what he could do. Stopping Gatta was surely an unlikely feat even for Sigismondo.

'You will do as you always do: keep your ears and eyes open as well as your mouth. I'm taking Gatta something he'll be glad to see.'

Benno, relieved to hear they were certain of a good reception from Gatta, said no more. He was finding it hard to forget that village.

It was late afternoon before they saw the tents. They were pitched on a hillside facing Mascia, which crowned the hill rising out of the valley's centre. Westering sun shone redly on the great walls and towers, and glinted off the big guns ranged below, their snouts pointing at the town but silent now. Huge dents in the masonry, and patched battlements, showed where they had tried to breach the defences, but no gaps as yet offered a chance for men to storm it.

The only activity, as they rode forward, seemed to be in the camp. Smoke rose from fires among the tents, horses

18

neighed, but the city crouched on its mound, stubborn, without a sign of life.

A guard soon barred their way. He handled his pike as though he would sooner use it than hold it.

'Declare your business.'

'I've something for Gatta he's been waiting for.'

The guard found it easy to glance contemptuously over Benno, but had a problem dismissing Sigismondo's general bearing. 'He's expecting you?' Meant as a sneer, it turned into more of a question.

'Who's this?' It was the voice of authority, even though it was light and mocking. Benno, turning, let his jaw drop a further half inch. The man who had ridden up, on a roan that pranced sideways under his controlling hand, was bare-headed and his scalp gleamed like silk, the twin to Sigismondo's under its hood. The face however was hollow cheeked, with a pointed chin and a wide mouth – a mobile face but with hooded eyes. He was smiling. Benno was not reassured. 'Visitors with *presents*? Gatta *loves* presents.' Something in his voice suggested to Benno that such presents should best take the shape of severed heads tied up with ribbons. 'Come with me.'

They followed the man with the bare scalp through the camp, threading among the bivouacs and the tents which varied from well-weathered pavilions to patched brown canvas held up by sticks and looking like oversized cowpats. A circle of men sitting on billets of wood, playing cards, scrambled to their feet as Sigismondo's guide rode through their circle, waving his hand in friendly fashion as they scattered. Men were busy cleaning weapons, pushing carts of supplies, whipping horses that dragged hurdles piled with gunstones, gathered round fires cooking and eating. Troopers pulled back a labouring horse and jumped to its head to keep it out of the way as the man led on. Benno had a sudden vision of him riding in battle on a carpet of dead faces.

The big pavilion was striped green and gold. Gilded tassels hung round the eaves, the flap tied back to a pole showed a lining of scarlet silk. Another pole, with a banner that flapped in the breeze like a captive bird, was stuck in the ground next to the opening and two soldiers, their helmets and jerkins studded with steel, were on guard. Benno was thrown the reins of both Sigismondo's dun and the tall roan as their guide dismounted and led the way in. Benno was left grateful he didn't have to go in and face Gatta himself.

Gatta was busy. He was having a bath. Steam filled the inside of the pavilion like a local fog, and the red silk walls seen mistily through it seemed to be dripping blood. Two sweating pages had buckets of hot water, replenishing the water in the half vat where Gatta lay. When Sigismondo and his guide came in, a pair of broad hands gripped the linen-draped sides of the tub and Gatta pulled himself forward to stare at them through the steam.

'What the devil? Have they surrendered?' It was not a serious question and he sat back again, watching them. At first glance he did not live up to his nickname. There seemed little feline about the large face and heavy shoulders until the build of a tomcat came to mind. Then the gaze of the half-slitted eyes seemed more intimidating.

'A stranger with a present, Gatta.' The bow caricatured a court flourish; the man in the tub ignored it. His half-closed eyes were examining Sigismondo very carefully.

'You were right to bring him, Michelotto.'

Sigismondo smiled suddenly, and Gatta heaved himself upright again, sending a wave of herb-scented water to the ground. A page came forward, arm braced for Gatta to lean on should he wish to rise. He ignored it as he had ignored Michelotto's bow, and beckoned Sigismondo to approach. As Sigismondo moved forward, Michelotto drew a knife, a matter-of-fact precaution since Gatta was unarmed, that only held menace because of the man who did it.

Gatta's curiosity was professional. 'Where have you fought?'

'France, Scotland, the Low Countries, the Holy Land. And other places.'

Gatta was silent a moment, splashing the water idly over his raised knees with one hand. His hair was streaked in dark wisps over his forehead and behind the ears where the soldier's cut, shaped to the helmet, left the thick neck bare.

'What is the present?'

'The plans of Mascia. Showing the underground ways.'

A tidal wave slopped to the floor, splashing Sigismondo and the page who hurried to offer his arm again. Gatta clambered out and allowed himself to be wrapped in linen, not taking his eyes from Sigismondo. He was bulky, with no fat, a body built to take the weight of armour.

'Where did you get them?' A wet hand gripped Sigismondo's wrist.

'From a dead man.'

'Convenient.' Michelotto had been shifting from foot to foot, restless for action, perhaps to be hanging strangers. 'Dead men aren't talkative.'

Gatta flung up a hand towards him. 'Be quiet, Michelotto. Let him speak.' The pages were working on him, patting and rubbing him dry through the linen, Gatta grunting and flexing his shoulders.

Sigismondo's deep voice continued. 'He attacked me on the road out of Viverra, crying *Michelotto!*' Gatta and Michelotto laughed together, Michelotto clasping both hands on the hilt of the knife and shaking it, as if the joke particularly pleased him. 'I found the map on him and thought you'd pay well for it.'

'*Pay?*' Michelotto stepped back, raising his hands in pretence of surprise. 'You're in Gatta's camp with his men all round. Why should he *pay?*'

Gatta was being wrapped in a green velvet gown, now that the damp linen had been peeled off him. A folding stool of carved wood inlaid with ivory was placed for him. He brooded.

'This man you killed. Where was he going?'

Sigismondo shrugged. 'He only said the one word.'

21

Neither of the man had any reason to disbelieve him and both were amused, but only a foolish man would rely on their credulity. One of the pages, at Gatta's elbow with a silver flagon, was gestured towards Sigismondo.

'Sir, some wine. Show me this map.' Gatta might take the leisure to have a bath, but here was business. A page produced a folding stool, and silver goblets, then both pages swiftly set up a table on trestles. Gatta leant his arms on it and waited. Michelotto was paring his nails with the knife and whistling under his breath. Outside, horses whinnied and stamped. A distant trumpet made Gatta turn his head sharply and Michelotto move to look out. He came back, waving a negating hand.

'A false alarm. They thought a sally-port was opening.'

'It shows they weren't asleep.' Gatta tapped the table. 'This map, sir. If it is worth it, you shall have your money.'

Sigismondo produced the flattened scroll from inside his doublet, and unfolded it. Gatta trapped one end of it with his sword, which a page had put on the table when the trumpet blew. It was a workaday weapon. Its weight and size said much for Gatta's shoulders.

'That's the Prince's seal.' Gatta's blunt finger pointed. His gaze switched towards Sigismondo – strange eyes, almost yellow. 'This has come *from the Prince?*'

Sigismondo once again shrugged. 'I've no doubt it was stolen from his archives. This plan is old, the fortifications go back more than a century, I'm told.'

'It was the old Prince, this one's grandfather, that had the towers built. This could have been stolen from him.' Michelotto came to look over Sigismondo's shoulder, his knife too close for comfort.

'What does the writing say?' Gatta had followed the bearings of the dotted lines showing the passages, with swift understanding. Now he screwed up his eyes at the written lines beneath. Knowing how to read and write was a luxury for a soldier, the letter Sigismondo had seen on the Prince's desk had no doubt been written by a secretary, and the sprawling signature was perhaps Gatta's sole literary accomplishment. 'The plan is plain enough.' He spoke with satisfaction, leaning back to finger the sword as though impatient to use it. 'We're close in two places, if this map is right, though Lorenzo could have burrowed away for months and never struck them. These numbers give depth, do they not? And the words?'

'The writing adds nothing to the plans.' Sigismondo's hand brushed the scroll dismissively. 'It gives the architect's materials, such as lining and reinforcing stone, his calculations and estimates of how long the work should take.'

'Ah, then now . . .' Gatta made a sound in his throat very like a purr.

Michelotto said, 'Antonio Carlotti and his rat Scala know these tunnels existed. They believe they were blocked off years ago and are no threat. That pair of foragers we caught two days ago told us so, in the end.'

The purr became a laugh. Gatta slapped his hands down on the map. 'We've got them! *We've got them!* Michelotto, send Lorenzo to me. His sappers must start at once. We'll kiss that rat Scala good morning.' He turned to Sigismondo as Michelotto instantly left. 'You, sir.' His hand tapped the plans. 'You had a price?'

'You know what these are worth to you. I leave the price for you to decide.' The deep voice was quiet, undemanding. To ask nothing would have aroused the most active suspicion; to ask too much was equally unwise.

Gatta brooded and finally said, 'If I take Mascia with the help of this map you shall have a bag full of the gold we take there. Two, if you help me further.'

'How may I do that?'

'Fight for me.'

4. "Heads You Win."

'They do themselves well in this camp.' Benno was still licking his fingers from the dish he had been allowed to clean after waiting at his master's shoulder during dinner. Roasted meat had been plentiful, the wine of excellent quality. What Benno was drinking, now they were back in the tent allotted to them, was rough country wine, but he swallowed it in enthusiastic gulps.

'Some do. Those at the top. If you were an ordinary soldier you'd have dined on beans.'

Benno stoppered the leather bottle, and placed more sticks on the fire. Their tent was only a bivouac. A couple of reluctant solders had been invited to leave by a smiling Michelotto and had removed their baggage in a hurry. Coarse canvas lashed to poles kept the night wind off, while the little fire warmed them on the open side. The squat towers and walls of Mascia, dark against a sky in which the moon swam in soft radiance, caught his attention. 'Bet *they* haven't had beans.'

'Antonio Carlotti has a pack of his hunting dogs in there. He'd sooner start on the townsfolk than sacrifice them. Lucky the household with plenty of rats.'

Benno adjusted the saddlebags behind his back. 'Prince Scipione has plenty of enemies, hasn't he? They were on about it, last night at Rosaria's. There was Landucci, that was taking his cities before this Gatta got hired to take them back;

25

and now Count Carlotti. People reckon the Prince deserves it, though.'

Sigismondo was reclining with his arm across a saddle. He stretched out his legs towards the fire. 'You mean, because he dabbles in alchemy.'

'*They* said, magic. What is alchemy?' Benno picked his teeth with a piece of twig, waiting to be educated.

Sigismondo laughed.

'I can tell you what alchemists want to find. What I can't tell you is how.'

'Haven't they found it yet, whatever it is?'

'I think we'd see the signs. Unbelievably rich men are far to seek.'

Benno sat up. 'He's looking for *treasure*? But he's a prince.'

'M'm-hmm . . . who needs treasure more than princes? Do you think captains like Gatta come cheap?'

'But what about the magic?' Benno spat out a bit of twig and flicked it and some extraneous straw from his unkempt beard. 'Last night they were talking *devils*.'

'People talk devils about anything they don't understand. You should know that by now. If you're looking for the Philosopher's Stone, which is what Prince Scipione is doing, then that involves fire, and fire suggests Hell.'

'This fire here doesn't suggest Hell,' Benno protested, holding out his hands to it. 'What is it that's special about the Prince's fires?'

Sigismondo grunted. 'You'd have to see them to know.'

'You've seen them?' Benno turned and stared, but Sigismondo was closing his eyes. 'You've seen the Prince?'

'Good night, Benno.'

Usually, Benno fell asleep as promptly as if someone had knocked him unconscious. That night he was aware of the life of the camp around them, of people moving, horses stamping, men coughing, snoring, stirring restlessly. One cried out as if in nightmare. Benno had his own private nightmare.

26

There was to be an attack on the city. He had gathered as much from the talk at table in Gatta's pavilion. Sigismondo was to fight for Gatta, though Benno could not fathom why. From what little he had found out about his master's past, he knew that Sigismondo had fought as a mercenary in countries Benno had only just heard of. There were scars, when he stripped to wash, that proved it.

It wasn't this which worried Benno. He had seen Sigismondo fight and thought it was a shame for those who would meet him tomorrow. His worry was, would he be required to fight too? It had never happened yet, but this was a war and perhaps things were different. Fighting was all right if you were saving your skin by it – he was ready to do that – but voluntary fighting, even supposing you were paid for it, was not attractive at all.

When he did fall asleep he dreamt of devils pursuing him with a rolling boulder – the Philosopher's Stone.

Sigismondo woke him when the world was still in darkness. He lay there, heart pounding.

'I am off to a Mass for those fighting today.' His master spoke quietly, close to his ear. 'There's bread and wine for you in the saddlebag. Look after things here . . . There may be a sudden noise before long and it seemed to me you had sooner not be woken by that and find me gone.'

His voice smiled. Benno, in utter relief that he was not to fight, sat up, Biondello tumbling awake off his chest, and reached for the saddlebag that had been his pillow. A movement of air, and he and his dog were alone.

Battle is by nature chaos. The loud noise Benno had been promised was a dawn cannonade concentrated on a weakened wall to the north. Long enough after this for the garrison to have been drawn to the north, a bricked-up door in the citadel was blasted open, a neglected door in an old house was broken through, and both openings disgorged streams of men.

27

Gatta was at the citadel. He found Antonio Carlotti in bed and took him prisoner, then started on the garrison.

Michelotto danced out of the old house into the street with Sigismondo at his shoulder and headed for the walls.

The condottiere Scala had a well-trained band and they fought hard as soon as they realised that the men coming on to the walls from the city side were the enemy, but a sizable number never made that discovery. The gatehouse was virtually taken and the drawbridge lowered. An old captain made a try at disabling the portcullis gear, but a thrown axe put an end to that.

Although the light in the sky was stronger, down by the gates under the tower there was only torchlight. Scala's men fought to defend the gate, in a confusion of noise and shadows. Finally there were too few of them to prevent the invaders laying hands on the great bars to heave them from their sockets.

Suddenly a giant swept in among them, heading a troop, an agile giant with a great sword he swung from hand to hand to get the best purchase for his blows, a giant who howled like a wolf. He struck hands from the bars. He stood in the vaulted gateway whirling his sword, his feet planted among screaming crippled men. No one approached. In the moment of surprise his troop fought Gatta's men back from the gate out into the street. Sigismondo crouched by the wall. He studied the man for a long moment: the whirling sword, the great shoulders, the triumphant yelling face. If this man was Gatta's 'rat', it was certainly not in the physical sense. Sigismondo came under the sword with his own sword sweeping high and visible in the torchlight in a parrying stroke, and his left hand brought the axe up unseen under the giant's chin. The same movement carried him full weight against the falling giant, but he leapt aside from the body and his voice resounded in the archway, '*Gatta! To me!*'

Gatta's men swarmed from the gate-towers, treading down the wounded, lifted the great bars and drew back the bolts.

The men waiting outside poured in, yelling 'Gatta!' and Gatta himself on a tall bay warhorse came down the street to the gate, cutting down fleeing men of the garrison. The gilded cat crouched on his helmet seemed ready to spring, to sink teeth and claws into the faces lifted to it. A sweep of the sword and the faces were fewer. As he came to the gate no one opposed him. When Prince Scipione hired a condottiere, he knew what he was doing.

'Where's Scala?' Gatta held his fouled sword clear, and pushed up his visor with the back of his wrist. He turned a sweating face, the eyes brilliant with excitement. 'We haven't got Mascia if we haven't got Scala.'

Michelotto was off, jumping corpses, slashing at a rising enemy, while Gatta's horse circled and pivoted. Howls and shrieks still rose, but more distant, with the clash of weapons. It was evident that resistance was done, that Gatta's men were free to stave in doors and barrels and start the rape of the town.

'You asked for Scala?' Michelotto straightened up, his voice ringing back from the arch above. 'Catch!'

Gatta caught the flying shape out of the air, as Michelotto pointed to Sigismondo, who stood nearby with his axe resting on his shoulder. 'He gave him to you.'

The head of Scala hung from Gatta's hand. He brought it towards him, blood trailing sluggishly over his armour, and pressed a kiss to the forehead under the matted hair.

'Mascia is ours at last.' He flourished the head, scattering red drops, and grinned at Sigismondo. 'You shall have gold, and more. I have my present for Venice . . . A pike, someone, where's a pike? Mascia shall see the height to which a rat can be raised.'

He rode off up the street with a pikeman at his stirrup and Scala's head bobbing near his own.

Some hours after that, on the road to Viverra, Benno was pursuing the point. 'What was that about *a present for Venice*? Isn't he sending Scala's head to the Prince?'

He had been witness to its wrapping, standing behind Sigismondo in Gatta's pavilion. Pages had swathed the object, definitely the worse for wear after its outing on the pike, in spices and layers of cloth and silk, had placed it in a fancy velvet-covered box; and it had been dispatched with an escort bearing a letter to the Serenissima. He had been right, after all, about presents of severed heads tied in ribbons.

'Gatta will bring Antonio Carlotti with him when he comes to Viverra in a day or two. That's a good enough present with Mascia thrown in. Gatta's entitled to his perks. There's a lot of peer rivalry among condottieri.'

'But why to *Venice*?'

'I thought you kept your ears open better than that. This is the story: Scala was hired by the Venetians against the Pope's troops last year, but as the Holy Father offered more money, he changed sides, hey, quite *suddenly*. The Serenissima have been very anxious to get at him ever since. It's a pretty present from Gatta.'

Scala's head, after its triumphant parade round Mascia, had toured Gatta's camp, for the commissary, the camp followers and the wounded to admire. It was a vivid lesson in the importance of being on the winning side in a war. Benno was proud that his master had provided this edifying sight. The reward, three heavy bags of gold, travelled now behind them on mule pack, guarded by two of Gatta's soldiers who were properly respectful of Sigismondo. Benno knew that his master's services had provided him with bank accounts in various cities, but these financial arrangements were a mystery savouring of magic to him.

He preened. 'Gatta gave you all the credit, didn't he?'

'Gatta can *afford* to give away credit. He's earned plenty of it on his own account. The Prince is lucky to have him.'

Benno, batting away flies as the horses picked their way past heaps of manure flung outside the village they were approaching, asked, 'If Scala could rat on Venice . . . I mean, is the Prince sure Gatta . . . ?'

'Condottieri live by their reputation. They sign contracts. Scala was an exception but, yes, there's always the possibility.'

'The Prince'd best keep paying Gatta a lot of money, I should think. He'd better hurry and find that stone you were talking about.'

Sigismondo's hum was prolonged.

This village had not been touched by the purveyors to Gatta's army. Its inhabitants reacted with no more than wary curiosity to the men riding through. A woman ran to snatch up a toddler from the horses' path, and with the child on her shoulder stood watching. The soldiers called out cheerful, rude invitations as they rode. What would the villagers do if they knew of the gold that was passing through, enough to buy a dozen villages? But Benno had seen what happened to villages that forgot their manners.

Viverra's towers were on the horizon before Benno thought he could introduce his next question, though it had been irking him all the way from the camp.

'Why wouldn't you let Gatta tell the Venetians it was you killed Scala?'

Sigismondo put a finger to his lips.

'It's called diplomacy. Gatta liked his present to come from him without acknowledgements to anyone else.' He smiled. 'And the Venetians will get to hear.'

'So Gatta sent you to bring the good news to the Prince instead? People who bring good news get rewards, don't they?'

'Don't become greedy for gold, Benno. Look where it got Scala.'

There were more people on the road leading to Viverra's south gate than they had seen before. These were not traders or carnival crowds. Chanting mingled with groans and cries. Some had taken dust from the road and smeared it on their heads; some beat their breasts, one man down on his knees was knocking his head on the ground in penitence.

'What's happened?' Benno was anxious. Had the Prince

died so they'd never get their reward? Was the plague . . . he stopped thinking.

Sigismondo pointed.

A man, tonsured and cowled, was forging through the throng towards the city gate; Sigismondo and Benno made way for him as best they could in the crush. Above them, on the pole he carried, and packed with clay to keep it steady, jauntily rode a skull.

5. Vanity of Vanities

Benno had to shake himself free of the horrible idea that Scala's head had somehow burst from its parcel on the way to Venice and hurried here to find them, shedding its flesh *en route*. The skull that grinned ahead of them looked yellowish and shiny, as if it had been divorced from a body for some time and liked the freedom. Benno crossed himself.

Sigismondo turned in the saddle and shaded his eyes, looking back over the road into the distance.

'What is it? Who's coming?'

'That skull's a promise as well as a warning, Benno. From what I know, Viverra is shortly going to hear a sermon; or many sermons. Having the plague not so far away makes people remember Hell fire.'

The wailing of the crowd that pressed round their stirrups was loud enough to make even Sigismondo hard to hear, and Benno was not entirely sure that he caught what his master said as they were swept through the gates on a tide of *Miserere*. He understood he was being told to stay and listen to the sermon, not come to the palace. Benno was aware that he made a poor impression on the gentry in spite of the new clothes acquired in France, but he had been looking forward to catching a glimpse of this prince who was searching for a magic stone that made riches. However, if the skull was anything to go by, the sermon wouldn't be short of drama. Benno was ready for fun of any kind.

33

There was no mistaking the 'Wait here' when they reached the palace gates. The crowd was thickening, drawn by the chanted *Miserere*, and by the skull that had caused a few shrieks as it bobbed past first floor windows on its way. Sigismondo and Gatta's men went in at the palace gates, taking Benno's horse. Sigismondo mounted a long flight of steps and disappeared through a great archway, above which was carved the civet cat, rampant, of Viverra, and a princely coronet. The crouching gilded cat on Gatta's helmet had looked more dangerous.

Inside the palace, the letter with Gatta's seal got Sigismondo speedily forward. Guards uncrossed their pikes, curtains were lifted, doors opened, until a last pair of doors let Sigismondo into an audience chamber and the presence of the Prince.

Prince Scipione was listening to music, his family and court gathered about him. Two lutanists on the steps of the dais bent their heads close to one another as they harmonised as if, in order to concentrate on the intricacy of their music, they must exclude their own awareness of listeners. Above, on the dais, were three chairs of state, blue velvet fringed with bullion. The Prince, in the centre, in mulberry velvet with sleeves of gold damask, looked frail and ill at ease. He glanced up quickly as Sigismondo was ushered in, and a page crossed the room to tell him the newcomer's business.

He raised a hand to still the music.

'From Mascia?'

It was as if the whole company drew breath and turned all attention on Sigismondo, who came forward to sink to one knee on the lowest step. The deep voice was clear in the sudden silence. 'Highness, Mascia is yours. Ridolfi has taken it, Scala is dead, the Lord Antonio Carlotti prisoner.'

There were joyful exclamations. Sigismondo, invited to rise by the Prince's gesture, bowed and handed Gatta's dispatch to a page to take to the Prince.

'Your name, sir?' The Prince took the letter and paused,

his tired eyes looking under slightly raised brows at
Sigismondo, who, bowing once more as he identified himself,
gave no sign that he was not a stranger to the Prince.

'You are Sigismondo *of Rocca*?' The speaker, leaning a
little forward in her chair of state, splendid in gold and green
brocade, could only be the Princess herself. Her face was a
long oval, the dark eyes large, the nose narrow, the mouth
small and full, her air coolly confident of her beauty. Piled in
a luxuriance of braids and ringlets, twisted with pearls, her
hair was dark red: the true Venetian red.

'I was able to do the Duke of Rocca some service, but I
am not his subject.'

'Whose subject are you?'

'With respect, Highness, I am my own man.'

'Why do you come from Gatta?' She twirled a pendant,
gold set with pearl stars, that hung to her waist. The Prince
read his letter, paying no attention to his wife's questioning.

'I come from Gatta, Highness, because I have been
fighting for him at Mascia. A soldier of fortune seeks
employment where it offers.'

'So you might have fought for Scala?' The Princess
smiled and the courtiers took this as licence to laugh
discreetly. Taking the side of the Prince's enemy was a joke if
the Princess thought it was.

The Prince had finished the letter and was looking
vaguely round. 'He's bringing Carlotti here in a few days.
Gatta dragged him out of bed.'

This, demonstrating the surprise of Gatta's attack and
presenting to every mind the picture of a naked man in shock,
was genuinely entertaining; the Prince himself smiled and
laughter was loud. The elderly woman with grey hair, in the
third chair of state, the Princess Dowager, asked, 'What will
you do with Carlotti?'

The Prince dabbed at his nose with the piece of linen he
kept in his sleeve. 'We shall debate that in council, madam.
We must take advice on it.'

Profound nodding among a group of older men showed

they were councillors, but the Princess sat back impatiently, her eyes still on Sigismondo.

'A waste of time. Carlotti is a manifest traitor. *My* advice is to hang him.'

The Prince employed his piece of linen to mop his brow under the purple velvet cap. 'It will be decided . . . hostages perhaps—' He flickered a glance towards a young man nearly at the forefront of the courtiers, and was again embarrassed. 'Sigismondo, you shall be rewarded. This is good news indeed.' He rose, his wife and mother rising too, and as all bowed and curtsied he left by a side door, followed by a single page. Sigismondo guessed that the Prince would shortly be in his laboratory, and perhaps would send for him later there.

Meanwhile, he had another of Gatta's errands to perform.

Benno, instructed to listen to the expected sermon, passed the time of waiting by buying and eating some pork fritters. Establishing himself on a mounting block and letting Biondello wander – for he was a dog not given to straying far – he struck up acquaintance with a large penitent who, with a face like a bull that has run against a barn door, might have done quite a lot to be penitent for. Now a sudden excitement ran though the crowd, a jostling for better places that made Benno stand up on his block and scoop Biondello to safety. There was confused shouting of a name. It seemed the waiting was done. The friar carrying the skull got himself up on the rostrum where city proclamations were made, and Benno wondered if for once Sigismondo was wrong and the sermon would be given by him, but all he did was to raise the skull for another menacing survey of the crowd, and to shout, 'Repent! For the Kingdom of God is at hand.'

What in fact was at hand was another friar, skinny, with disorderly white hair obscuring his tonsure in the brisk breeze, being helped on to the rostrum by many willing hands. He carried a crucifix, and his first action was to extend it towards the crowd, evoking a long-drawn-out groan for mercy, and a great activity of hands in crossings and beating of breasts. The man beside Benno hit himself such a thump that only one of his build could have taken it without toppling on to the people behind him.

'Repent, dear children!' It was a voice carrying but not strident, thrilling but with a curious gentleness in its cadences. 'I am sent by God to bring you to Him. Oh keep in mind, dear children, the Death who waits for us all.' Here the attendant friar, with his air of cheerful ferocity, twirled the skull to take in everyone within the range of the dark eye-sockets. 'Death waits for you, each one, at the end of the street—' Quite a few turned nervous heads '—in the tavern, in the market, perhaps in your beds this very night.' A woman nearby burst into violent sobs. 'Not one of you can escape Death.' The friar paused and looked out over them all with dark eyes that glittered; he had the hollow cheeks of the ascetic, and a face of almost agonised compassion. He raised a long thin hand. 'Death – Death lasts but a moment. Death comes, and is gone. Oh my friends, it is Hell that lasts for ever. Think, think of those flames, the unceasing flames; smell your flesh burning – for God does not let the body of your soul be destroyed as your earthly body is; feel, feel those flames now, flames that burn and devour not, for unimaginable years upon years of torment! For if you die as you are now, with sins on your soul, in a country at war, in a city where men feud and women deck themselves in vanities, where the Prince communes with wizards – then the flames of Hell will devour you for all eternity.'

He paused again, while the crowd's moaning rose in intensity and the attendant friar dipped the skull at each quarter in illustration of Death's imminence. Then the preacher raised the crucifix once more, looking up, his white hair blown into a halo. 'Pray, dear children, pray, pray for a change of heart. Look not to earthly princes for your safety but to the Prince of Peace Himself. Put not your trust in magicians! Let Christ rule your city.'

The moans changed note. A more positive, hopeful

sound arose. What having Christ as ruler of their city in fact meant was probably obscure to them all, but the bold declaration that their own Prince was a liability seemed to meet with widespread agreement. Benno sucked his teeth: all this time, there in the palace, Sigismondo was bringing news of the return of Mascia to its rightful owner the Prince, and out here it looked as if Viverra was to be lost to a far more awkward opponent than Antonio Carlotti. Benno stared at the friar. If this was God's own condottiere, how could anyone tackle him?

'Oh give up your sins, my children! Lechery, sloth, gluttony, avarice, wrath, envy, and that worst, most heinous sin of all, vanity. Women! You, who in your natural weakness are most prone to this, give up, oh give up your vanity! What will your love spells, your songs, your masks, your ornaments avail you when Satan seizes your soul? Will your paint and your false hair look fine when you come to this?' Obediently, his attendant dipped the skull to the pointing finger and Benno, gaping and shuddering with the rest, wondered for the first time if the sermon had been carefully rehearsed. 'Women, women! Remember it was by you that man first fell! Did not Eve rob Adam and all his sons of Paradise for ever?'

The sobbing woman at the foot of the mounting block here almost collapsed. She was held up by the crowd as she wailed, and women all round were shrieking. The large man nearest to Benno thumped the woman beside him to express his opinion of her cheating him of Paradise. In front of Benno a woman was rocking to and fro, hands clasped to her fine lace cap from under which flowed quantities of golden ringlets. These had already attracted the lustful attentions of a little dark man pressed hopefully against her, who divided his gaze between her and the preacher.

'Burn, burn your vanities, dear children, before Satan burns you! Your Prince entertains the Devil but you must cast out the Evil One from you for ever.'

The attendant friar, handing the pole with the skull to a member of the crowd, who looked stunned and not wholly pleased at the privilege, began busily to construct something on the rostrum, while the preacher presented the crucifix towards a pretty girl in the front.

'Take off your paint, dear daughter. Be rid of those tresses before the Devil pulls you down to Hell by them. You do not wish to be rid of them; I see your unwillingness; does that not show you, dear child, how much they are dear to you? That they are dearer to you than is our crucified Lord? He longs, how He longs, to see a pure soul, stripped in all its humility.'

His target was perhaps not best chosen, for although she tried to scrub her face with her silk apron, and undid a ribbon from her abundant hair, she seemed to have no more to offer. A concerned matron on her left made a strong effort to help her: fastening her hands in the braids of hair she tugged, but she caused only wild shrieking from the girl.

Others were more forthcoming. A velvet cape was passed over the heads of the crowd, a lute with cherry ribbons made a jangling journey to the rostrum.

'Give, give up your vanities! Each one is a handle for the devils to draw you from God!'

Someone had been carrying song sheets, others cards, weeping women sacrificed chains and brooches, a full head of hair went from hand to hand like a curly lapdog, a gauze scarf or two was sent forward. This crowd, on a weekday and fairly impromptu, had no great fineries or possessions about them. That would come later. The preacher intoned a penitential prayer in his thrilling voice, the crowd chanted with him, the attendant friar steadily and skilfully added the offerings to his little edifice. Benno wondered where the wood for the framework had so suddenly come from, which was being draped with scarves and ribbons and which supported the lute but now the friar looked in his scrip and produced a painted cut-out of a devil, with horns and pitchfork, which he attached to the top of the pile in a split stick, and it was evident that the whole show was well prepared.

'And now, my dear children, forgive each other as God

will forgive you if you truly repent and change your ways. Beg for His mercy, and each one of you give your neighbour the kiss of peace.' The preacher raised the crucifix on high and led the shout of '*Misericordia!*' which echoed from the house fronts, startling the pigeons into explosive flurries overhead and making people in other parts of the city hurry to their windows.

The kiss of peace involved Benno in being crushed to the bosom of the hefty penitent beside him, while Biondello, put for safety inside the front of his jerkin, squirmed and kicked as the kiss landed on Benno's head. He was released in time to see the little swarthy man in front grabbing opportunity and the neighbour with the golden ringlets. One moment before, her repentance had got the better of vanity. He pursed his lips for a smacking kiss and had to deliver it to a woman bald and scabbed of scalp, who brandished her ringlets and cap for sacrifice. Everywhere kisses resounded, peace was invoked and the preacher, clasping the crucifix to his breast, looked down at the crowd with tears shining on his thin cheeks.

Beside him, the friar had produced tinder and flint, and the fire caught quickly, ribbons twisting in the flames, smoke billowing out from the lute, and the devil on top rippling in the heat as though he writhed to get away. The purification of Viverra had begun.

Sigismondo meanwhile was witness that the message concerning vanity had not penetrated to the palace. He was closeted with Ginevra Matarazza, lady-in-waiting to the Princess, widow of Gaspare Matarazza, mistress to Gatta. Only the self-confidence of the Princess could have invited such comparisons to her own beauty as those that Ginevra offered. Ginevra was a small woman, delicately rounded in every part, and all gestures, all adornments, showed what value she set upon capturing attention and love.

The room was only big enough to contain a bed, on the cushioned platform of which she had arranged herself; a brazier; and Sigismondo. Behind him a window, half of it shuttered, looked over the main courtyard of the palace, and in the window hung a cage. Linnets or finches were too ordinary for Ginevra Matarazza; her cage held a parakeet of brilliant plumage, that sat malevolently regarding Sigismondo with shoulders hunched and its head on one side.

Ginevra regarded him with a very different expression.

She too held her head on one side, with her lips parted, watching his mouth as he spoke as if she strove innocently to understand what he might say. At the same time she gave the impression that it would be too intellectual for her pretty little wits to grasp. The parted lips were carefully painted, and smoothed with oil to make them glisten. She clasped her fingers round one knee, while leaning forward, all attention; a pose that compressed her bosom in its low bodice. The unnatural, silvery fairness of her hair was accentuated by the half-veil of silver gauze pinned to the braids, as was the whiteness of her skin by the indigo silk of her dress. There was no difficulty in imagining why Gatta had chosen her to amuse his leisure hours.

'You have something for me, sir?' She interrupted his description of Gatta's speed and dash in fighting, which might be expected to interest her. She had a soft, caressing, child's voice.

'*Whore!*'

The exclamation came not from Sigismondo, who almost started at the screech close behind him, but from the parakeet. So far from taking it as an opprobrious comment, Ginevra lifted her clasped hands and giggled. 'Take no notice, sir. Perro makes everyone laugh.'

At this point, jealous of the attention achieved by the parakeet, a lithe little monkey emerged from a fold of the bed curtain, ran down Ginevra's arm and bit her hand.

She screeched to rival the parakeet, and beat at the monkey. It ran up the green silk curtains to the tester and clung, rocking with it, to the cords that attached it to the ceiling hooks. It gibbered and made faces as Ginevra sucked her hand.

41

A basin, and a ewer draped with a towel, stood on the bed platform. Sigismondo poured water and, taking her hand, induced her to bathe it.

'Oh! It stings.'

'The wound isn't deep. I have a salve.'

Her wrist drooped bonelessly as he let go of it to look in the purse at his belt, and she leant against him, inert, as if half fainting, while he produced a small horn box of ointment. He dried the hand and smoothed some ointment on the puncture marks, while she winced and made little protesting whimpers.

He took out another small box, this time of repoussé silver, and laid it on his open palm.

'What is that, sir?' She began to revive, looked at the box, and raised her eyes to his. 'Is that for me? What is it?' She stretched out for it, her whole body instantly alive. 'Did Gatta send me that?'

Sigismondo brought his hand within reach, smiling. She struggled for a minute with the clasp, but as he did not offer to help her she got it open, and then cried out and was perfectly still, gazing at the brooch, a cabuchon sapphire set in a star frame of table-cut diamonds; till very recently the treasured possession of some rich Mascian.

She lifted it from its nest of red velvet and tried it against her bodice, now here, now there, looking down to judge the effect and then at Sigismondo for the same reason.

Suddenly her eyes focused past him to the window. Her mouth opened, she dropped the brooch and screamed.

A skull looked in.

The parakeet, backing along its perch from the intrusion, was lost for words.

6. "WHO IS THIS MAN?"

Ginevra's screams at once brought her maid running in, and Sigismondo left her hysterics to be treated with a competence that argued they were not unknown. He knew who must have arrived at the palace preceded by that inquisitive skull, and he had not so far seen the preacher himself. How would the man be received by the palace? If Benno too had found his way in, he could give an account of the sermon. Sigismondo had caught the bellow of *Misericordia* from the square, though Ginevra, happily absorbed with Gatta's present, had showed no signs of hearing it. Surprising, was the preacher's confidence in coming to the palace; more surprising, that he had been let in. Bishops and Cardinals were welcomed in palaces, nomad fanatics were not.

A corridor led past Ginevra's room along the length of the main apartments of the *piano nobile* and at the end overlooked both the marble entrance hall with its staircase, and the courtyard. Sigismondo leant on the balustrade to look into the hall.

The Prince's major-domo had evidently received instructions to admit the preacher, but was banning the skull. The preacher, tall, imposing even in this setting of marble and gilt, stood apart. His hands were clasped over the crucifix which now hung from his neck; he smiled faintly as though he had abstracted himself from the argument. Authority prevailed: the attendant friar, almost stamping

43

with rage, strode out to lean the pole against a wall outside, where the skull stared sarcastically, mocking the idea that death did not visit palaces.

It was, naturally, the first thing spotted by a party of horsemen who came suddenly clattering into the courtyard, hallooing and yelling to each other in high spirits not at all dampened by sight of the skull. Indeed, it seemed to raise them further. One, after drinking from a flask that hung at his saddlebow, drew his sword and, with a hunting call, slashed at the pole while he made his horse prance and circle. The rest shouted applause. A slash toppled the pole and the skull, held by the pitch, lay in the gutter grinning up.

Far from sobering the party, this provoked guffaws and wild challenges. Flagons were passing from hand to hand.

The one that had felled the skull looked about eighteen or less, with dark hair in a fashionable frame of curls, his cloak and doublet banded with scarlet silk. The chief of the others, who had been egging him on and making his horse circle, now took a hunting lance from someone and aimed it at the skull. He was much the same age, his clothes embroidered in gold and lined with sable, his hair straight to his shoulders, dark Venetian red.

Inside the hall, the major-domo left the friars to themselves and prepared to receive the hunting party when they should choose to dismount and enter. The preacher had to restrain the younger friar from rushing out in defence of the skull. Sigismondo saw that a hand on the sleeve and a steady glance sufficed. This man knew something of true authority.

By now the game in the courtyard had reached a climax. The young man had speared the skull through an eyesocket and lifted it, seized the pole – which broke off short just below his hand, tribute to the sword's sharpness – and detached the spear. Brandishing the skull, he urged his horse up the shallow steps and into the hall, where the noise of shod hooves cracking the marble resounded, bringing a covey of women out on to the landing above the staircase.

44

Sigismondo drew back into a window. The Princess came through the women and stood looking down at her son.

'Is this your property, Father?' The young prince was making his horse trample round the preacher, and thrust the skull towards him. The attendant friar shrank out of the horse's way but the preacher held his ground, composed, even gently smiling as the skull approached his face. 'You could be a pair, you two!'

Certainly the preacher, with hollow cheeks and sunken eyes, had a more than passing resemblance to the skull. Some of the ladies tittered. Unexpectedly he reached out and wrenched the trophy from the young man's hand, turning it to face him. 'A pair, my son, to you also. You will come to this in the end. Do not think I am nearer to Death than you. He rides beside you always, no matter how far or fast you go.' His voice rose effortlessly above the clash of the hooves, and the tittering stopped.

'Who is this man? What does he do here?' The Princess too had a voice that could carry, light and elegant as it was. She stood, not far from Sigismondo, her hands hanging at her sides, coolly undisturbed by the commotion below, relaxed and sure of herself, like the preacher. Although Sigismondo was several feet away, the scent she wore, mingled jasmine and musk, reached him without even a gesture to waft it.

'Highness.' The major-domo was a man used to the ways of courts, an adept at smoothing troubles away, but even he was disconcerted by the trampling of hooves and the difficulty of reasoning with the rider. 'He is called Brother Ambrogio. I understood that Your Highness wished him to be admitted?'

'I gave no such order.' She sounded mildly amazed; and it did not to any observer seem likely that she was a woman who would send for such as Brother Ambrogio. Her son had by now dismounted and thrown the reins to a waiting groom. The animal jibbed at going down the steps and needed some urging.

The young prince was joined by his friend, and they both, after bowing to the Princess, stood staring at the preacher as if hoping for amusement. Brother Ambrogio passed the skull to the attendant friar for custody and stood silent, his air of detachment daunting even the two drunken young men. The prince hooked an arm over his friend's shoulder and they both very slightly staggered.

'Who asked you to come here, Brother Ambrogio?' The Princess descended the stairs, perfuming the air and drawing her women after her. It did not escape Sigismondo that it was she who was coming to the preacher, not the other way round. 'Whom do you seek here?'

Brother Ambrogio gave his gentle smile. 'I seek no one, my daughter. It is God Himself who seeks the souls of all that are here. If He has led me here it is with a purpose. Does not the Devil live here too?'

The young prince found this extremely funny. 'Show us where he lives and we'll get him for you, Father. That'll make a catch for you to boast of in the market place.'

Brother Ambrogio turned his smile to the prince. 'He lives in you, my son. And the world knows that he walks with your father the Prince.'

The silence that fell after this was succeeded by an indignant outburst from everyone except the Princess. She simply extended a hand towards the door.

'Throw them out.'

The major-domo advanced, his gold-tipped staff indicating the door too. The young prince took hold of one of the preacher's arms in its sleeve of coarse frieze, and his friend hurried to take the other, Brother Ambrogio making no resistance. The friar behind him struggled violently with three servants, hampered by his care for the skull.

The noise and excitement were abruptly broken into by the appearance of the Princess Dowager at the stair-head. She clapped her hands to draw attention, and called down.

'Let Brother Ambrogio alone. He is here at my invitation.'

7. "Is He for Me?"

Benno had indeed managed to get into the palace in the preacher's wake; not because the gate porter thought Benno was anything to do with the spiritual revival of Viverra but because Sigismondo had already pointed him out as his servant when they arrived that morning. He came in humbly, cap in hand, Biondello out of sight under his arm and under his cloak, hoping not to attract the preacher's attention.

The sermon in the square had not failed to move him. He had searched his soul for vanities to give up, for something precious to him to be surrendered, and the only thing he could think of was Biondello. It was true he now had two new tunics, and shirt and hose, bought for him by Sigismondo, but that was only so that he should not disgrace his master when waiting on him; in a sense the clothes were his master's property more than his own. Clothes and appearance meant nothing to Benno. That full wig of curly hair, however, travelling over the heads of the crowd towards the bonfire had made him think at once of the woolly little dog inside his jerkin. He had no real idea of the preacher turning on him and pulling out Biondello as fuel for the next bonfire, but he had an obscure feeling that he might he putting Biondello before worthier objects or causes, whatever they might be.Perhaps, if any of the gold Sigismondo had just acquired came his way, he ought to give it in alms.

With all this in mind, he hung back when the two friars

49

were admitted to the palace, and lurked inconspicuously in the courtyard, hoping to slip in when the major-domo's attention was distracted. After one friar stamped out to prop the skull against the wall, Benno found himself on the periphery of the game played by the hunting party, anonymous among the grooms and footservants who accompanied them. He seized his chance when the young prince's horse was led out, and made himself an unobserved witness of the commotion inside.

Both the Princesses made a deep impression upon him. The Princess Isotta was everything he had ever thought a Princess should be: beautiful, wonderfully dressed, and dignified. He particularly admired the way in which she ordered the friars thrown out. It had happened to him so often that he was a connoisseur of such commands. When the grey-haired Princess Dowager clapped her hands for attention, she had Benno's at once. Here was a lady who, while she was no longer in competition with the other in the beauty stakes, could certainly make her wishes respected. Benno did not miss the younger Princess's glance of irritation when the Dowager descended the stairs, the curtseying ladies making way. The preacher strode forward to meet her and there was a murmur when, instead of giving her hand to be kissed, she took his and raised it reverently to her lips.

'You honour us, dear Father. May your stay here bring blessings to us all.'

There was some exchange of glances at this, some rolling eyes at a prospect of tedium, others malicious at a prospect of entertainment. Benno, studying from close at hand the jewels on the flowing black velvet, the gold net over the grey hair, wondered if the old lady had any idea what she was letting herself in for. By his reckoning, she was wearing enough vanities to provide a tidy bonfire all on her own.

He watched while the friars were led away to be given food and lodging. The Princess Isotta (after a word with her son, who nearly fell when his friend removed his support to bow at her approach) gave the barest inclination of the head

to the Dowager and swept back up the stairs, collecting her
ladies who were finding it hard to repress giggles as they
whispered. At the stairhead, Princess Isotta paused and,
glancing to her right, beckoned. Benno was pleased to see
Sigismondo step from behind a pillar and bow.

It was not an easy job to keep his master in sight. Benno
knew he himself would not be allowed into the Princess's
presence, but he must be at the door when his master should
emerge and look for him and his report on the sermon; the
Prince's search for the Philosopher's Stone was not about to
gain Brother Ambrogio's backing. The ladies proved an
obstacle from the start, clustering after the Princess, one
imitating Brother Ambrogio, adjuring the others to remember that Death was right behind them. One girl, in the rear,
glanced back and, seeing Benno, gave a faint shriek; luckily
the major-domo was still in the entrance hall, supervising the
cleaning up after the young prince's horse and lamenting the
chipping of the marble, or Benno would have found himself in
the courtyard in record time even for him.

By the time he had got up the stairs without offending the
ladies by following too closely, the head of the little
procession, and his master, were out of sight. He hoped by
following at a distance to locate where Sigismondo was.

The last lady in the train, having become aware of
Benno, made shooing gestures as she disappeared around a
corner; he broke into a trot to catch up. A door to his left
opened and out shot an exceedingly pretty young woman,
who cannoned into him and fell back, gasping. Benno
clutched at his cloak and began to apologise.

Ginevra had that day seen worse sights than Benno, so
she was not unduly overcome. In any case, her eyes were
attracted instantly from his face to the little dog now revealed.

'Oh! How adorable! Is he for me?' Ginevra's immediate
reaction to anything she coveted was to visualise it as a
present. She pulled Biondello from under Benno's arm and
pressed kisses on his head. Unfortunately, he had had one of
his rare baths only yesterday, and his wool was as appealing as

a lamb's. 'Oh! I'm late and I'm sent for! Oh, the darling!' As Benno stood, his arms out to receive Biondello, she hurried off, cradling and caressing the little dog, who thrust his head out for a moment over her elbow to look back.

Benno had half expected something bad to happen to him, ever since Brother Ambrogio's sermon had made him feel so guilty. He had never expected this.

The young prince and his friend had reached his apartment, a suite of rooms very modern in the new antique style, with Corinthian pilasters and, in the prince's bedroom, a fresco of a hunt. He lay supine on the bed now, contemplating this.

'Good sport today.' He stretched and yawned. 'You got that old devil finely. What tusks!'

His friend was having his doublet and shirt removed, while a page brought a silver basin from a shelf and another carried in ewers of steaming water. Stripped to the waist, he showed surprising muscle for an eighteen-year-old; he ran his hands over his upper arms and shoulders exploringly. 'I'm going to be stiff, I can tell you. It was all I could do to hold him.' He stood to be washed, while the prince still lay on the bed and the pages waited for him.

'Donato. Who were those three men you spoke to on the edge of the wood? Proper villains they looked. I was going to send Ladro over to see them off. Were they begging?'

Donato had, for an almost imperceptible moment, stopped dashing water over his face. 'What men?'

'At the edge of the wood. The tall one – very tall – and the one with that ridiculous sword. Looked like robbers to me.' The prince raised himself on one elbow and pointed to a cup on the table, which was hastily filled and brought to him. 'What on earth did they want?'

Donato towelled his head briskly, turning his curls into a luxuriant halo. He spoke muffled in the towel. 'Oh – money, of course. Begging, as you said. Unemployed soldiers, I suppose.'

The prince swung his cup towards the page for more. 'Idiots, then. There's war enough to keep every soldier in the world employed, even fools with swords too big for them; his grandfather's, I suppose, though people are starting to use those again. Why don't they hire themselves to Gatta?' He got up languidly, and not too steadily, to let the pages start undressing him. 'You heard what they were saying at the gate, that he's taken Mascia? The report must have come while we were out.'

'Another victory for that proud bastard.' Donato had his clean embroidered shirt put on and a page worked round him tying his points. 'Lucky for your father, though. Again.'

Prince Francesco was silent as they washed him, because of the bitterness in his friend's voice. They could hardly discuss Gatta's last victory: it had been over the Count Landucci, Donato's father, and was the reason Donato lived here, hostage for his father's good behaviour. After a moment the prince found another subject.

'That ragamuffin friar! One of my tutors was a friar but he didn't wear such wretched stuff as that. My grandmother has no idea what she's doing. He'll have all her jewels off her and given to the poor.'

Donato drank wine while his hair was combed. 'I didn't think her Highness your mother looked delighted.'

'Not her style at all. When she tells my father, the fur will fly. When I'm married, Donato, I hope my mother won't interfere. She's bound to outlive my father, years younger; and he's always ailing.'

It was Donato's turn to be silent. A page held his blue brocade doublet ready, but he stood as if in a dream. The prince washed his face, splashing water on the floor and holding out a blind hand for the towel. 'When I rule here, Viverra and Landucci shall be friends, I tell you. We'll make our pact – and you shall marry one of my sisters.'

'I shall never marry.' Donato's voice faltered with emotion. 'Never. You know I can never marry the one I truly love.'

Francesco had, for the moment and in the pleasure of a new idea, forgotten. He had forgotten, because he did not really believe, the drunken confidence Donato had made the night before: the only woman, Donato had affirmed with tears in his eyes, the only woman he truly loved was the Princess Isotta.

8. A WIND STRONG ENOUGH?

'You must tell me, sir, about the siege. All my ladies are anxious to hear.'

The Princess surveyed her ladies, sitting on floor cushions and, though with pretence of embroidery and ribbon-plaiting, studying Sigismondo either openly or under eyelashes enhanced with oil and soot. Strangers who resembled Roman emperors – and not in the cold marble in which one always saw them, either – and who had shoulders like Atlas to carry the world, were not frequent at court. The shaven head aroused the usual speculation. One lady devised, on the spot, a theory she was on edge to impart: that the stranger had taken a vow not to let his hair grow until his loved one relented. She herself would not have made him suffer for more than a token week or so; possibly a day. Then when he answered the Princess, what a voice! It was made for murmuring compliments and persuasions in one's ear! Several determined to make a play for him. After all, Ginevra had already got her claws into Gatta, who brought the same whiff of glamorous danger into dull court lives.

'Your Highness, I have no wish to disappoint you, but there is little to tell that is fit for the ears of ladies. Fighting is the same the world over, brutish to see, disgusting to describe.' A page, at a sign from the Princess, had brought a carved folding-stool, and Sigismondo, acknowledging her graciousness, sat, hands on knees, smiling slightly, the shaven head respectfully inclined, as conspicuous among the spread skirts of the ladies, in his fine linen and tooled black leather jerkin and thigh boots, as a bull in a flower bed.

The Princess raised her thin arched eyebrows. She recognised a refusal to do as she asked, however politely phrased. She had been smoothing back the hair of her youngest daughter, a pretty child of eight, and now she turned her round and thrust her towards her waiting nurse. 'You are a philosopher, sir, to be a fighter by profession and to describe fighting as disgusting.'

'Fighting itself is not disgusting, Highness. Although it may not be Christian to admit it, to save one's life by taking another's has its moment of glory.'

The Princess made a brief, amused pout. 'You had best not allow this Brother Ambrogio to hear you. He has come, her Highness the Princess Elena tells me, to purge the palace of sin and strife. Those who live by the sword and claim for it moments of glory are not likely to be in his favour.'

'Even though, like Ridolfo Ridolfi, they restore his Highness's rightful cities to him?'

Sigismondo's question, however innocent it seemed, raised several others, but they could not be pursued at the moment. A little commotion at the door attracted more attention than had been meant. Ginevra, attempting to slip in unseen, caught her half-veil on the tapestry door-curtain and, encumbered by a little dog she carried, could not free herself. A page detached her. She curtsied to the Princess, the movement sending blonde ringlets sliding down her neck to seek her *décolletage*.

'Your pardon, Highness. I was – I was ill.'

The eyebrows arched again. 'You seem to have recovered. Was it news from Mascia restored you?' The brooch sent by Gatta shone on Ginevra's bosom as only a large sapphire surrounded by diamonds is capable of doing.

The ladies, making way by drawing in their skirts for her to reach her accustomed place, whispered and nudged, while she picked her path, sat down, and struggled to hold Biondello kicking in her arms. The Princess was amused. 'Your little dog has lost an ear. Was it wounded in Mascia? Is that the best Gatta can do for you?'

No one could resist this invitation to laugh. Ginevra examined Biondello's head in dismay and, finding its lack of symmetry confirmed, released her hold. Biondello flung himself off her silken lap and pelted over the skirts strewn in his path, to leap up at Sigismondo's face. Sigismondo's hands closed round the furry body.

'He seems to know you, sir.' The Princess's implication was plain: that Sigismondo, who had disappeared from view after delivering his news of the victory, and Gatta's letter, to the Prince, had in that time added his own present to Gatta's. Ginevra's efforts to adjust her bodice and put up the wandering locks of hair encouraged everyone to suppose the present had been given in return for services rendered. Sigismondo smiled, and scratched Biondello under his ear.

'Soldiers both, your Highness. The dog is mine.'

Ginevra put a hand to her mouth, surprised, and rueful at having jettisoned a wounded warrior. She had no chance to make another claim, however. A page had come in with a message for the Princess. The artist engaged to paint the frescos in the Prince's new chapel begged to know if the Princess were now at leisure; she had promised him time to make studies for her portrait on the altar triptych.

'Let him come.' The Princess picked up the mirror on its gold chain at her waist, and considered her reflection with the detachment of one viewing a masterpiece of no personal connection. The mirror flung up light into the long oval of her face, made luminous the perfect pallor of her skin, created a glitter in the large dark eyes. She touched, but did not rearrange, the artfully disordered curling tendrils allowed to break free to frame her face, softening the line of the smooth red braids. She let the mirror fall, folding her hands as the painter entered.

Leonello Leconti was accustomed to seeing beautiful women, from closer than this view across the room, and very often wearing fewer clothes or none. Nevertheless, announced by the page, he stood still and stared. The Princess's regard summed him up. He was a man who might be as handy with a dagger as with a paint brush. His eyes, round as an owl's, had intense concentration. His beard was no more than an emphasis to the wilful mouth and strong chin. He was wiry, even perhaps athletic.

At last he came to his manners and bowed, and advanced over the ladies' skirts with as little regard for them as Biondello had. His assistant was more careful – a cowed youth burdened with a portfolio, a board, a folding stool and a box of charcoal.

'How should I sit?'

Leconti took the portfolio, pulled it open and extracted a sketch, which she studied for a moment; then she moved to turn her right profile towards him. As she gave back the sketch, it was seen to show the Princess, in profile on her knees to one side of the main panel opposite Prince Scipione. A lady intercepted the sketch and it was passed round. The main panel between the portraits represented St Francis raising from the dead a boy who had fallen from a high window. The face of St Francis strongly resembled Leconti, so either it was cheaper to use yourself as a model, or Leconti fancied himself to have saintly attributes.

Judging from the way he was looking at the Princess, indicating by tilting his head how he wanted her to hold hers, he was deceived in that.

She made no further effort to arrange herself but seemed already composed, looking at the archway of the window, with its lunettes of burgundy and blue, while Leconti placed the stool, sat, and took the board with paper pinned to it. The cowed assistant handed a stick of charcoal, and then drew back, earning more black looks from the ladies although he avoided their dresses, just because he was a cowed assistant.

Leconti began, with rapid defining strokes, to put down his outline of the Princess's profile. As he looked at her now, his gaze had altered. It was a stern, professional one, his eyes seeing her, then the paper, swiftly up and back again.

'This Scala.' She spoke without turning her eyes, but she addressed Sigismondo. 'You saw him. What was he like?'

Sigismondo hummed. 'Very large, Highness. A giant among men.'

'The poor fool Carlotti supposed himself invulnerable, no doubt, with such a defender – thought he would hold Mascia against Gatta and then go on to conquer Viverra. Why did he not learn from what happened to Landucci?'

'No doubt he imagined himself both stronger and better armed than Landucci, Highness. Some men do not learn from what is before them. The craving for power is like the craving for wine – or women.' Sigismondo smiled benignly at the assembled ladies. 'It blinds men to reality. They see only their dreams.'

'Did Gatta kill Scala with his own hand?'

Sigismondo, all eyes except those of the artist and the Princess upon him, shrugged. 'Your Highness, I was busy at the time. It is possible.'

The Princess turned her head, the artist's hand stopped in mid-stroke.

'*Possible*? If Gatta killed him, all his men would know – those who saw would tell of it.'

A loud affirmatory sound arose, Ginevra nodding her head with conviction, her lips firmly together. Her lover was a man people would notice, whatever he did.

Sigismondo might have been going to cast a further obscurity upon the matter, but he was saved from answering by the entrance of the young prince and his friend Donato Landucci. The ladies rose, some scrambling, some with the grace of long practice; Ginevra caught her foot and stumbled against Donato, who set her right with unexpected indifference.

Prince Francesco came to kiss his mother's hand and cheek and, as he straightened up, she looked him over carefully. In his silver brocade he was a very beautiful young man, with pale skin and large eyes like hers but with a wider mouth and cheeks more hollow. The dark red hair framed his face. With something of the same air of cool detachment he returned her glance.

To Sigismondo, who knew human nature, such an air could well be the cover for violent passions, the more violent for being always concealed. The question for Prince Scipione might be, did his wife conceal such a passion for anyone who could be a danger to himself and his state? The Princess had shown an interest in Gatta's exploits; that might be innocent. She had shown a pleasure in mocking Gatta's mistress. The two, together, might be an insubstantial straw that showed the way the wind blew. If such a wind did blow, it might be strong enough to blow the Prince out of Viverra; and that was Sigismondo's business to detect and to prevent.

'You dine with us tonight, my son?'

'I dine with friends in the city, alas.' The regret was light and false, his eyes said he was looking forward to spending the evening away from his family and the eyes of the court. The Princess did not allow a frown to spoil her face.

'Your father wished to speak with you.'

'His Highness may command me at any time.' Unspoken was the corollary that any time was better than now. Behind Francesco, Donato's gaze never wavered from the Princess. He carried a small box of woven wood tied with scarlet ribbons. One of the ladies saw it, hastily looked at the floor, pursed up her mouth and shook with suppressed giggles. The young prince bowed again to his mother and was turning to leave when two pages snatched back the tapestry curtains at the door and Prince Scipione himself came in.

He looked round at everyone standing, with a vague glance that appeared to flicker over Sigismondo without recognition, and did not even acknowledge his wife and son.

Taking a few steps forward into the crowded room, the Prince, with no more ceremony than if he had been an ordinary person, crumpled to the floor.

9. Bishop's Move

Sigismondo had reached the Prince before the women had time to get a grip on the situation and start screeching. The Prince lay doubled up, clutching his stomach, his face white and sweating, and as Sigismondo knelt beside him he retched. No more than a little foam appeared on the crooked mouth. His son was kneeling by him and put a hand on his.

'Father, what is it? The fumes again?'

'Of course it's the fumes.' The Princess Isotta had pushed her women aside and now looked down at her husband's writhings, as composed as if she still sat for her portrait. 'It's always like this. You can't play with fire and not get singed.'

'It is the work of the Devil.'

No mistaking the thrilling tones of Brother Ambrogio, raised above the noise and confusion. He stood in the doorway, the Princess Dowager visible past his shoulder, yearning to get at her son but holding the preacher in too much awe to be able to push past him.

'We must get him from here, to his bed.' Sigismondo's deep voice was calming, heard under the hubbub rather than over like Brother Ambrogio's. The Princess Isotta seemed more concerned, however, with the preacher's challenge, and she advanced and confronted him.

'You should seek the devil in your own heart. It is pride that has brought you here to this city.'

Dark eyes deep in their sockets glinted as if she had

struck fire from flint, but Brother Ambrogio's smile was wholly compassionate. 'Don't deceive yourself, my daughter. The pride in your own heart prompts you to say this.'

Sigismondo had by now picked up the groaning Prince, who clearly weighed light in his arms. Striding forward, he let his burden force its own way. Preacher and Princesses fell back as he carried the Prince under the door curtains and, ushered by anxious pages, on down the corridor to the Prince's bedchamber. The young prince seemed as if he would follow but his mother spoke to him and he turned away down the stairs. The one who did follow Sigismondo was Benno, who had already collared Biondello flashing out past Brother Ambrogio like an exorcised demon. No one, in the confusion of the moment, prevented Benno from joining the servants in the Prince's bedroom and watching his master lay the Prince on the bed, from where the fur coverlet had been swiftly removed by the pages. The doctor had been summoned, and he arrived in a hurry, two assistants scuttling after with a carrying-box of phials and jars, set up at once on the bedside chest.

'Grave. Very grave.' The doctor, shaking his head and feeling the Prince's pulse, pulling his eyelids down to examine his eyes, was taking out the usual medical insurance against death of a patient. 'Very serious indeed.' The graver the illness, the less likely could it be expected of the doctor to find a cure and, if he did or if the patient recovered of his own accord, the more prestige and the higher the fee. 'It is another of his Highness's attacks and a severe one.' He realised suddenly that he was addressing a stranger across the Prince's twisting body. 'Who are you, sir?' he demanded with a stare so outraged that it suggested Sigismondo alone might have precipitated the attack by his mere presence.

'I was sent to his Highness with news of Mascia.' The simple statement made no attempt to explain why he was at the Prince's bedside now, when the news had been delivered hours ago. The doctor, confused, felt that some point had escaped him. He busied himself ordering preparations for a blood-letting, while he pressed linen to the Prince's brow and temples, and tetchily demanding a basin as the Prince retched again. Sigismondo, after a moment when he leant over the moaning Prince, nostrils flared and mouth parted like a cat taking an elusive scent, withdrew into the shadow of the bed-curtains. Now at last pages thrust open both double doors and the Princesses entered, the mother more agitated than the wife, and came to opposite sides of the bed. Brother Ambrogio was not with them – perhaps tempted to stay and give the ladies an impromptu sermon on their not inconsiderable collection of vanities.

'How is my son? What are you doing for him?' The Dowager Princess smoothed back the fine damp hair sticking to the Prince's forehead, bending lovingly over him and unconscious of Sigismondo within a foot of her. The doctor made a series of tutting noises designed to signal his fears for his patient and, respectfully, of any interference in his treatment. Prince Scipione himself provided a counterpoint of groans, and a climax by suddenly throwing up into the bowl skilfully held by an assistant. This made the Princess Dowager step back, almost into Sigismondo without yet noticing him, and it also provided a striking reception for a swarm of courtiers who, evidently having heard further sensational news of the Prince's state – the word 'dying' audible among their murmurings – were anxious to be present at an event that promised so melancholy a thrill.

'Your Highness, I beg you. The patient must have quiet.' The doctor turned to the Princess Isotta instinctively as a source of authority, a point appreciated by the spectators of the power game between the Princesses. 'If he does not have complete peace I cannot be answerable.'

'*Peace!*' The word was echoed, with drama, from the doorway. Princess Isotta, her hand raised to order everyone out, for once risked encouraging lines on her perfect brow, and frowned. Brother Ambrogio was making yet another grand entrance. 'Peace! The Prince needs peace for his soul above all else. Let us all pray that he will find grace to renounce the works of the Devil before his soul is called to account before the Eternal Throne.'

Making his way forward, the preacher unceremoniously pushed those in his way to their knees. At the bedside, the doctor feebly resisting, he raised the sweating, moaning Prince until he was propped against the high brocade pillows, a position which did seem to ease his pain a little. Then, with surprising tenderness, he drew off the worn leather gloves the Prince was wearing and, casting them away on the floor, he pressed the Prince's hands together and, holding them gripped between his own, raised his voice, drowning all protest.

'Almighty Father, sweet Lord and Saviour, behold this sinful lost son of Yours and have mercy on him in this hour, this hour which may be his last. Chase the Devil from his heart and from his royal dwelling, purify his soul and his city. Oh, cast out from him sinful desires, restore to him that innocence of wonder at Thy works which does not seek to enquire into the manifesting of Thy creation. We, sinners all, beseech this of Thee, through the sacred blood of Thy Holy Lamb shed for us.'

All those present had, without option, knelt, and now uttered acquiescence – save for the Princess Isotta who merely stared coldly at the preacher. Sigismondo, kneeling in the shadow of the curtains behind the preacher, with head bent in respect, held between his linked hands one of the gloves the preacher had thrown down. His lowered glance saw that it was stained and eroded with acid, the surface scraped and ripped, even burnt here and there; his nose told him from the pungent chemical smell that it was undoubtedly worn in the laboratory and that the fumes were quite capable of making the owner ill.

His nostrils caught another smell in the air: incense. A door beside the bed, probably leading to a private stair, opened. Preceded by an acolyte with a censer and followed by others with candles, a large, imposing priest, in embroidered chasuble and stole, paced into the room: the Prince's own confessor. He was followed by the young prince, showing that he and his mother thought alike on the subject of Brother Ambrogio.

No one kneeling now had their eyes shut or raised to heaven. All were alert to what might be the next move in another power game.

'My daughter—' The Princess Isotta had come swiftly forward to kiss his ring, the amethyst which proclaimed the Prince's confessor to be no less than Bishop Ugolino of Viverra. The voice, rich and harsh, was accustomed to command. The face, now turned to stare at Prince Scipione supported by the preacher, would not have disgraced a boarhound, albeit one of a plethoric nature; the eyes bold and bloodshot, the jaw heavy. This was not a man to welcome any stranger on to his territory. 'The prince told me his father is in danger. *Who is this?*' It was a stentorian question. One or two of the courtiers kneeling at the back got up to obtain a better view.

What happened next surprised almost everyone. Brother Ambrogio, releasing the Prince's hands, straightened up to tower over the Bishop, only to bow profoundly and reach to raise the Bishop's ring to his lips.

The Bishop, his glare softening, permitted the act of tribute, while his free hand gestured at Prince Scipione, and addressed the room. '*All* will leave, save the physician. His Highness must not be disturbed by anything.'

'Anything' appeared to include the Prince's family, but Princess Isotta had brought the banishment upon herself by summoning Bishop Ugolino and she was satisfied since it included Brother Ambrogio. Her arm round her son's shoulders, she left the room without casting another glance at the man on the bed. He, now that his hands were freed, pressed them once more convulsively to his midriff and doubled up. The doctor, under the glare of the Bishop who had restored his authority, was trying to bleed the Prince; his assistant, having got rid of one bowl, had produced another which he tried to fit to the Prince's arm. Sigismondo slid discreetly from the shadows without attracting the Bishop's attention, and followed the skirts of the Princess Dowager, who was weeping and being consoled by Brother Ambrogio. The courtiers, getting up from their knees and preparing to follow, were only prevented from whispering by the ranging glare Bishop Ugolino sent over them. Ginevra, as usual, required special assistance to regain her feet, assistance which two young men were assiduous to supply. She still contrived to stumble, and to send to the floor a marquetry box standing on a painted chest by the door. Pretty confusion was so much a custom with her that it was taken for granted. Her little accidents never took the form of mislaying jewellery or forgetting what her friends owed her at cards.

'Your Highness. May I speak with you alone?' The young prince was glad to be released by his mother, although he gave Sigismondo a startled glance as he went on his way. The Princess moved into an alcove, where a window looked over an inner courtyard. She turned the dark gaze on Sigismondo, consideringly.

'What is it?'

'Your Highness, I believe the Prince is being poisoned.'

10. ROUND ONE TO THE DEVIL

'Didn't she believe you?' Benno's walk was interspersed with trotting steps as he tried to keep pace with Sigismondo across the palace gardens. Ahead, in the beginning of early autumn dusk, loomed the old castle. Benno had taken a good look at the Princess, and he thought that if anyone was arrogant enough to believe his master was wrong, she'd be the one. Sigismondo was unruffled, as usual, and stopped in his stride to bend to a sweet shrub that bordered the path.

'Why should she? The Prince has had these attacks before. Each time, away from his experiments, he has recovered. She grants that he is being poisoned, but poisoned by the fumes in his laboratory.'

'Could they do that? When I saw him I thought he'd die on the spot.'

'I expect that the first time it happened, everyone thought so.' Sigismondo was strolling now, a sprig of the shrub held to his nose. 'Yes, there are chemicals whose smell alone can make you ill – in learned terms, they exude a noxious vapour – but I am no alchemist to tell you which ones they are.'

Benno's faith in his master's encyclopaedic knowledge was such that he instantly discounted this as modesty. He turned to check on Biondello, who was capering about the grass snapping at flies. A thought occurred to him. 'Will we get ill if we go in? I'd better leave Biondello outside . . . Why

69

don't the people working there get sick? Aren't they there all the time? 'Tisn't just a pastime for them like it is for the Prince. Is it just because he's princely?'

Sigismondo hummed, on almost the same note as a bee that fell out of a late flower and zoomed away. 'You've put your finger on it, Benno. Yet we may find that they do fall sick. Workers are easier to replace than are princes.'

'You said there's an alchemist there, looking for the Philosopher's Stone. If he's there all the time, with being the expert, and if he keeps getting ill, you'll know, right?'

They had reached the great door to the ruined tower where Sigismondo had been let in before. Benno picked up Biondello and tucked him under his left arm, crossing himself with his free hand. Sigismondo had not said what might be poisoning the Prince, if it wasn't fumes, so questions about it had better wait. In Benno's mind alchemy, although practised by princes, was likely to be the Devil's work. Brother Ambrogio had been quite specific about it.

A page was waiting inside. He had been playing knucklebones – there was one he'd failed to pick up – during his interminable wait. He bowed when he saw the seal the Princess had given to Sigismondo, and gestured them through the wicket. He accepted a coin from Sigismondo to look after the little dog. He found his post a lonely one and was delighted to make a fuss of Biondello, who responded with his party trick of walking backwards on his hind legs, which Benno called 'learning to be a courtier'. Benno looked back jealously as they turned the corner, but he was distracted from all other thoughts by his first whiff of the giant's fetid breath along the stone passage. He immediately accepted the theory that smells could produce deadly illnesses.

There were differences from Sigismondo's last visit which Benno did not know. The gnome with the leather apron appeared much sooner, not at the curtained door but at the foot of the worn steps, sitting with legs asprawl, holding his head. A thread of blood ran between his fingers. Sigismondo took the steps fast.

The curtain hung askew, and beyond it came not the sound of the great bellows, but a hectoring voice.

The fires still burnt in the firepots and furnaces, the smoke eddied, but the workers so busy before among the flames and glowing vessels were now idle, all staring at a figure who had climbed on a stool to harangue them. Sigismondo and Benno knew the thin face, the light brown hair, the eyes showing the whites all round them, the rictus of wild enthusiasm, the coarse brown robes of the friar, companion of Brother Ambrogio.

'Repent! Your works are accursed! Your time has come! Your patron is dying, struck down by God for his part in this evil! You will be destroyed and your vileness with you! Repent! Flee this devilish place and pray for forgiveness!'

The friar was having a splendid time. His rhetoric might not have the flow and polish of Brother Ambrogio's, his voice, reedy and shrill, failed any comparison, but he was not really aware of this and his conviction gave him energy. Spittle flew as he shouted, and his gestures had hitched up his cowl which in turn teased up the fringe of hair left by his tonsure so that it stood on end. In the swirls of smoke, and lit by a vessel of greenish liquid bubbling over a fire, he looked like a conjured spirit, a vision of madness.

'The Prince is not dying.' The statement was flat, unexpected, and brusque. The alchemist had come forward, in his sacking gown, holding dividers in a gloved hand. He looked like a hawk, with his beak of a nose, deeply lined face and sharp black eyes. Benno had expected a wise, white-bearded old man. This man was vigorous, clean-faced, and had hair, black as Benno's own, cut pudding-basin style above his ears. 'The Prince will recover. He always does. Who let you in? You've no business here.'

He put down the dividers on the trestle table, among great books and retorts and stubby cut-down quills, and he reached out and gave the hem of the friar's brown tunic a brisk tug.

'Devils! You are all devils.'

The alchemist gave another sharp tug and the friar, caught off balance in the middle of a gesture, whirled his arms furiously to keep upright, failed, came off the stool and hit the table, sending a large tome and a glass jeroboam to the floor. As it shattered, the alchemist lifted the friar bodily and ran him away from the shards. The floor smoked and bubbled; a wizened little man ran forward with a box from which he flung powder. The flagstones fizzled and smoked again and after a minute or so the surface calmed.

The friar pointed a shaking finger. 'The Devil's brand!'

'Balderdash. A chemical reaction of no interest. Fortunate that there was little left in that vessel—'

'Meddling with the works of God! Impious wretch!' Either his narrow escape from burning or his belief that the whole thing was proof of the Devil's malice made the friar tremble, and the alchemist gazed with contempt, turning down the corners of his mouth.

'Impious to explore God's works? Why else has he given man intelligence? You may choose to shut your eyes when you say your prayers, but I choose to keep my eyes open and not stumble through the world as ignorant as on the day I was born.'

Benno's nose had been prickling with the smoke and the pungency of the spilt acid. He now cataclysmically sneezed. The alchemist whirled round, and his eyes showed that he at once recognised Sigismondo. 'Has the Prince sent you? Does he wish to see me?'

'The Prince is under his physician's orders and may see no one.' Sigismondo offered no reason for his presence there and stood, at ease, while Benno's sneezes ricocheted off the walls.

The alchemist now became conscious of an idle workforce. 'What are you all doing? Luigi, the fire! How often have you been told that the heat must be constant? Piero, the pump! Never let me find you neglecting it again.' His glare swept round, and they all swiftly turned to work with an alacrity which argued that the alchemist had either the gift of inspiring or the art of punishment.

The friar had been dumbfounded at the alchemist's counterattack. Possibly he had not often tangled with articulate, educated men. He stood gazing as the fires glowed violently under the bellows, and the terrible stertorous gasps of the pump brought back the heartbeat of the laboratory.

'You – you will regret this! Wait till Brother Ambrogio comes!' With this feeble threat, uttered with bad timing as the giant expelled a breath, the friar pushed his way out, taking care, Benno saw, not to get too near any of the apparatus. Round One to the Devil.

'And now, sir—' The alchemist retrieved the tome that had been knocked to the floor, smoothed the ruffled pages and tenderly examined the spine. He propped the volume back on the book wheel, open at what seemed to Benno, wiping his wet eyes, to be magic diagrams. 'Are you here from curiosity, or some other motive?' The sharp black eyes examined them both, and although Benno gaped vacantly he had an uneasy feeling that the man was not taken in.

Sigismondo exhibited the seal. The alchemist shot a glance at it.

'From the Princess. So?'

'To enquire into the possible causes of his Highness's attack. He has had many such?'

The alchemist pulled a face of resignation. 'This is not the first. His Highness forgets warnings. We all of us know to avoid inhaling certain substances, but his Highness does not remember. He is interested, he comes closer; I can turn from supervising a vital process to find he has been hanging over another for far too long. Nor has he our immunity.'

'So you and the others do not fall ill as His Highness does.'

'We are human, sir, although we are said to do Devil's work. There are accidents.'

Sigismondo hummed and nodded, accepting this. He picked up a discarded glove lying across a paper of diagrams on the table. 'You have to remember to protect yourselves at all times.' The glove was worn through, even more scarred than the ones Brother Ambrogio had taken off the Prince's hands. It retained a scrap of former elegance, an arabesque of stitching on the back, that argued this had belonged to the Prince too.

The alchemist's laugh was more of a bark. 'His Highness can forget to change his gloves, but now he usually wears them. A bad burn taught him.' He moved towards Sigismondo, pausing to watch an assistant pour something from a glass flagon into the liquid in a crucible warming over a charcoal firepot. Sigismondo came forward, and crouched to watch the liquid turn dramatically from purple to red.

'You are interested in the science, sir?' The alchemist paused, his hands clasped behind him, and raised a speculative eyebrow at Sigismondo. His tone held a mild degree of sarcasm.

'I know it is a mystery and that the terms you use mean more than one thing.'

The alchemist shot out a hand and drew Sigismondo away from the crucible and the assistant by the sleeve. Under the thud and gasp of the pump, his voice took on urgency. 'What do you know, sir? What terms do you speak of?'

Benno, pinching his nose to suppress more sneezes, edged up behind the alchemist, although he did not expect to understand.

Sigismondo looked faintly surprised. 'Why, that the Philosopher's Stone is a symbol for what all wise men seek, self-knowledge. That the purifying by fire, the formation by pressure, is the physical manifestation of what the spirit must endure if the essence it seeks, the pure gold that is its true nature, is to be created.'

The alchemist nodded sharply. 'You know. But do you know also—' and he spoke words in a language incomprehensible to Benno '—as it is in Heaven, so on earth. If the pure gold of the spirit is indeed to be found, it will be echoed in this world by material gold. Is it not so?' He had come close and was looking up into Sigismondo's face, as though for reassurance. Sigismondo looked down gravely.

'Have you found it so, Doctor Virgilio? You have made gold?'

The alchemist drew back, and his eyelids narrowed. 'The Prince has told you so?'

'His Highness and I have not discussed the matter. If you have made gold, Doctor Virgilio,' continued Sigismondo smoothly, 'then you are of infinite value to any who employ you. Before the Prince of Viverra became your patron, who was fortunate enough to enjoy your services?'

The black eyes stared unflinchingly into Sigismondo's.

'My former master,' said Virgilio with clipped clarity, 'was Rodrigo, Count Landucci.'

11. Taking Your Eyes Off Something Can Make It Disappear

The city of Viverra was agitated as an anthill after the sermon of Brother Ambrogio that noontide. Those who had heard it were altered by the experience. Most felt that they should do something towards leading a better life; the immediate difficulty lay in deciding what a better life involved.

Quite a few considered that people in general, and neighbours and family in particular, should accept their obligation to behave in a more Christian manner. Indignation and high words followed when they discovered that their neighbours and family expected this obligation to start with them.

Some had been impressed enough to decide of their own accord to sacrifice vanities. False hair, face washes, ribbons, rouge, various pieces of padding, and jewellery and fine clothes were taken from chests and cupboards and put aside to offer on the next bonfire – for they had been promised more bonfires.

The more devout, alarmed by the preacher's threat that the Prince was damaging their chances of Heaven by his meddling in the Devil's arts, speculated on the chance of a royal conversion, and the less devout laid bets on it. Not a great deal was generally understood about the nature of the Prince's pastimes, but now it had been made clear that they were infernally inspired and moreover were not, comfortably and simply, his own affair.

People who as a rule made their living out of the failings of others, such as the sellers of false hair, ribbons, musical instruments, brocades and fine cloth, and the innkeepers, wine merchants, card sharpers and brothel owners, were cautiously reluctant to welcome Christ as the ruler of their city, rather than the Prince. They had doubts about the relative tolerance of the two rulers. The more sage and worldly wise among them believed it was only a matter of waiting it out. Brother Ambrogio would move on to other cities and new congregations, and customers would return, doubtless with appetites refreshed from having been denied.

Some citizens, whether or not they had attended the sermon, were prepared to spend the evening in their usual way, unhampered by thoughts of the next life when this one was still requiring attention. The young prince, satisfied that his father was having no more than one of his usual attacks, arranged with his friend Donato to visit a house of assignation on the riverbank just below the walls of Viverra. In time gone by, the river had swept against the living rock on which Viverra's walls were built, but the river's outward curve and the heavy degree of silt it carried had combined to make an alluvial bank below the rock, and in slow succession graziers, market gardeners, cottagers, a smith, a baker, watermen, a chapel and a brothel had arrived.

The brothel was not one the friends had patronised until now, but its reputation was excellent – if that was the right word – and they were expecting to enjoy themselves. The effect of the wine they had drunk during and after their return from hunting was wearing off now, towards evening. The prince in particular felt himself to have been unfairly sobered by having his father collapse at his feet, so they set about remedying this, which in turn led to a friendly argument about who was likely to engage the attentions of the prettiest girl.

Donato asserted that the prince had only to appear in his fine clothes, be recognised by his red hair, and get preference over anyone regardless of their natural attractions. Prince Francesco denied it, laughed, drank more and ordered his page to change his clothes. He would wear Donato's, Donato should wear his, he would put his betraying red hair under a cap. They would see who got the prettiest! Their pages, changing their masters' clothes for at least the third time that day, did not show by the slightest expression that the prettiest girl in a whorehouse would go to the one who could afford the best, which was the prince. Any madam would see to that.

The groom who looked after Donato Landucci's horses heard from his page that there was more work ahead of him. After rubbing down and feeding those that had been on the hunt, he had now to saddle up another and ride out of the city that night, and no doubt catch an ague waiting by the river. He grumbled to his mate, Prince Francesco's groom; to Ladro, the prince's huge bodyguard; and to the girl he was angling after, pretty Bonaventura who was a palace seamstress.

As a direct result of his grumbles, three men in Viverra made hasty plans of their own. Funds were the first item discussed, as at least two members of the trio had not the least idea in the world of economy and their leader had been having his work cut out restraining their expenditure on wine and women, and this though they were perfectly happy with the cheapest of both, and though Fracassa, who was good looking in a rather awful way if you could see under his hair, often got his women, like Bonaventura, free; but the two were aware there was money, which meant they could spend it. Recent extra expenses had cut into the purse, and Aldo made a point of driving a hard bargain with the owner of the boat they went to hire. In fact they paid, having not hired a boat in the city before, the full value – the owner, having looked them over, concluded they were the sort of villains likely not to bring the boat back at all, even if they were not fools enough to sink it. Luckily they had no need to hire horses as well, their destination being so close to the city gates. Aldo insisted that Fracassa stay with the boat, though he did not give his reason: a fear that Fracassa would be somehow tempted during the first part of their plan into using his sword, a weapon even more formidable to his friends than to his foes.

As dusk fell, therefore, the young prince in Donato's clothes, under a cloak much less elaborately embroidered than his own, which was on Donato's back, made his way accompanied by his bodyguard, his friend and their grooms, out of Viverra. He saw no need to tell anyone where he was going. It was true that he had listened to warnings from his mother, his grandmother and his tutor that his father had enemies, any of whom would be delighted to kill him. The only enemy of his father whom he had ever met, or at least the son of such an enemy, was the young man of his own age who had become his best friend, preferred above the young men about court who were his official companions. Besides, he was not really very anxious that those who might criticise his behaviour should know that, while his father lay ill, he proposed to amuse himself in a brothel. It was not as heartless as it might seem, he told himself, for if he were to go into sackcloth and ashes every time his father fell harmlessly ill, there would be no fun left. And there was no need to worry. Ladro was a giant, of immense strength. He was sensibly taking Ladro along.

Donato, not quite as drunk as Prince Francesco, having a stronger head as well as a tougher physique, was delighted with this opportunity to play the prince. A hostage is constantly reminded of the powerlessness of his situation; once he has given his word of honour that he will not abscond, he is treated like a guest, which is not, all the same, like being treated as a prince in his own home. He was a proud young man living among his father's enemies, his father mentioned only in whispers and behind his back, and with smiles because his ambition to conquer Viverra had been so ignominiously crushed. Donato could not look forward to the arrival of Gatta. It was because of Gatta that he was a hostage, because of Gatta that his father was not by now Prince of Viverra.

Tonight at least, acting the prince, he had every intention of forgetting what the future might hold.

The future had cached a few surprises for both of them up its sleeve.

The first was not plain to them at the time. As their pages had known, the madam of the house, with a nose as keen for money as a pig's for truffles, was not for a moment deceived by Donato's clothes or by Francesco's air of meekness compared to his friend's swagger. She allotted her prettiest and most skilful girl to the pale, beautiful young man with the cap that hid his hair, and soothed the splendidly dressed one with compliments, the best wine, and the next best girl. She had noticed at once that the huge man who accompanied them as bodyguard kept his eye on one of the pair alone. It was a factor the young men had never considered, as neither of them had ever looked at Ladro. She smiled, flattered, and knew that gentlemen may have their jokes, may dress up as they please, but you don't guard the unimportant.

Prince Francesco got the best room, too.

He was deliciously entwined there barely twenty minutes later, and his cap in danger of being removed, when there came a scratching at the door. He was annoyed, firstly; then he thought he might have forgotten to tip somebody, or they were bringing more wine. These expeditions in disguise created more problems than a prince normally had to contend with. The message that reached him, however, hoarsely whispered through the cracked boards, made him start from his embrace and get to his feet by the door, rapidly doing up his clothes.

'. . . Message outside, sir. Come from your father, I think he said; or about your father.'

The prince was galvanised. A bucket of water in the face could not have sobered him so fast. His father was dying. The night he himself leaves the city and visits a brothel his father chooses to die. He did not wonder how he had been found. His household, in such an emergency, would of course betray where he was. He must in a moment tell Donato, but meanwhile he hurried to the outer door, where he understood the messenger to be waiting, while the inn servant ran off in answer to a shout for wine. Francesco passed the madam, who was receiving new customers and had no eyes to spare for the young man going outside, probably to relieve himself. He had already paid, anyway, she had seen to that. Ladro, whose proper business it was to keep an eye on the young prince, had both eyes on something else, a girl whose bosom was as out of proportion as it was out of her dress. The grooms were in the shed called a stable, playing morosely at dice.

So that when the young prince stepped outside into the moist dusk of the river bank, there was no one there to protect him from what happened.

What happened was rapid. One man pinioned his arms, the other thrust a sack over his head and down to his elbows. The sack had once held flour and some immediately found its way up his nose. Blinded, he bent forward in an overwhelming sneeze. A noise was the last thing the pair with the sack needed and, more inspired than prudent, the second man headbutted the prince in mid-sneeeze as he swung forward. Pio was used to being told he had nothing but wood between his ears, and the effect of his action proved it to him. The prisoner sagged to the ground in his sack at once.

'Idiot!' Aldo hissed, his face contorted in exasperation. 'I didn't say *hit* him. Suppose you've killed him?'

Pio, himself dazed by his blow, looked vacant. Aldo bent and, his hands under the victim's armpits, frantically urged Pio, 'Take the legs! Come *on*! To the boat!' He was ridden by the image of Fracassa alone in a boat. The possibilities for disaster were unlimited.

When they got to the end of the wooden jetty, however, the prisoner limp between them, the boat was in the appointed place, and nothing had happened to it or Fracassa. He had put his sword on the deck at his feet, as its weight on his back had all but pulled him into the water when he handled the pole. They got the prisoner into the boat and laid him down, adjuring each other to make less noise. Fracassa managed to push off from the jetty without sinking them. There was no sound of discovery or pursuit from the shore. They were doing well.

All the same, Fate was being generous with surprises that night, and they were not to be denied their share.

They had got clear of the towering shadow of Viverra's walls and were fairly off down stream, by the light of a young moon. The chill of the night breeze stirred the reeds into suspicious rustles and brought the damp smell of mud and decaying vegetation. Aldo had been chafing at their slow progress; now he had time to think of their prisoner's comfort and safety.

'Get the sack off. He could choke.' His voice rose suddenly from a sharp whisper to a sub-shriek as he remembered Pio's nutting. 'He could be *dead*.' He tore at the fastening of the sack, ripped a nail, swore, and with Pio's help dragged the sack away. With it came the prisoner's cap, and the long hair spilled out, dark in the moonlight but unmistakably straight. Aldo and Pio stared at the face, the eyes still shut and the features obligingly defined by the pale rays from above. Fracassa stopped poling, and leant forward to see.

The reaction of all three was, after that one moment, immediate. Aldo snatched up the discarded sack and he and Pio, without exchanging a word, rammed it down again over the prisoner's head. Fracassa stepped back in alarm and lost the pole.

They drifted to the bank a mile downstream. Aldo and Pio between them heaved the prisoner on to dry land after Aldo had prudently relieved him of several objects. Fracassa had been scrabbling on hands and knees and nearly knocked his sword into the water as well, and now located the spare pole. He thrust off from the shore and they were away.

Back at the house of ill fame, the girl abandoned by the prince had fallen asleep waiting for his return. Wine and exertion had overcome Donato, who also slept. It was not until dawn that Ladro, roused from the sumptuous bosom of his girl to escort the young gentlemen back to the city, discovered like a conjurer's audience that taking your eyes off something can make it disappear.

12. The Palace Sleeps, or Doesn't

While the young prince was having more of an adventure than he had bargained for, the city slept as peacefully as it could. Many were experiencing the pain, like spiritual gout or chilblain, of awakened consciences, and lay weighing up the enticements of this world against the appalling price exacted for them in the next.

Their Prince was rumoured to be at death's door. This time Death might open it and usher him very possibly to the torments of Hell. It made many think of their own end and, although none of them could be accused of indulging in alchemy, everyone had been guilty of something or other. There was the additional chance that Brother Ambrogio was right, that their Prince's sins would be visited on their own heads. Some felt indignant that the Church had not made any fuss about this before, and others were indignant that Brother Ambrogio was making an issue of it now. If the preacher were right, it might have been better for everyone's souls if Count Landucci had conquered Viverra last year or Antonio Carlotti this, since neither of them was known to be an alchemist. Gatta, who had been seen as the hand of God protecting Prince Scipione from his enemies, now looked like the Devil's instrument making sure he continued to burden his subjects' souls with his wicked sacrilege. There were probably not more than six among the hundreds of Viverrans who knew what alchemy was, but the whole city was aware tonight that it was ungodly and could damn them all. One or two muttered that, in saying Masses in gratitude for the Prince's past recoveries, they had been addressing them to the wrong source; Satan surely had the greater interest in the Prince's continued rule.

Prince Scipione, too ill to know, or care, whether he had his subjects' prayers, was being conscientiously tended by his physician. His inflamed eyes had been treated with an infusion of marshmallow, recommended by both Pliny and Dioscorides as a demulcent and emollient. The same herb, for the same reasons, was used as medicine for the Prince's cough, his throat being as irritated as his eyes. Although the doctor could have continued the use of marshmallow for the Prince's griping flux, or comfrey which his own master had prescribed in such a case, he preferred a decoction of cinquefoil, since it was customary to flavour it with sugar or honey, and the Prince, with his sweet tooth, was more willing to receive the medicine as a result. Honey could also be added to the infusion of sage he was administering for the Prince's headache. Then there was oil of agrimony for the Prince's hands, which the removal of his gloves had shown to be worse afflicted than the doctor had ever seen them. However, his masterstroke was, he considered, the infusion of angelica root, *archangelica officianalis* which, as he remarked to his assistant, would not only serve to eliminate the toxins in the patient's body but also be a sovereign remedy, by its nature, against the Powers of Darkness which must have made their entry with the alchemical fumes.

The Princess, visiting the Prince's bedside before she retired to sleep, found that he had been made as comfortable as possible. The doctor himself, with cushions at his back in a chair drawn up to the bedside, had prepared himself to watch all night by his patient; his assistant was busy preparing some mixture with a pungent but not unpleasant smell, in a little long-handled pot over the fire in the great chimney. The fire had been lit, although the night was not cold, to drive out night dews which might be harmful in a sickroom. Princess

Isotta stood looking down at the pale face, and at the crooked mouth which tried to smile at her though the Prince was obviously too weak to reply to her enquiries.

'All is in the hands of God, your Highness.' The physician did not add, *also in mine which gives us hope*. 'The Prince is already quieter and free from purging, his illness follows its usual course and we must pray that rest, and the remedies I am applying, will restore his Highness to his former health.'

The Princess did not reply. Her husband's former health had never, even at the best times, been robust. She might be wondering if at last she were to be a widow; if there were to be two Princesses Dowager and, more importantly, if her son would be responsible or strong enough to keep Viverra against his father's enemies who would become his own.

Gatta was riding toward Viverra. Would the temptation be too great?

Before she left, she bent and kissed the Prince's cheek, sweeping the embroidered sheets with the dark red ringlets that hung before her ears. Then beckoning her lady-in-waiting who stood near the door, she took from her a little woven box tied with ribbons and, regardless of what other objects she displaced, set it down on the chest by the bed next to a jar of leeches. The doctor bowed as she swept out. He waited a minute before he investigated the contents of the box. Comfits! He might have known. Of course it was a charming and kindly gesture but, as he explained to his assistant, quite mistaken. Prince Scipione must have only the lightest and most regulated of diets until the poisons had left his body. His sweet tooth, so indulged by his wife, must be satisfied by the honey added to his medicaments.

Then the Prince's mother came to see her son. Her visit was carefully timed to succeed that of the Princess Isotta, pages reporting when that lady had returned to her rooms. The Princess Elena had no intention of sharing her son with his wife, nor did she want interference when she was questioning the doctor. She was still anxious about the final outcome, for every one of these attacks must weaken an already feeble constitution. What trouble she had had in rearing him! Yet what comfort in the knowledge that his spiritual as well as his physical health was now being attended to! It was an inspiration direct from God to invite Brother Ambrogio to Viverra, to the palace, to see if he could not turn her son away from the infernal pursuits which were endangering his soul and his State.

Not having heard Brother Ambrogio's sermon earlier that day in the square, she was not aware that he had already increased that danger by representing her son to his subjects as a liability.

She tenderly stroked his forehead, and her hand encountered the stickiness of the holy oil. Bishop Ugolino had given her son the Last Rites . . . If this night should carry him from the world, surely it must therefore be to a better one. He would have made an act of penitence and be in a state of grace if that act were sincere; and if it was sincere he would, if he recovered, give up this wicked alchemy for ever.

It was her own fault. He had inherited her nature, which she had even encouraged in him. Always she had been inquisitive, always wanting to know the reason for things. Many times she had been scolded by her nurse, her governess, her mother, for watching people at their work and asking questions unbefitting a princess. The proper thing to do was to glide through it all thinking of nothing but oneself, like her beautiful daughter-in-law.

Princess Elena made an angry little face at the thought and turned. The doctor stood attentively in front of his inviting chair, and she picked up one by one all the objects and bottles and boxes laid out on the bedside chest, and enquired in minute detail as to their use and how likely they were to be wanted tonight. She stood for a while watching her son asleep. She knelt and prayed, attempting with no more than her usual success to put everything, in faith and true resignation, into the hands of God; and then she left the exhausted doctor to his patient and retired to rest.

Gradually the palace slept, although others beside the doctor were awake. Brother Ambrogio had found his way to the chapel and was praying before the altar, the light of the vigil lamp warmly gilding his haggard face. Two priests, by command of the Princess Dowager, were kneeling in constant prayer for the Prince's recovery, and from time to time they risked a glance at the preacher, envying his power of saintly absorption.

The younger friar, Brother Columba, a little downcast at his experience in the laboratory, about which he felt it best to keep silent to Brother Ambrogio, knelt back in the shadows. He felt he might have trespassed upon territory earmarked for later and more public cleansing. He accused himself of pride, and had deliberately hauled up his robe clear of his knees. The unyielding marble was very cold, and as he tried to offer the pain in expiation of sin, he also felt satisfaction that the alchemist, when he died and realised himself to be in the Devil's power, would know misery beside which this fleeting penance was a paradise.

The alchemist was also in the thoughts of Sigismondo and Benno. The Prince's steward had found them a tiny room at the far end of the servants' quarters, where from the window they could see the lights burning in the tower rooms of the old castle across the park.

'Is he poisoning the Prince?' Benno was still chewing on a piece of cake he had pocketed from the food provided by the steward. It was a Sienese speciality, Sigismondo said, and was rich in fruit and spices, and his opinion of the Sienese rose with every mouthful. 'Doctor Virgilio? If he worked for Count Landucci, could he still be working for him in secret? He said the Prince forgets to come away from the fumes. Couldn't he just not tell him? Or make some really bad fumes just for him?'

Sigismondo did not answer for a while and Benno thought he had asked too direct a question and would get no answer. Finally Sigismondo turned from the narrow window saying, 'Put the shutter up. It was Prince Scipione who took

Doctor Virgilio from the Count, the Prince who offered him money to work for him instead. A man like Doctor Virgilio is apt to have only one loyalty – to his search for truth.'

Benno sucked his fingers lengthily, while Biondello at his feet gazed up with mistaken hope. He was a dog with a long wait before him until he got to Siena and had a chance to eat *panforte*. 'You really think he's looking for this stone, then. I thought he could be a fake. But he got all worked up when you said you understood his terms and so on. Isn't he just looking for the stone so he can make gold? I mean that's not mysterious, it's only magic.'

Sigismondo laughed. 'As simple as that. Don't forget it's called the Philosopher's Stone. You heard us say that the search for the material, physical substance is paralleled by that for the spiritual.' He relented at Benno's sudden look of vacancy. 'You look for gold, you find it in man as well.'

Benno's face cleared. He thought. 'You mean the Prince isn't messing about with devils at all? He's trying to be *good*?'

'Mm'mm . . . I don't think we can say for sure what Prince Scipione's motives are. The only thing we do know with certainty is that the two of them are fascinated by what they're doing and that the Prince would be glad of a lot more gold. And now we are going to sleep.' Sigismondo rolled over on the pallet, adjusted his cloak round him, and closed his eyes. Biondello, taking the command to himself, obediently jumped up beside him, circled, and snuggled down, laying his head across Sigismondo's thigh and rolling his eyes towards Benno before puffing a little sigh and following Sigismondo's example.

Benno realised he was no wiser about who was poisoning the Prince than he had been before. He put out the candle and curled up on the floor, accepting Biondello's wise choice in preferring to be off it. If someone were poisoning the Prince, Sigismondo would find out, perhaps in time to stop the Prince dying if he was lucky. Soon, Benno slept.

In a room only a little larger than theirs, though with a high ceiling and far more crowded with its curtained bed and bedside chest – itself filled and crowded with possessions – slept Ginevra Matarazza. A silken bedspread was drawn up to the white shoulders, golden curls lay on the tasselled pillow, thick lashes rested on her cheek, her mouth was parted in as delicious a pout as any she achieved when awake. One hand beside her face had relaxed its grip and the sapphire set in its star of diamonds glittered in the night light. The salve Sigismondo had applied to the monkey's bite had left a stain on the sheet, the marks on her hand still looked raw and inflamed. The monkey, long ago forgiven and kissed, slept at the foot of the bed, his chain rattling faintly as he twitched. The parakeet had its head under its wing. All this anyone who looked in at the door might have seen; invisible to view was what lay under the tasselled pillow. Ginevra's latest acquisition was, like the brooch sent by Gatta, too recent to be relegated yet to her store of treasures in the chest: a pair of gold-embroidered gloves, of the finest doeskin, gold-fringed, scented with sandalwood and musk. With the perfume of these stealing into her nostrils as she slept, Ginevra wandered happily in her dreams, being decked by the returning Gatta in a rainbow of jewels.

13. "She's Dead!"

Of all the people who slept in the palace that night, not one was destined to sleep much beyond dawn. That was the time that Donato arrived and sent a message to the Princess that her son was missing. His distress when she admitted him to her presence was such that he was very nearly unable to appreciate the unusual vision of the Princess dishevelled. Her disarray was so exquisite in his eyes as to have as much effect as careful adornment in any other. With dark red hair in thick twin braids on her bare shoulders, the linen sheet held to her bosom with one hand, she presented a picture that stirred Donato for all his anxiety and fear. She, for once, had no care whatever about how she looked.

'Vanished? *Outside the city*? Where was Ladro? Did you not think of his enemies?' She stopped, and he saw from her eyes the recollection that she was speaking to the son of one of them. 'Why are you in his clothes?'

'It was a joke . . .' This was not the time to explain nor was there need, the two young men being known for their jokes. The Princess did not bother to ask any more about yet another foolish escapade. Her son must be found. He could be abducted, held to ransom, murdered—

She sent for the captain of the palace guard. Horses were saddled, men sent clattering through the streets in the half-light to go out and scour the countryside for tracks, traces, to

93

arrest everyone at the brothel, to question all dwellers on the river bank. The corridors of the palace and the public rooms soon filled with incompletely dressed gossiping courtiers and servants. The Princess Dowager came to see her daughter-in-law, swathed in blue linen damask with sable at the hems.

'Why am I the last to be informed?' For comfort, the Princess Elena held, pressed to her bosom, a small elderly lapdog whose indignant eyes stared out from an arrangement of little grey pouches, a mirror of the face above. 'What measures are being taken? My son must not be told. It would kill him.'

She managed to give the impression that the Princess Isotta was only waiting to run and deliver the fatal news. The agitated Donato had gone to his rooms and the Princess was dressing. Another thought roused the Princess Dowager and she glared over the dog's head. 'How do you know that boy has told the truth? What if he bribed Ladro – what a useless lump that man is – and poor Francesco is at this moment being taken to Landucci? Have you thought of *that*?'

'Why, in that case, would Donato have come back to tell us? He'd be on his way to his father too, not returning here to be hostage still for Landucci's behaviour. I had, naturally, thought of that.' She gave her mother-in-law one of her famous enigmatic smiles, which drove the Dowager back to her own rooms, though on the way she stopped to look in at her son, check that he had not been told, and interrogate the doctor minutely. Prince Scipione had passed a good night with the help of a little valerian, and was able to smile at his mother and ask what the commotion was. That she burst into tears and then bravely wiped them away and smiled, he luckily ascribed to her relief in seeing him better. He lay with the peaceful sensations of convalescence – one of the most pleasant of human conditions – listening to the birds outside in the gardens, and the more distant first sounds of the awakening city. That his mother had come to see him so early, he ascribed to how ill he had been, and he put his hands

94

together and gave thanks for being so much better. God had been good to him. Perhaps He had listened to the prayers of that burning-eyed friar who had swept in last night and, he vaguely remembered, had held his hands together as he held them now. It might be his luck was turning. His subject lords would cease to rebel against him. He might find the Philosopher's Stone.

By the time Princess Isotta was dressed she had thought over the situation. The disappearance of her son was an emergency calling for someone of the standing and experience of Gatta. Her husband's councillors and courtiers were useless in such a business. Gatta, daily expected, had not arrived, but there came to mind that other man who had experience in helping the great with their problems and who was not far to seek.

Sigismondo, roused by the disturbance in the palace, had just finished the extensive and tricky operation of shaving when the Princess's page arrived. Benno had combed his beard with his fingers, and had his second best tunic on, in honour of the palace, and thought he would try his luck at getting close to the Princess Isotta once more, having found in his whole life nothing more worth gaping at. He picked up Sigismondo's gold-braided short cloak, officiously draped it over his shoulder and arm, as a serving page might do, and followed his master.

'What is your counsel on this?' The Princess Isotta, surveying the man before her, felt inexplicably less desperate; her outward calm became a little easier to sustain. If her son had not already been killed – and he was surely too valuable a pawn in the game of power to be thrown away so lightly – then this quiet listener was certainly the man to get Francesco back.

'Your Highness is already doing all that can be done. As Count Landucci's son has returned then, I agree, it is unlikely his men have taken Prince Francesco. With your permission, Highness—'

He took his leave. There was no point in questioning the

95

Count Donato further about the exchanged clothes, a disturbing element until events should reveal themselves. Sigismondo, hired by both Prince and Princess of Viverra, unbeknown to each other and for different tasks, set about the immediate one. Gatta had put it out of his power to spy on his intentions for the moment, so he could bend his energies to working for the Princess.

He heard in the guardroom that a boat had been hired by a stranger last night for, the boatman understood, romantic purposes. Sigismondo sat his horse outside the palace for a moment as if sensing the magnetic forces in the air, and then set off. It was Sigismondo who, a mile out of the city, stopped a cart jolting slowly towards the gates and woke the young man curled up asleep half under the sacking that covered onions in the back. The peasant driving his oxen had not the slightest idea of the importance of his passenger, who had been too ashamed both of his state and how he had arrived at it, to admit his identity. It was as well, for he would scarcely have been believed. The young prince blinking up at Sigismondo looked exactly like someone who has been butted on the forehead, half suffocated (twice), been thrown on stones, fallen in river mud and been beaten quite severely about the head and shoulders. All of this had happened.

When he had been dumped in haste from the boat, the sack still on his head and shoulders, he had fallen on mud and stones, half concussed and struggling to breathe while he tried to extricate himself from the sack whose strings gripped just above his elbows and seemed to have no knot.

Washerwomen came down at dawn with their baskets of dirty clothes to wash in the shallows and beat on the stones. They saw in the half-light and the wreathing river mist something like a living boulder rise up from the bank at their feet, a thing with a monstrous head, peaked at the sides like a demon's ears, lunging at them with uncouth noises, flapping and clawing with short clumsy arms. Most of them ran, shrieking. Brother Ambrogio, whose sermon they had all at least heard of, had frightened the devils out of Viverra but not far enough. One, more courageous, stayed long enough to set about the devil with the paddle she beat clothes with. Then she ran off screaming at her own temerity.

When he finally freed himself from the sack, the young prince was feeling far too ill to draw attention to himself or to demand help. After lying sprawled on the stones, he had crawled up the bank and lain for a time, breathing deeply, in mud which was very cooling to his bruises. The world was still showing a tendency to move round him and slip down behind his right shoulder, and he lost consciousness for a while. During this time, the palace guard was searching for him and two soldiers had interrogated the owner of a hut and a pig further up the bank, but they did not examine the shore for unmoving objects that by now blended with their surroundings. Had they been able to interrogate the pig, they might have got a more helpful answer, for that animal, trailing a long tether from its off hindleg, and ever curious in its quest for food, had wandered down to the bank and stuck its snout enquiringly into the young man's ear. It was probably this stimulus that shortly enabled him to regain his wits, and stagger as far as the road and the passing cart.

'He's yours, is he?' said the carter. 'I let him up because there's nothing in there he can spoil. Oh – thanks to your honour. Made a mess of his good clothes, he has, and drunk as a lord.'

The young prince was in no condition to ride a horse, and since he was patently content to lie in the cart, as was shown by his lapsing back on the onions and closing his eyes, Sigismondo adopted this discreet method of returning the young man to the palace. The prince became aware of their entrance under the city gate, where the echo of hooves and feet and voices under the archway roused him, for he stirred, became alarmed and besought Sigismondo confusedly that a Lady Lucia should not see him in this state. Sigismondo had not intended that anyone should see him; at a side door of the palace he hauled him from the onions and got him in, a little muffled in Sigismondo's cloak and then, the need for discretion being almost at an end, carried him to his own room, so that his pages might improve his appearance before his mother, to whom Sigismondo now reported, should see him.

The Princess Isotta was not anxious to know the squalid details of how and where her son had been found. Her relief at his return was mingled with anger born of the anxiety he had caused.

'Why does he never listen? He takes nothing seriously. He and Donato Landucci are like children together.'

The complaint was that of all parents since Adam looked at Cain and Abel, but these were modern times. Once the nurse no longer sewed leading strings on their clothes, children were dressed as adults and looked to adulthood as a time of real freedom. A young man of seventeen like Prince Francesco could have been leading armies for the last four years or so. The Princess had something to complain of.

'Your Highness, he will find his place some day.' Sigismondo's deep voice was confident. Of course, it was true. Everyone found such a place, even if it was the gutter – not so far from a cartload of onions. Nevertheless, the Princess was comforted and only a short while later, after she had given Sigismondo her hand to kiss, and a ring of pearls from her finger as recompense for his trouble and his discretion, she was able to regard with equanimity her damaged son presenting himself in her chamber. Below the dark red hair, the bruise on his brow dealt by Pio the bonehead was taking on hues of deepening browns and purples on the fair skin. The blood from his scalp wound had been carefully washed away, and salves applied by the doctor called from the father to tend the son. All the same, in spite of fresh clothes and restorative cups of wine, he was not looking well. The Princess's maternal feelings for once evinced themselves openly.

'What did they do to you?' She embraced him, and lifted the hair from his most visible bruise. 'Did you get a good look at them?'

98

'They put a damned sack over my head.' The prince, not unnaturally, was indignant. 'I couldn't see a thing.'

'And before they put the sack on, Highness,' Sigismondo's voice slid into the exchange too diplomatically for either of them to feel it an intrusion, 'was it quite dark?'

Prince Francesco considered. 'One of them seemed to loom over me, that's all I saw. Then I was pulled round and this *sack*,' his voice took on disgust, 'came over my head. Then I was hit.' His finger gingerly stopped short of the bruise. 'They took the sack off later, or I think they did, on the boat – I was giddy but I think it was a boat. I could hear boat noises: water and creaking. I'd passed out, I think, when they took it off, and I was just coming round, and they put it back on.' He extended his hands, palm down. 'All my rings are gone, and my purse and neck chain. Donato brought back my hat with the brooch, though.'

'So it was robbery after all.' The Princess, relieved, sat back in her chair. 'Ladro shall be flogged for this. Why was he not at your side?'

The prince flung up his head, conscious of his share of the blame. 'I shan't give you such cause for grief again, madam,' he announced grandly; and he might have gone on to make further and rasher promises if he had not been interrupted. One of the Princess's ladies ran in, squealing as though chased by rats.

'Your Highness! Oh forgive me, your Highness! It's Ginevra Matarazza. I went to call her for duty because she hadn't come, and *she's dead*!'

14. In Search of Truth

The Princess rose to her feet, the young prince stared, Sigismondo acted. He was by the weeping, trembling girl's side, an arm round her shoulder. He looked across at the Princess.

'By your leave, Highness, this should not be noised abroad.' He did not add: Gatta is returning; what involves his mistress involves too much else; keeping Gatta sweet must be a first concern of those who employ him. 'May I go and see what is to be done?'

Permission was instant. The Princess knew at once how delicate the matter was, and as women in the anteroom who had caught something of the news began to raise their voices, she was at the communicating door at once and forbade their rush to Ginevra's room.

Sigismondo needed no direction to find Ginevra's room but, when he went in, it was as well he had seen more than a few worse sights. All the same, it was pitiable and he crossed himself as he stood in the doorway. Benno, at his heels, got pushed back and heard the click as Sigismondo bolted the door.

What space there was between him and the bed was strewn with things he had to pick his way over – silks, scarves, ribbons, embroidery, gloves, gauze veils, sleeves, velvets, silk plaits the colour of Ginevra's hair, jewelled collars, earrings. Her treasure chest stood open. She herself, in nothing but a scarf of Persian silk so fine her skin glowed through it, lay face down on the bed. One hand gripped a fistful of the green silk curtains that had been ripped from the tester hooks and drooped in a drunken swag across the pillows. There was vomit on the floor and the brocade cover and the room was pervaded by a stomach-turning smell. There was no sign of the monkey. The parakeet, disturbed, stamped up and down his perch and climbed the bars of his cage in the window. Sigismondo stepped over pieces of a broken hand-mirror. The parakeet let out a squawk which brought the monkey's head peeping from the half-tester above. Two pairs of eyes watched Sigismondo without comprehension as he gently raised Ginevra. She slewed round in his arms, the scarf slithering to the floor like a serpent, and her head fell back. Her eyes stared up at him as if in terror but they did not see. He closed them gently and held them closed for a moment. Ginevra had begun her bad luck for breaking a mirror, in another world than this.

Suddenly a hammering came on the door, followed instantly by a boot crashing against the lock. The door canted inwards, missing Sigismondo and the naked Ginevra by inches, and Gatta stood there, staring.

'Whore!' The parakeet had perfect timing.

Gatta was across the threshold with a dagger in his hand before he picked up the smell, and it stopped him. Sigismondo had laid Ginevra on the bed again, and there was that about him, standing with his hands at his sides and no move in defence, that arrested Gatta too.

'I found her like this. She has been poisoned.'

Gatta slowly put up his dagger in its sheath, looking round. 'Poison . . . ! Has she been robbed?' The disarray suggested it, the empty coffer with treasures scattered, but too many treasures were left on the floor and the bed to argue a successful thief. Sigismondo in respect drew up the brocade bedspread over Ginevra as she sprawled almost voluptuously, hair straying, limbs spread, as if to welcome the warrior from the wars.

'I think not robbed. One of the Princess's women found her like this.'

Gatta crunched across the shards of mirror, caught his foot in a streamer of scarlet silk, tripped, plunged forward and fended himself from falling on his mistress with a fist either side of her head. The heavy face swung abruptly towards Sigismondo, darkening. 'Why was the door locked? What were you doing here alone?'

'The Princess sent me to find out what had happened. I locked the door to keep out gawpers and gossips.' The deep quiet voice was convincing. Gatta came upright and relaxed. He reverted to what Sigismondo had first said.

'Poison. Because of the purging . . . But who would do that to her?' He touched one of the blonde curls that lay across her forehead, gently with one finger. 'She harmed no one. She was a child.' He sank on the bed beside Ginevra and, unexpectedly, gave a loud sob. Tears began to find their way down the lines of his face. 'Just a pretty child, greedy for love.' He twined his fingers in the fair hair. Sigismondo, making his way among the evidence that, if she had been greedy for love, it wasn't the only thing she was greedy for, found the little washbowl and jug on the far side of the bed platform, and occupied himself in cleaning the crust of vomit from her lips and cheek. He crossed her hands on her breast over the rosy brocade, and then paused, turned the hands over and examined them closely. Gatta's head came sharply up.

'You see?' Sigismondo held one of the hands towards him, the one with the monkey bite. It was swollen, not only round the bite but all over, and covered with a rash, oozing and raw. Gatta was going to take the hand to see it better when Sigismondo said swiftly, 'Don't touch!' and put it back on her breast. He bent to the basin and, pouring more water, rinsed his own hands and dried them on the linen towel put out for the woman who would not use it now.

'The poison's on her hands?'

Sigismondo pointed to a pair of gloves, the doeskin,

103

perfumed gloves fringed in gold that had spent the night under Ginevra's pillow and now lay, half inside-out, the discoloured silk lining showing, thrown across the little room. 'On those gloves, I would say.'

'Who would do it?' Gatta had flushed, anger spurred by grief. To have his mistress murdered, quite apart from personal sorrow and the loss of his own convenience, was a blow to his self-esteem. Someone had dared to destroy his known possession. The big shoulders hunched. 'I shall find the one who did this and take him to pieces, slowly.'

For a moment he contemplated this, while spreading her hair on her shoulders. Then his nose wrinkled, he looked round and stood up. 'Her woman must clear up all this. Come with me to the Prince.'

'The Prince may not receive us. He has been close to death.'

Gatta, stepping round the cockeyed sagging door, turned a savagely amused face to Sigismondo following. 'The Prince will see us. He has been as close to death before, as near to losing Viverra.' It was impossible to tell if he referred to the past dangers from Carlotti and Landucci or to a present one from himself; Gatta was confident of an audience with his employer even on his deathbed. If Prince Scipione were to die, of course, Viverra would very likely fall into Gatta's capable hands. Neither the Princess Isotta nor her son were popular in the city, both being considered arrogant; and the Princess's aloofness emphasised in the common people's mind that she was a foreigner from the Veneto.

Gatta's greatest rival for the rule of Viverra might, if Brother Ambrogio had his way, be Christ Himself. It was to be doubted that Gatta envisaged the competition.

Benno had been suffering. When Sigismondo bolted the door he did not take it as a reflection on his ability to repel interruption; he was well aware nobody expected him to stand up against authority. However, it was another matter to see authority in the form of Gatta come striding down the corridor. Benno thought of tapping on the door to warn his master, but in the same moment thought again, and moved off at an unhurried amble, clicking his fingers to Biondello. Nothing could have been more compromising than to be seen signalling Gatta's arrival. There was a useful pillar not far from the door and Benno slid behind it with the skill of an experienced eavesdroppper. When Gatta hammered on the door, Benno did wonder whether he should have tried to give earlier warning by letting Gatta find him outside and shout at him a bit. He reflected that his master was not easily taken by surprise and could talk or fight his way out of anything. He wouldn't be still alive otherwise.

Now, after straining to hear what was said, but not daring to go closer, he was relieved to see both men emerge without any damage done. Sigismondo, who seemed always to sense his whereabouts, looked directly at the pillar and beckoned, while Gatta set off down the corridor towards the royal apartments.

'Get her woman and tell her to have it all cleaned up; then wait for me outside the Prince's chamber.' As Sigismondo strode after Gatta, Benno noticed he was carrying in his belt a pair of very fine doeskin gloves with gold fringe and threadwork. He wondered who could have given him those.

The Venetian Ambassador was visiting Prince Scipione. The doctor's injunction that his Highness was to see no one had been unexpectedly overridden by the Prince himself, who was feeling remarkably better. He was propped up now on bolsters, his face no paler than usual and his eyes certainly brighter. His hair, very fine and unusually glossy for a man in his forties, had been combed neatly and flowed almost to his shoulders under the linen nightcap. He had resisted being bled again and had knocked over the jar of leeches. The doctor, recognising a stage of convalescence, gave way. Alienating the patient was no way to secure his health; princes must be allowed to choose for themselves how ill to be. It was most likely wise not to seem too ill in front of an ambassador – allies had been known to change sides if they believed the power they supported was on the wane.

'I am delighted to see your Highness on the road to recovery.' Nothing could be more keen than the melancholy eyes of the Venetian Ambassador, almost hidden under heavy lids. The Prince, meeting their gaze, was aware that a report of his appearance, and possible relapse, was already composing behind those melancholy eyes. He made an effort to control the twitch of his mouth and managed to turn it into a crooked smile. The Ambassador's voice went mellifluously on, 'I would have presented myself before this to offer my congratulations on the restoration of Mascia. How fortunate is your Highness to command the services of such an eminent and able condotta as that led by Ridolfo Ridolfi.'

The Prince read into this that the Serenissima would be delighted to command Gatta's services themselves, and that they also wondered where he found the resources to pay someone so redoubtable. He made pleasant acknowledgement.

There were many undercurrents here: the Venetian Republic was on notably poor terms with the Pope; the Holy Father was waiting to see if he should replace Prince Scipione with a stronger man to hold the Papal state of Viverra for him; the Venetians were waiting to see if their support for Prince Scipione would manage to disappoint the Pope in his plans for a replacement, but if the Prince went under they would leave him there. At the moment, Gatta's success and present loyalty tipped the scales in Prince Scipione's favour. Gatta, at all costs, must be kept happy.

The eruption of a spectacularly unhappy Gatta into the Prince's bedchamber was enough to give most patients a relapse. The doctor's protest went for nothing so he retired to the far side of the great room where, like Pontius Pilate, he washed his hands of the whole business in a brass basin held by the inferior assistant.

Also like Pontius Pilate, Gatta was in search of truth.

'She's dead! Ginevra is dead! Who has done it?' No

106

factor of morality was involved, everyone knew of the relationship. The Venetian had sent a report to the Republic in which the Lady Matarazza's charms were listed, together with a speculation upon her acquisitiveness and the chance of bribing her to influence Gatta. The Prince pointed out the presence of the Ambassador, and Gatta gave the rough outline of a bow and went on speaking. Both ambassador and prince were absorbed by the account Gatta gave them of his mistress's death.

'But this was a dreadful thing for you to find. It shall be investigated at once. Who discovered her? Did you?'

'One of her Highness's women, I'm told. I found this man with her.' Gatta gestured at Sigismondo, still by the door, who bent his head in acknowledgement. 'He believes she was poisoned by a pair of gloves.' The Venetian Ambassador was shaking his head. Gloves! An old device. The Republic had employed it now and then. A very hit-and-miss method, there had been grave disappointments – and a few successes. This man whom Gatta had found with his dead mistress, what had he been doing there? Among the things to be sure of before he made his report was more about this man. He looked very like a description the Ambassador had received of the agent who saved Rocca for its Duke and who had been active lately in France. Men with shaven heads were not so rare, Michelotto della Casa was one in point; but the Ambassador had taken note of the strong features, the hooked nose, the full yet secretive mouth, and the unmistakeable look of power – the more interesting for being controlled. This was a man to watch.

'A pair of gloves!' The Prince pulled himself up on the pillows, a page racing across the room to help him. He waved the young man away. 'Where are they? Who gave them to her?'

Sigismondo took the doeskin gloves from his belt and showed them. 'I would not advise your Highness to handle them. The poison will be in the lining, of course, but it's well to take care.'

Gatta took the gloves from him, turned them over, flicking at the golden fringe. 'These did not come from just anywhere. They're fit for a prince. They shouldn't be difficult to trace. Can you find who poisoned her?' This was a direct question to Sigismondo, delivered as if no one else was present. 'I will reward you well.'

It did not escape the Venetian Ambassador that Gatta made his request – his demand – without reference to his employer who might be supposed to be the fount of justice in his own principality.

'It may be possible.' Sigismondo guessed that his accent was being analysed by the Ambassador, and knew that no conclusions about it could be made. Italian was one of his many fluent languages and yet, as was evident, it was not his native tongue. The caution of his response appealed to the Ambassador, but not in the least to Gatta, who seized Sigismondo by the front of his jerkin and came close.

'*Find him.*' Some of Gatta's teeth had been broken in past fights, which lent a certain vicious strength to his snarl. Sigismondo's calm did not waver.

'Or her?'

This answer made Gatta slowly release him and step back, looking thoughtful. The idea of some woman jealous of Ginevra's charms and, perhaps, of one particular conquest she had made, was both likely and enhancing to his self-esteem. He nodded. 'Do what you can. His Highness will wish it.'

The Prince did not dispute this estimate of his wishes. He had slipped down a little on his pillows. He was paler, and a line of sweat gleamed under his hair. 'Indeed. I give you full powers. Full powers.' His mouth twitched. The Ambassador wondered if he were to be treated to another attack. It would be a chance to get a full description the physicians at home could use for diagnosis and prognosis of the Prince's condition.

At this point the doctor, who had clamped his spectacles to his nose and watched from where he stood, saw the point

108

had been reached where he must exercise his authority or be blamed should something go wrong. He gathered all his courage and, reminding himself that he held degrees from Salerno and Padua, and that the men here might be able to bring down kingdoms but were helpless before things he understood, advanced.

'His Highness—' He bowed to each, separately and rapidly. '—His Highness must rest.'

A look of profound relief came over the Prince's face. The Ambassador at once, with apologies for taking the Prince's time and strength so unconscionably, withdrew.

'Sigismondo.' The Prince spoke. Sigismondo, going out after Gatta, turned and came back. The doctor, pouring a dose, made no objection. This Sigismondo was the man to soothe his patient: quiet, unobtrusive, with a voice made for the sickroom. He was approaching with the cup when the Prince with surprising vigour ordered him out of earshot. He retreated, holding the cup, to show that he went only under protest.

'Sigismondo . . . those gloves.'

'Highness?'

'Those gloves are mine.'

15. The Next Target?

'These gloves belong to your Highness? There is no doubt?' One does not lightly suggest to a sovereign prince that he could be mistaken.

'The bullion fringe. I remember.' The Prince's hand, in which the tremor was more marked than ever, went to his forehead and brushed at it, as if trying to erase rather than to evoke memory. 'They were in the marquetry box by the door. Where the gloves always are.'

'Who puts them there, your Highness?' The hand was waved fretfully before his face. 'Oh, pages, pages, I suppose. They are for me to wear in the laboratory. They are handed to me, or I pick them up, when I have to discard a pair. Her Highness does not like me to burn and scar my hands.'

Sigismondo leant nearer, his voice audible only to the Prince. 'Her Highness sends the gloves? She has them made for you? She sent these?'

'She makes sure there are always gloves there. It is her custom.' He paused and looked across the room at the doctor, still holding the medicine cup and clearing his throat significantly. 'These were too fine. I did not take them, and wore the old pair. I meant to speak to her . . .'

The implication of his words struck him now. He fixed his gaze on Sigismondo in horror. 'No. No, not her.' His eyes closed. He slid down the pillows as if collapsing in on himself.

Sigismondo at once supported him and looked to the

doctor, who was approaching. 'You must leave, sir. You see his Highness cannot talk.'

Sigismondo left the semi-conscious Prince being clucked over, having a quill put between his teeth to take the medicine he could barely swallow, as ignominiously as any horse given a drench.

Benno stood outside, Biondello safely in his bosom. Although the pretty lady who had snatched his dog was dead, he was taking no more risks carrying Biondello under his arm in this inexplicable place where anyone might take a fancy to him; Benno had been taught a lesson in his own helplessness in such a situation. The dog had grown sturdier since Benno acquired him, though no larger, and it was less convenient to carry him as he used to do, but he must.

He had thought about Biondello's temporary loss being a sign from Heaven that he should sacrifice the dog as his one luxury but, if he were looking at signs from Heaven, then it was also a sign that Biondello had been restored to him and the abductor so terribly punished. No doubt the pretty lady – and Our Lady have mercy on her – had done other things, much worse, to deserve death, but surely helping herself to things not hers had something to do with her fate?

As it happened, Sigismondo agreed with him.

It was time for the noon meal, not a good time for making enquiries anywhere. They left the city by the gate Prince Francesco had used a few hours before in his disguise of onions, and they found a small inn by the waterside, catering mostly for fishermen and river traders. They had an excellent meal of slices of polenta grilled on the open fire, and eels marinated in vinegar, rosemary and garlic. They finished with fritters of mountain chestnuts, and took another flagon of rough wine outside to sit on a bench and stare at the river. Biondello had eaten himself to a standstill on a mash of bread and sausage to which Benno had treated him in thanksgiving and, after sitting at their feet for some somnolent minutes, had scarcely the energy to wander down to the waterside for a drink.

'Mmm . . . she must have stolen the gloves in the confusion when the Prince fell ill. I saw her stumble and knock a box off the shelf. While they were helping her to her feet she must have picked up the gloves and whipped them out of sight, in the folds of her skirt, I dare say.'

'A magpie, like. You should have seen her make off with Biondello. Whipped *him* out of my hands and left me gaping.'

Sigismondo's wide smile showed he appreciated that this might involve no serious change in Benno's expression. 'I think she took what she could when she could. Perhaps many of the treasures in her room were not hers . . . Gatta was her biggest catch. With those gloves she would never have thought she was stealing her death.'

Benno looked solemn. 'I bet it was up to Brother Ambrogio. He told people yesterday that death was waiting for them. Him coming here could have brought it on, right?'

There was no arguing with superstition, and Sigismondo didn't try. Benno had not seen Ginevra's hysteria when the skull peered in at her window. He poured more wine and raised his face to the autumn sun.

'I'm not sure that Brother Ambrogio had much to do with what had been going on in the palace before he came.'

Benno waited – while Sigismondo bent to pick up a stick of frayed wattle lying by the bench and tossed it into the water – to see if this remark would be followed by revelations of what in fact had been going on. All that happened was that Biondello, taking the piece of wattle as an invitation to heroism, launched himself into the river to save the stick's life. Benno risked a direct question.

'Someone's been trying to nobble the Prince for some time, then? Was it his gloves all along?' He scratched his beard ruminatively. 'Then why did the poor lady die straight off and he doesn't?'

'Mm-mm. There could be a number of reasons.'

Biondello toiled up the path, having taken exercise somewhat early after his blow-out on sausage, and laid the stick diplomatically between Benno's battered boots and

Sigismondo's tooled leather. Mission accomplished, he backed a few feet and shook his wool in all directions, including them in the peripheral spray. Sigismondo laughed, and continued, 'She unluckily had an open wound on her hand. It gave the poison a path to her blood—'

'But the Prince's hands are all messy.' Benno was so absorbed that he interrupted. 'Why didn't the poison get to him as quick?'

Sigismondo shrugged. 'I think the Prince has been absorbing poison from somewhere and he's acquired some sort of immunity.'

Benno's jaw dropped. After a moment he said, 'He's *got used to poison*?'

'There was a king in ancient times, by name Mithridates. He knew people would try to poison him to gain the throne and so he prepared himself for survival by dosing himself a little at a time with various poisons. The body can learn to live with dangerous things. It's shock it doesn't like.'

Losing a head for instance, thought Benno. 'But then, if someone's trying to kill him they must be tired of waiting for him to die. *Wouldn't* they get excited each time he collapsed! But what about the fumes? Don't they have anything to do with it?'

'Hey, who knows? I'm not a doctor. One thing I do know, Benno: few things go wrong without at least three reasons. You can get away with a mistake or two and then, pff!' He flicked a finger and blew. 'The next mistake and you're gone. Perhaps the Prince can take so much – and then the fumes make him ill. He always gets better away from the laboratory but then he only wears the gloves he's supplied with *in* the laboratory.'

'Who supplies the gloves, then?'

'He says, his loving wife.'

Benno choked and coughed wine on to the ground. 'The Princess?' He scrubbed his eyes and wiped his beard. 'She's trying to kill him? What for?'

'Hard to say. It would seem to deprive her of position and security.'

114

'Her son would be ruler then, wouldn't he? And she'd be like the old lady. Not much fun. Though she could get another husband pretty fast. And her son doesn't look like he could manage, I mean think of holding his own against people like Gatta. Gatta would have him for dinner.' Benno could see Gatta licking his lips, a large cat after a dish of cream.

'Or the Princess might be the one Gatta would prefer to dine on.'

Benno cogitated. 'You mean he fancies her?' He stared at the river, then turned to Sigismondo. 'Could he have put her up to poisoning the Prince? It'd have made him hopping mad when his lady love got the gloves by mistake.'

'It was a mistake on her part, certainly. But *he* told me to find out who had provided the gloves. Did he think it would be hard to discover?'

Benno studied Sigismondo. Gatta didn't run a successful condotta by making mistakes about men; he couldn't suppose Sigismondo would fail to carry out a task. This partisanship led him to suggest, 'D'you think he thought that if you found out it was the Princess, you wouldn't dare say?' Benno's knowledge of the world had increased since he met Sigismondo, but he had never thought it was a sensible move to accuse the great. It wasn't even safe to know they'd done wrong. You could end up sharing a pit with some snakes and not a lot of time for regrets.

Sigismondo shook his head 'He may not have known where the Lady Ginevra got the gloves. More than one court lady may have been jealous of her catching Gatta as lover . . . It's time to get back to Viverra.' Sigismondo rose, as two men in the ragged sacking tunics of fisherfolk came up towards the inn from their seagoing boat. They carried a dripping creel and smelt of herring, and approached in silence, intent on their thirst. A boy, left on board, watched as his masters went into the inn and the two strangers and the small dog took the path to the city gate. What freedom, to do as you like and not have to worry about anything!

Benno, following Sigismondo, had suddenly started to

worry about something. If his master was known to be investigating the source of the gloves that had killed the Lady Ginevra, would he not be the next target of the poisoner?

16. Paint, Prayers and Problems

Leone Leconti was used to having people watch him paint. It was not a thing that he cared for, but patrons were fond of looking over his shoulder – after kindly ordering him not to stop working – and they would comment to their friends, relatives and admirers on his subject, his treatment of it, his technique and his use of colour. Well informed on the first of these, as they had usually chosen it, they were invariably ignorant about the others, while set on appearing expert.

So he would continue to mix his paints, carefully ground and prepared by his pupil, and apply them while hearing a description of what he was not doing, to the impressed murmurs of his patron's entourage. He had to please, and as he was both a competent painter and, by now, an experienced and sometimes inspired one, he knew he could please. Even patrons who had no taste at all and could not begin to appreciate his gifts were proud to have obtained his services and he received almost as much praise and money as he felt he deserved. He was engaged in a number of commissions for Prince Scipione who, although it was not his major interest, showed discrimination in art; and Leconti was hopeful that the pay would rid him of most of his debts and also enable him to buy the finest suit of clothes the city could provide.

At the moment he had several problems. There were purely technical problems connected with his work, of course, but patience and application should solve them –

except that he despaired of catching the essence of the Princess's beauty.

There was the problem of the Prince's illness. All very well, this talk of attacks having happened before from which the Prince had recovered, but for a little time when Leconti first heard the news he saw his fine suit of clothes disappearing into the distance. He had once worked for a patron who'd died in the middle of having his portrait painted; his successor not only did not want it finished but refused to pay for it *because* it was not finished. This rankled still. It made Leconti nervous. Although reassured that the Prince was indeed better, he yet felt apprehensive that his splendid suit of clothes – already ordered, being stitched with silver braid by a tailor in a back street here – might prove harder to get than he had thought.

This was in his mind because of the man looking over his shoulder, a critical observer. Brother Ambrogio was at least silent, hands clasped before him, examining the work. Leconti had prepared a panel for the final stage of the Princess's portrait.

The central panel of the triptych was already done, and stood against the wall ready for the gilding of the border. The right-hand panel, showing the Prince, was almost finished. The centre panel did, on the whole, satisfy Leconti. The boy miraculously restored to life sat up on his bier, arms raised to St Francis floating above, whose bleeding hands blessed, whose body lay horizontal on the air. Leconti was particularly proud of the way he had dealt with the saint's robes so that they seemed airborne on a divine afflatus. As background he had painstakingly rendered the city square, with the façade of the palace and the cathedral recognisable in every detail, and a few city dignitaries thrown in for a consideration from each one.

The Prince and Princess, as donors of the altarpiece, had their natural places secured for them on the folding leaves either side. Leconti had placed the Princess Dowager, in rose brocade, her grey hair in a net of pearls, in devout rapture at

118

the head of the bier facing the saint. The young Prince Francesco stood behind her, looking out of the picture with an air of indifference, as though miracles were a trifle déclassé and had, in any case, nothing to do with him. The Princess's daughters – he had made a terrible journey in the height of summer to paint the eldest, fifteen years old, at her husband's home – were grouped round him, the two small girls with their eyes fixed on the flying saint as though longing to pick up their skirts and join him in the sky.

'Did you ask God for inspiration before you painted the face of the blessed Saint Francis?' The acute question showed Brother Ambrogio had not missed the likeness to the artist himself. Leconti muttered something ambiguous in reply. It was lucky, at least, that his painting had, by virtue of Prince Scipione's naming his firstborn after the saint, been of St Francis.

Brother Ambrogio was silent. He had swivelled to watch Mario the pupil, a wet rag tied over his nose and mouth, hard at work by the trestle table grinding colours. He swung back, and pointed a skinny finger at the dish of butter-yellow paint on the small table at Leconti's elbow.

'That looks fit to eat. What is it?'

'Orpiment, Father. A Venetian pigment. We use it also in illuminating – with blue, it produces a divine green.'

'All colours are divine, my son.' The reproof was almost absentminded; the preacher bent his head towards the glistening yellow, fascinated, and approached it with his finger as if to dip and taste. Leconti thought he was very likely fasting and was drawn by instinct to something so edible in appearance. He knocked the probing finger aside.

'Don't touch, Father. It's arsenic sulphate. Poison. You'd be reporting to St Peter far sooner than you might want to.'

Brother Ambrogio withdrew his finger and clasped his hands before him again, smiling a little. What a face, thought Leconti as he blended the green tone for flesh on his palate; wish I'd had him for a model when I did that St Anthony for

119

the Duke of Rocca. Those hollow cheeks, sunken burning eyes – and yet the wonderful kindness of that smile! Another St Anthony one day, please, Heaven? I'll ask him if he'd sit for sketches. Someone is sure to want a St Anthony, they're a legitimate way of getting in a few naked women as temptations. That smile would be far more interesting as a sign of true rejection than the usual tortured grimace. If I could get away with it I'd put Princess Isotta's face on one of the naked demons, to pay her for haunting my mind – sinuously writhing, dropping a last veil like Salome before Herod.

He paused in front of the formal, kneeling shape and imposed her figure, stripped in his imagination . . .

Brother Ambrogio might have sensed this heated vision. He suddenly fell on his knees, taking Leconti by surprise, his brush dropping from his hand.

'O most dear Lord!' said Brother Ambrogio in his low, thrilling voice, 'Look down with pity on this man so cumbered with vanities! Purify his mind and heart that the work of his hand may be to Thy glory and not to his. He must use poisons. Let not the poisons of this world bring him in the latter day to the everlasting fires of Hell.'

Brother Ambrogio crossed himself, stood up and, directing at Leconti a smile of singular sweetness, left the room.

While Leconti painted and was prayed for, Sigismondo pursued the matter of the gloves. It was far from diplomatic to ask the Princess if she had tried to poison her husband, and it was necessary to use tact in questioning the pages concerned.

Emilio, a page of the Princess's household, always put the gloves, her gift, in the marquetry box at the door of the Prince's room. Then it became the responsibility of Basilio, page to the Prince, to anticipate when his master was about to visit the laboratory, and bring the gloves from the box. What actually happened, Sigismondo heard, was that usually one couldn't judge when the Prince, a man of impulse who often

did not himself know where he was going next, was about to
visit the alchemist. Basilio and the others had often got it
wrong, running after him with gloves he didn't need, not
providing them when needed. Once panic had prevailed
when the Prince went off across the park and the box was
empty. After a quarter hour of chaos, it was ascertained that
he had helped himself to the last pair.

All the pages to whom Sigismondo showed the gloves
agreed they were far too fine for use in the laboratory. Plain,
strong leather was the rule – fine leather, fit for royal hands –
and no gold stitching or bullion fringe. It was absurd.

'Might there have been confusion with other pairs of his
gloves? These are such as a prince might wear riding, for
instance.'

The page in charge of the Prince's wardrobe looked at
the gloves carefully, Sigismondo keeping them in his grasp.

'They do not belong to his Highness; nor have I seen
them on anyone at court.'

'When his Highness returned from the laboratory and
fell ill, he was wearing gloves. Brother Ambrogio removed
them. Yet there was a pair already in the marquetry box.'

Basilio, the Prince's page, said he had remarked to
Emilio that the Prince's gloves showed signs of wear.

'And so *I* put a fresh pair in the box.'

'*I* would have taken the old pair as usual; and burnt
them.' Basilio wrinkled his nose to register the disgust with
which such objects were destroyed.

'And Emilio gets the new gloves from . . . ?'

'They're delivered every month from a glover in the city.'

Sigismondo, attended by Benno, set out for the glover's.
There were a few of Gatta's men on the streets, bedizened
with loot of Mascia, who hailed Sigismondo as they passed.

The glover was bewailing the altered mood in the city,
and the idea that gloves were a luxury. He was not sure if the
gloves his workshop was producing for the rich of Viverra
would be paid for, although ordered, now that people were
cautious of being seen in finery. There were bands of children

121

and young people roaming the streets – he had heard that they ordered an innkeeper to shut up shop and, when he refused, had wrecked the place and staved in all his barrels.

'They collect what they call *vanities*, sir. I have heard that pairs of my gloves – recognisable by their quality alone – sewn with seed pearls, if your honour would believe – are on that bonfire on the city square.'

The glover was almost too distracted to give his attention to the gloves Sigismondo produced.

'No. Not mine. Not even from this city. That's *Venetian* work.'

17. MICHELOTTO!

Sigismondo and Benno, emerging from the glover's, caught the sound of distant shouting. Gatta's men, roaming the streets in their finery, were looking for drink and girls. They had found shut-up wine shops and barred, silent brothels. Bystanders informed them as they hammered, amazed and indignant, on unresponsive doors, that they need not expect to find occasion for sin in a city declared by Father Ambrogio to be under the rule of Christ.

Some of the soldiers, who had been drinking before they left camp, were sobered by this news. The majority, although they had certainly heard of Christ, were entirely ignorant of Brother Ambrogio. They had been fighting for the Prince of Viverra when they took Mascia, not for Christ. Where had this Brother Imbroglio been when they were spilling their blood for Viverra? What about a bit of gratitude from the citizens they had saved from Carlotti?

'You've damn well been paid for that!'

The ungrateful citizen shouting this earned himself a faceful of pig dung scooped up from the street. This might have made a good start to a riot if the leader of the soldiery, remembering Michelotto's smiling orders to them to keep the peace in the city when he permitted them to leave camp, gripped the dung-flinger by the shoulder and marched him off.

All might yet have been well if they had not met the

posse. Brother Columba was taking full advantage of a leading role in the preacher's campaign now that Brother Ambrogio was engaged at the palace. He had used his considerable energy to recruit the teenage gangs of whom the glover had spoken. They toured the streets, banging on doors and bullying the occupants of houses into surrendering treasured possessions – entering and pointing out what they considered luxuries but which, as most of them came from poorer families than the ones they visited, were old and familiar belongings. Only one or two of the householders courageously threw them out. False hair and, once or twice, real hair as well, had been grabbed, ribbons torn from ladies, especially those at bosoms or lacing bodices. A lute taken by force had been smashed over its owner's head; a card party had seen their cards confiscated and their dice pocketed, and had not dared to protest, such was the city's mood. The city police, the marshal's men, sat tight in their headquarters, and shut the doors. Either it would all blow over, or the Prince would order them out and they would have to take steps of some sort; meanwhile there was wine and cards, perhaps the only packs in the city that were not under threat.

The gangs also stopped people in the street and demanded their jewellery and fine clothes.

Gatta's men had more than a sufficiency of both.

'Give to the Lord!'

A boy of about fifteen whose unusual height and breadth made him a natural leader of the purity gang that accosted the soldiers, held out a confident hand.

'What lord?' It was a genuine question. The soldier had fought for quite a few lords in his time. 'Reckon he owes *us* if he's your prince – hi! You stop that!' A double-linked thin gold chain he had personally lifted from a fat burgher's wife in Mascia was being pulled at. This oaf must be taught a lesson.

The young oaf in question had less than a second to triumph at snatching the chain from the soldier's neck. He was felled by a blow that sent him sprawling into his fellows and scattered their burdens of clothes, hair, cosmetics and cards all round them. A scavenging pig, startled, received a full head of hair between its ears and ran away from itself, ringlets streaming either side of its snout. Stones were thrown, one catching a soldier on the ear and spattering his newly acquired silk doublet with blood. People streamed in from an adjoining square, where they had been listening to one of Brother Columba's inflammatory sermons, ready to fight for their new Prince, Christ, as savagely as any Crusader.

This was what Sigismondo and Benno heard as they went down the dark alley leading from the glover's towards the house Gatta had been given by the Prince, which Gatta was now inspecting. Sigismondo was going to report lack of success so far in tracking the poisoned gloves, for diplomatic reasons suppressing their Venetian provenance, information it was the Prince's right to hear first.

'Shouldn't we see what the shouting is?' Benno asked.

Sigismondo genially shook him by the shoulder. 'There is trouble wherever you may go in the world. You don't have to go after it. If you can't avoid a fight then choose, if you can, what moment to enter it.'

Benno remembered this piece of wisdom quite soon.

Gatta was pleased with the noble proportions of his new house, bought by the Prince when the man who had commissioned it went bankrupt. He received Sigismondo very cordially, and took him into the big reception hall where glaziers were at work still. The high coved ceiling was probably to have been filled with a tangle of mythological beings, but all that floated against the blue empyrean was a solitary eagle.

'So someone meant the gloves for the Prince?' Gatta's enemies were, after all, the Prince's enemies, so his plan of dismembering them with his own hands needed no alteration. He had quickly grasped that Ginevra must have stolen the gloves, and he had to wipe away a tear at the pathos of it. He accompanied them to the street door and at the top of the steps embraced Sigismondo like a comrade-in-arms.

This embrace was watched with keen attention by three men in the dark entrance to an alley.

Aldo, Pio and Fracassa, after dumping the young prince ashore in the early mists of that morning, had poled upstream quarrelling in violent whispers. An accusation of stupidity from Fracassa had provoked the retort Pio understood best. Fracassa, taken off balance by the impact of Pio's skull on his brow, flew backwards into the river, losing the second pole. The boat, helpless in the current, revolved slowly as Fracassa, gasping and shaking long wet hair from his face, tried to grasp the gunwale while Pio tried to stamp on his hands. It was Aldo who tripped Pio with the scabbard of Fracassa's sword and, while he floundered in the bilge, hauled Fracassa on board. His threats to damage both of them finally calmed them down. Rude shouts from men rowing upstream, coarsely urging them to control their boat, united them at last in common hostility; as did the realisation that they were drifting downstream again.

Pio stated that Fracassa, already wet, should swim and push the boat ashore. Fracassa stated that Pio should swim and butt the boat to shore with his head. Aldo observed that the pole was drifting along within reach, and this was almost true. Fracassa refused to let anyone try to hook it into reach with his sword, and they were assisting Aldo, with the longest reach, to stretch out to his utmost to grab hold of it when the boat jarred into a willow root and everyone fell.

Aldo could not swim, and that was how he found he could stand up in the water, which came nearly to his armpits. His fall had floated the pole further away, so he waded towards it and immediately discovered a deeper channel in the stream bed. Fracassa fastened a hand in his hair as he went down and kept his head above water, although he was not wholly appreciative or grateful. His protests and Pio's comments clashed with Fracassa's bulletin on the pain in his arm and shoulder, but their manoeuvres had sent the boat hard against the bank and they got themselves, floundering, sliding and arguing, ashore. They sat there for a short while, explaining to one another what ought to have been done, but at last Aldo roared that their task in Viverra was not accomplished. There was a silence. He remarked that it would warm them up to walk.

Finally he got to his feet and set off in the direction of Viverra. Six yards off, he half turned and pointed out that it was he who was carrying the money.

By the time, therefore, that they found themselves watching Sigismondo take leave of Gatta, their clothes were certainly almost dry, although their feet hurt from walking in wet boots and their appearance had led a generous soul near the city gate to offer them money, which they had not refused.

As Sigismondo and Benno set off along a narrow street in the direction of the palace, the three set off with a simultaneous impulse in their wake, once more united in enmity. The ferocity of their silence was almost palpable.

The two ahead were not hurrying. In fact they stopped a hundred paces up the street, and the shaven-headed man pointed out to his companion a mechanism for raising sacks of grain to a loft. High, over the loft door, was a double pulley, from which beside the loft door hung a long sack, the height of a small man, a counterweight. A double line ran down the wall to a hook, a large business-like hook, at present secured in a ring perhaps four feet from the ground, and below this, another pulley wheel jutted from the wall, with a ratchet.

The two were occupied with this mechanism during the short time it took for Aldo and the others to approach. The shaven-headed man pointed and gestured, the other nodded. A very small dog was investigating the gutter further up the street but, apart from that, the place was deserted in this somnolent time of early afternoon.

When the three were within ten paces Fracassa reached back for his sword. Aldo through his teeth muttered, 'No room, you fool!' Their prey was still oblivious, the crown of the shaven head tilted towards them as the man looked up at the dangling sack against the sky.

They charged. Aldo alone yelled out the man's name as he raised his dagger: '*Michelotto!*'

The man wheeled. He was holding a falchion, and his whole body showed that he knew what to do with it. He drove forward to meet them.

Aldo, fighting for all he was worth, knew he should never have forgotten that this accursed brute was a soldier. He knew he was in Fracassa's way, but saw Pio circling round by the wall. The man Michelotto saw him too, backed and swivelled, kicked Aldo in the knee and, catching Pio's short sword on his own blade, forced him backwards to the wall where the small man stood ready to stab him in the back. Aldo, stumbling to Pio's aid, heard Fracassa's sword come rasping out of its scabbard and, going for Michelotto, muttered again through his teeth, but this time a Hail Mary.

Pio, released by the vile brute Michelotto, soared suddenly, inexplicably, horizontally into the air. He sailed upwards, yelling as the wall scraped him, nearly cut in two by his belt. Fracassa's great blade swept. A huge pale object landed among them and disintegrated as Fracassa's blade sliced effortlessly through it: the counterweight, filling the air with chaff and a ballast of ancient rusty metal and bits of stone. Aldo sought for Michelotto in the flying chaff and found nothing; Pio came screaming down from above as the remains of the counterweight flashed upwards; Fracassa leapt through the cloud of chaff and, flailing a blow at the retreating Michelotto, tripped on a broken ploughshare and fell headlong precisely in time to break Pio's fall and be completely winded.

Aldo ran in pursuit of Michelotto until the man turned, facing him again in that competent crouch, falchion in hand. Then Aldo felt suddenly alone. He remembered his unfulfilled task in Viverra. He thought a private feud should not jeopardise it. He stopped, uncertain. The armed man, the scruffy servant who had hooked Pio's belt to the hoist, and the little woolly dog, looked at him. He took a step back, then another.

'Next time!' he said. 'You'll never—'

The chaff he was covered with got him in the throat. He coughed – was convulsed with coughing. When he at last wiped his eyes the street was empty.

'Third time lucky,' he vowed.

18. The Battle of the Bonfire

'Why didn't you kill them?' Benno asked. 'I thought you would.'

'The Prince empowered me to trace a pair of gloves, not to kill his subjects. I won't unless it can't be avoided.'

'They think you're Michelotto.' Benno felt an injustice here. He looked up at Sigismondo, who was drying sweat from his head and neck with a napkin from his belt pouch. 'Why didn't you tell them you aren't?'

'You think they'd believe me?'

'You're not the least like him, except your head.'

'The head must be the only thing they know about him. In war a man makes enemies he doesn't know he's got. I'll tell him they had another try.'

Sigismondo was looking ahead towards the city square. A sudden burst of noise had come from there, and as they turned the street corner and could see the whole square spread before them, Sigismondo took the gloves from his belt, wrapped them in the napkin and stowed them away. They were a vanity not safe in anybody's hands.

The turmoil was round the bonfire. As an edifice it was impressively high, and if it had been composed solely of vanities it would have argued an amazing preoccupation with frivolities and ornament among the citizens. However, a pyramid of wood supported the embroideries, the painted cloths, the cut velvets, the painted panels, the majolica, plumed hats, jewelled chains, gloves, kerchiefs, painted boxes, ballad sheets, music sheets, lace petticoats, lace caps, gold-braided jackets, books upon books, ribbons, laces, silk flowers, velvet slippers and gilt-studded chopines, Venice glass, carvings, gold chains, mirrors, silk sleeves, enamelled cups, velvet jewelled collars, gold-thread nets for the hair, painted or jewelled or embroidered belts and girdles, folios of drawings . . . and round this pile raged a furious fight.

Gatta's men saw no reason why, if these desirable objects were to be thrown away in a useless fire, they should not have them. They were going begging! Why, if such things were for the taking in Mascia, should they be burned in Viverra while there were people who wanted them?

The purity gang, the righteous children, were dedicated in defence. They fought for Christ against godless robbers. The city should be cleansed! Gatta's men had not drawn weapons. They flung the young defenders aside, used fists or, against the raging girls, the flat of a hand. They had begun almost in laughter, reaching for the pyre, grabbing prizes. Now the children seized billets of fuel; and here suddenly in the midst Brother Columba cheered them on, the skull riding above on its new pole as he alternately yelled anathemas at the soldiery and rallied his own troops.

Hit on the nose with a billet, a soldier caught up the boy who had wielded it and hurled him to the ground. A hand to his nose proved that it poured blood, and he swung his foot into the boy's side.

'Benno: tell Gatta. Go.'

The bonfire was being dismantled; but now men ran from the houses with fire-irons, axes, hammers. Their children were being injured. Sigismondo strode forward, pulled an infuriated soldier from the mêlée and would have spoken to him, but the man was shouting curses. Sigismondo let go and dived into the throng to get the younger children, at least, out of it. A soldier wrested the pole from Brother Columba's hands and used it to knock a prize from the bonfire. The skull cracked and shattered, leaving shards of bone embedded in the pitch. Young voices screamed underfoot, men attacked the soldiery. At once swords were out. The bonfire rocked and tilted, shedding finery. Brother Columba seized the pole from the soldier with astonishing force and laid about him, at friend or foe, yelling in Latin. Sigismondo stopped to pull a boy from underfoot, run him out of the fight and shove him towards a group of women shouting furiously on the steps of the town fountain. Other women, more active, raged through the fight with ladles and skillets and brooms. The citizens' knives were as effective at close quarters as swords. One burly man pinioned a soldier while another beat him up, until the hilt of a sword crashed into his face and he let go. Sigismondo saw another prone body, a bundle of clothes rolling and shifting under the feet, and forced his way through and bent to take hold. Some weapon came violently down on his back and for a moment he was on all fours over the girl's body. She had clasped her hands over her head and rolled up. He climbed to his feet, holding her; and heard Gatta's voice roaring at his men, then a tattoo on metal, a fast rattling rhythm that every soldier heard.

They began to back from the fight, on the defensive, towards Gatta. Some of the townsfolk and the gang youths pursued them triumphantly until they found themselves facing an arc of very determined armed men. Hands with cudgels and fire-irons dropped, fierce faces became unsure. There were defiant shouts, that dwindled.

Round the debris of the bonfire the ground was strewn with finery. To Gatta and Sigismondo it might have been reminiscent of Ginevra's room.

The wounded were being helped away. A thin, anxious woman took charge of the girl Sigismondo had been supporting, and he went to join the men round Gatta. At this moment a platoon of the city marshal's police came at a fast trot into the square and halted in a belligerent stance by the wreckage, and the marshal himself, a man resembling a

Michaelmas goose with spindly legs on which balanced a bulbous body, came forward.

Gatta advanced from his men's line, and conferred. He announced he would march his men back to his house. They would need, and would pay for, food, drink and entertainment. Gatta ended by saying, on an unmistakable note, that he was sure the marshal would see that this was provided.

There was a creaking, rending sound suddenly from what remained of the bonfire's scaffolding, which slowly tilted to one side and crashed to the ground raising a cloud of dust. It subsided, revealing Brother Columba, sitting with legs out before him, covered in dust, and clasping the broken top of his pole, with its ball of pitch and embedded jaw-bone and cranium, to his bosom. His head was bowed and his body racked with sobs.

Sigismondo and Benno took up their interrupted walk to the palace. Now that the place seemed safer, Benno put Biondello down for a run. 'It's been quite a day so far.'

'As you say: so far. Hey, you've done well. You sent that bandit nicely to heaven on the hoist.'

'Wasn't difficult,' Benno said. 'I just did what you told me. I didn't know which of them you were going to give me, that's all.'

'Not the one with the sword. That scabbard would've got in your way, for sure.'

Benno grinned, and kicked at a stone in the street.

'What happened at Gatta's house? You brought him fast.'

'I went in and said, "There's trouble, where's Gatta?" and the man pointed and I saw Gatta and I said, "Your men are all being attacked in the square," and he'd been eating and he grabbed up that plate he was drumming on and we ran.'

They climbed the palace steps.

Benno, behind Sigismondo, trying to be matter-of-fact but sounding very alarmed, suddenly said, 'You're bleeding.'

'Mmm. One of my more *dangerous* skirmishes, Benno.

We'll go to our room and you can wash it.'
So the battle of the bonfire ended.

19. THE EFFECT OF COMFITS

During all this time, Brother Ambrogio at the palace was giving occasion for sin.

He had been with the Princess Dowager when news came of her grandson's return, and they gave thanks for this together. The lady who had brought the good news was of that unlucky combination, pious and a great gossip, and she was moved to tell what she had heard from a page of Prince Francesco's: that he had been robbed outside the city while visiting a house of assignation. The Princess Dowager was not unduly surprised. Young men will be young men. She had brought up several of them herself, and she had heard that her grandson's pursuit of one of his mother's ladies had been in vain. He was naturally in need of consolation. She felt, however, that she ought to appear shocked in front of Brother Ambrogio, although she was really only resigned and pained. He put out a gentle hand to her head as she knelt.

'Sin, my daughter, brings punishment in this world as well as the next. Do not fear for this young man's soul. He has received a warning permitted him by God, and I will go myself to wrestle on the side of his conscience. The Devil shall not triumph if any word or work of mine can prevail.'

The Princess Dowager remained on her knees gazing after him as he strode from the room, already asking directions to the young prince's apartments. She was beginning to wonder what she had unleashed upon her family.

When her cousin had written rapturous accounts of Brother Ambrogio's work in bringing whole cities to God, it had inspired her to invite him here. Now her women told her that the friar's public sermon on his arrival yesterday had put the city against her son! Anxious though she was for Scipione to give up this beastly practice of alchemy and not lose his soul, she had hardly anticipated his losing Viverra. She began a series of Hail Marys, with the Intention of begging the Virgin to give her compassionate aid to Brother Ambrogio, that both son and grandson should leave their sinful ways and convert the city to heavenly harmony under their rule. Out of habit, she omitted her daughter-in-law from her prayers. Some people must be permitted to find their own way to Heaven or to Hell.

Thus at the hour of the siesta, while the city fermented uneasily under the raids of the gangs collecting for the rebuilt bonfire, peace of a sort reigned in the Palace. It was a hot autumn afternoon. Everywhere people dozed, even servants on duty, like a scene from an enchantment. There was to be a kiss for the beautiful princess too, though she did not know it yet.

Donato Landucci's feelings had been in turmoil since morning. The Princess Isotta had admitted him to her bedroom when he brought the news of her son's disappearance. He had thought and thought of that moment. He wanted to unburden himself to Francesco, but as the crux of the matter was that he longed to cuckold Francesco's father, while Francesco conceived the attachment to be wholly romantic, free talk was difficult. Going to his friend's rooms all the same, he paused outside the door and shook his head at the page who would have opened it, for he heard the unmistakable voice of Brother Ambrogio raised in supplication on the prince's behalf. Donato had no wish at all to intrude on anything with such potential for embarrassment, nor to be prayed for. His mood perversely hardened at the sound of that ardent voice. Brother Ambrogio, the young prince reluctantly on his knees beside him, prayed on, unaware that he was provoking a resolution to sin.

Donato knew the way from the son's to the mother's rooms. The interior of a palace is not guarded as are the outer doors, and no one suspected harm from the young Count's familiar presence. The lady nominally on duty during the Princess's siesta was taking a surreptitious nap of her own in the oriel of the antechamber. The door to the Princess's room stood ajar to let a breeze circulate on this sultry afternoon. Donato pushed it a little wider and paused on the threshold.

He was fairly confident. Wasn't he young, handsome, virile, all that the wretched Prince Scipione was not? The Princess knew of his devotion: his gifts, his poems, his gaze, all had told her – and there was that special assistance that by now, if calculations were right, would ensure his success. She had also sent him a message, thanking him for his consideration in bringing the news of Francesco's abduction himself. She had been, the message said, too disturbed by the news to appreciate his thoughtfulness, but wished soon to thank him in person.

She had sat up in the bed, that morning, barely covered. She had been 'too disturbed' at the time but – the words rang in his head – she 'wished to thank him . . .'

Donato slid inside the room and softly shut the door.

The Princess's bed hangings were still the summer ones of white linen, embroidered in scarlet with the civet cat of Viverra. They were drawn. No sound came from beyond them. The air was sweet, he breathed her scent of musk and sandalwood. He could hear his heart beating in his ears as he tiptoed across the floor. There was no trucklebed pulled out, no servant or lady lying there – she had arranged all for secrecy. She expected him. He reached the curtains and parted them.

She lay there, the green taffeta sheet clinging to her shape, her wonderful hair spread on the pearl-bordered pillows, her eyes shut. Either she pretended sleep or she had

139

grown sleepy waiting for him. He felt dizzy. Breathing hard, he shed his doublet, unlaced his points, peeled off shirt and hose and, lifting the sheet cautiously, slid in naked to meet her nakedness. He leant over her and pressed a kiss to her lips.

He had expected a burst of passion and he got it.

First came the blow, which left him doubled up and clutching himself. The huge dark eyes opening on him had held for a moment only shock, then came recognition and the blow. She sprang away from him, pearl-coloured against the curtains, more lovely than his imaginings, far more lovely than he could appreciate at that moment. She snatched up the sheet against her so that he writhed exposed.

She spoke, in a searing whisper. 'Donato Landucci! Are you mad?' She did not call for help. A wild hope entered his heart as the pain lessened, that this was how a tigress might make love. Did she mean to comfort him after all? He had been too abrupt, she had been too hasty; she had not, after all, expected him, that much was clear, and only now had she realised who he was. Now she regarded him and her lips began to curve into a smile. She was Venus Anadyomene, tresses dishevelled by the winds, one hand to the bosom half defined by waves of green taffeta. He blinked at her through tears, trying to respond to that smile, which had gone.

She pointed at his discarded clothes.

'Go. Never presume again if you want to live.'

Somehow he got off the bed, somehow scrambled into hose and shirt and doublet, aware of that blaze of scorn; somehow tied his points and got out of the room, cursing the woman who had led him to believe the Princess would welcome his embraces.

He got back to his room, flung himself down on his bed and wept hot tears into his pillow.

Back on her own bed, the Princess had put one slender hand to her face and was laughing silently.

Prince Scipione's doctor had permitted himself a siesta,

although he took it in a chair. The Prince was, thanks to his care, his doses and his strict diet, so far recovered that he had insisted on getting up. In a gown of crimson damask, and having exchanged his nightcap for a turban of black and gold twisted silk, he was wandering fretfully about the ante-chamber, considering whether to risk a journey across to the laboratory or to send for Doctor Virgilio for a talk on their progress. The sensation in his legs decided him. It would be humiliating to fall on his knees in the middle of the gardens. People might imagine he had become a devotee of Brother Ambrogio. His whole feeling about Brother Ambrogio was a desire to be left in peace. He had far too much on his mind to want friars cluttering up the place, just when Gatta had arrived and would need something more than a grand house in Viverra to reward him for taking Mascia. The Bishop was a churchman, but he had not this old-fashioned attitude towards intellectual curiosity. It was more than tiresome.

All the time, watched by two sleepy pages, he wandered between two travertine pilasters, exercising his legs, he was struggling with the greatest anxiety of all: did Isotta mean to kill him? Could it be she who had provided the gloves as usual? Yet, if she had, it did not make sense. To avoid suspicion she would have continued with the gloves he had always had, for she was certainly too intelligent for that mistake. It consoled him. And anyone at court passed that box at some time or another, or could do so without anyone remarking it.

Relief at being able to exculpate her made him stop and smile at a surprised page, and then as he turned to continue his exercise, he stopped and frowned at another; he was still left with the knowledge that someone – who could be anyone – wanted him dead.

As he was still alive, this person would undoubtedly try again.

'Stefano.'

The page, whose chin had reached his chest, started and

141

bowed. 'Go and fetch Doctor Virgilio. Don't stop and gossip on the way.'

Stefano had to step back in the doorway as the Venetian Ambassador, Signor Loredano, was announced. He had come to see for himself if the Prince's reported recovery were fact; the Serenissima must reconsider its whole foreign policy should Viverra fall into the hands of an untried young prince. The Ambassador believed that the news of Prince Francesco's escapade had been kept from his sick father, but unfortunately no profit was to be gained by disturbing him with the news now that the boy was found. Much more interesting was the rumoured poisoning of the Prince, and the inflamed state of the city itself. The Ambassador had been on his own private reconnoitre in a disguising hat and a plain stuff gown like any burgher's, and had mingled with the more respectable citizens and heard much of significance. It seemed to him that the influence of the palace was now weak. The explosive talk in the streets was enough to blow Prince Scipione out of Viverra. This, his masters must know. He smiled and bowed, with the greatest respect and concern.

'Your Highness! My congratulations on your recovery. So swift! The news will delight the Serenissima. Such resilience argues that the vital forces in your constitution are strong. But your Highness rejoices in the sign of Capricornus, which commands long life; and Mars was well aspected at your Highness's birth.'

The Prince's acknowledgement was inwardly a little sour. He thought of his natal chart being pored over for fatal flaws by the astrologers of the Venetian Republic. Their Ambassador had naturally come to spy on him, to find out more about the poisoned gloves too, no doubt. If only Sigismondo had come back from wherever his researches had taken him.

'Your Highness must rejoice—' the Ambassador accepted the velvet folding-chair, as the Prince conquered his own restlessness and took his own high-backed chair '—that Viverra has proved so religiously inclined. Brother Ambrogio is said to have worked wonders in the city. Penitence and good works everywhere!'

The Ambassador did not mention the good works in the shape of the beautiful objects he had seen on the bonfire in the great square – a lute of the most exquisite workmanship; inlaid panels; silk gauze woven with gold thread – nor mention that he had offered eighty thousand ducats for the whole collection. It was a move that could not but win. If the citizens had weakened and accepted, he would have known their spiritual pretensions could be dismissed and he would also have got a number of superb things at a good price. They did not accept. Therefore he believed the Prince was in trouble.

Had he seen the fighting that broke out not long after he had made his offer, he would have been very certain that the Prince was in trouble.

'Brother Ambrogio is not making a long stay,' said the Prince, hoping it might be true. 'He only came to pray with her Highness my mother.'

The Ambassador nodded comfortably. By now a page had brought wine. The Prince sipped without enjoyment. He craved something sweet, not satisfied by the honey in the medicines, which in any case never disguised the awful taste lurking beneath. He directed his page to bring the box of comfits from the chest by the bed. When the boy returned, however, with the woven box tied with ribbons, he wore a doubtful expression and whispered something in the Prince's ear. The Prince had opened the box and paused with his hand hovering over the sweetmeats. He shrugged and withdrew it, motioning to the page to take the box to the Ambassador.

'I am, alas, under doctor's orders. A strict diet as yet, until my system is purged of the effect of the fumes.'

The Ambassador enjoyed sweet things quite as much as the Prince did, but his spirit of natural caution kept him from all but the rarest indulgence. He permitted himself a treat now. He was savouring a piece of news an agent had just conveyed to him. The agent was placed in Gatta's army and had only now, in his role as mercenary, managed to get leave from Michelotto to enter Viverra. He brought a titbit as delicious as the rose- flavoured fondant the Ambassador was nibbling: Gatta had sent the head of Scala to Venice by secret messenger. That could only be a bid for the Republic's favour. Might it be seeking Venetian support should Gatta choose to take Viverra for himself?

'Quite excellent, these comfits, Highness. Are they of local make?' The Ambassador took the fringed napkin offered by the page but, not caring to miss a scrap of sweetness, licked his sugar-encrusted fingers before he dipped them again into the box, ignoring the offered bowl of rose-scented water.

'I've no idea. I often have them.' The Prince gazed sadly as the Ambassador took another. 'I am glad they please you. No, no, pray take as much as you wish.'

The Ambassador ate on, interspersing his choosing, chewing and sucking with delicately phrased inquisition about the conquest of Mascia. 'And the death of Scala! What a magnificent feat! I understand—' the eyes under their heavy lids glanced sidelong '—I understand that Ridolfo Ridolfi did not himself kill Scala?'

'Didn't he?' The Prince was surprised, and annoyed at showing it. He recognised that he had been teased with a bit of information he should have had. 'I've been too ill to receive a detailed report from Ridolfi.'

The Ambassador popped a confection of crystallised rose petals into his mouth. 'Indeed, Highness. No doubt Ridolfi will tell you it was one Sigismondo, who appears to be one of his men, who did the deed. His head was struck off at one blow, I believe.' The Ambassador found that the last comfit was flavoured with lemon. He dabbed the sugar from his mouth with the napkin. He said nothing of what he knew had become of the head. He had not got where he was by revealing all the cards in his hand.

Destiny, however, had plans for him that did not include further games of cards. The Ambassador talked and drank

144

with the Prince for a while longer, and then rose to take his leave at last prompted by a regard for his own health – the afternoon was oppressively warm; he felt queasy . . . Suddenly, as he bowed over the Prince's hand he bent further, toppled, grasping his stomach and, first groaning, then almost shouting, threshed on the marble at the Prince's feet.

Basilio, not waiting for orders, ran for the Prince's physician. At the noise, people entered and converged – pages, the Prince's chamberlain, Doctor Virgilio, the physician, guards. The Prince, who had stooped uselessly to help, drew back. A guard and the physician knelt by the Ambassador trying to calm him enough to see what the matter was. Doctor Virgilio knelt too, his hawk face intent. Then he rose abruptly and drew the Prince aside. His sharp black eyes still regarded the Ambassador.

His voice could barely be heard: 'He'll die. It looks like arsenic.'

20. "She Gave Them to Me."

'You'll never guessed what's happened!' Benno burst in, carrying a jug full of hot water which slopped with his haste on the tiled floor. He was still new to the task of valeting. Sigismondo, stripped to the waist, sat on a stool with a long cloth unrolled on the bed, from which he was selecting herbs and dropping them in the basin at his side awaiting the water. He raised his eyes and gave an interrogatory hum.

'—Surprise me, Benno, now's your chance.'

'The Venetian Ambassador's dying; he's been poisoned, just like that poor lady.'

The dark eyes fixed on him steadily. 'With a pair of *gloves*?'

'I don't think so.' Benno poured the water into the basin, and there came a mingled smell of crushed marigold and thyme. Benno crouched to whisk the water with one hand. 'No one mentioned gloves. Just he had a sort of fit at the Prince's feet, rolled on the floor and frothed, like. Poison, everyone says.'

'Who do they say poisoned him?' Sigismondo had been crushing comfrey root on the window sill, and now made a poultice with a pad of linen wrung out in the steaming water. Benno too soaked and wrung out a rag to clean Sigismondo's wound. He whistled when he saw it for the first time but consoled himself with the knowledge that Sigismondo had survived a lot worse. There was a long scar, for instance, curving across his ribs, where someone in the past had tried for his heart. He dabbed cautiously, finding that, although extensive, this was a surface wound.

'Who? Well, there's a sort of whisper the Prince did it, but that's not sense. He was with the Prince when he was took bad, but if I was to poison someone I'd take care not to be there. And I thought Venice was on the Prince's side.'

'Diplomacy is never simple—' Sigismondo grunted as Benno wiped off the last of the dried blood with too much enthusiasm. 'Venice supports the strongest. The Prince might not qualify at the moment.'

'Gatta does, doesn't he?'

Sigismondo handed over the poultice. 'Gatta would qualify as the strongest in a lot of places. At the moment, Gatta stands behind the Prince. As long as he's loyal the Prince has a chance.' He raised his arms to let Benno pass the roll of bandage round to hold the poultice in place. 'There's no telling what difference the Ambassador being poisoned will make. Venetians have minds like mazes.'

Benno, intent on the bandaging, watched by Biondello with his head on one side, said, 'They're not going to take it as friendly, are they?' He tied a flat knot he was proud of, and stood back as Sigismondo picked up his shirt. 'That glover said the gloves that killed the lady were Venetian. Could *they* have wanted to kill her for something?'

Sigismondo's gleaming head appeared from the folds of his shirt. 'Who can tell? But my sword is Damascus work, remember.'

Benno's forehead creased, and he scratched his beard. 'You mean it doesn't follow the Venetian gloves came from a Venetian?' Biondello gave one of his rare barks in approval of this logic. 'Though for all I know,' Benno added, 'you do come from Damascus.'

Sigismondo smiled. 'True. And all we know of the gloves is that whoever put them in that box must have expected the Prince, not Ginevra, to wear them. If it was the Venetians, it may be to clear the way for Gatta to take over Viverra. Don't forget the pretty present he sent to the Republic.'

Benno grimaced at the memory of the brocade-wrapped, ribbon-tied head. 'But the Ambassador wouldn't take what they meant for the Prince, would he? He'd have known.'

Sigismondo rolled up the herbs carefully, put the roll in a small leather bag, then tapped Benno's chest with the back of his hand. 'Remember to keep your mouth well open, my Benno; people will notice you can think.' He turned his head as someone approached the door and as they knocked he said, 'That will be a summons to the Prince, and more thinking. Biondello has the best of it.'

Sigismondo found the Prince alone in his room. The chamberlain and the formal guards were in the anteroom; the page who had brought Sigismondo retired with a deep bow, closing the doors.

The Prince was in his carved chair by the window, resting his head on one hand, his cap pushed awry. When Sigismondo was announced he put down his hand and straightened his back with an effort. His eyes were deeply troubled and the crooked mouth twitched as he spoke. 'You'll have heard what has happened to Signor Loredano. Everyone must have heard by now. They are saying I poisoned him. His secretary would not hear of his staying in the palace, ill though he was, but got a closed litter and took the poor man off to his house. He was full of suspicion.'

'What reason could they give, Highness?' The deep voice was calm and gave comfort. The Prince shook out his furred sleeves and sat up straighter.

'The Holy Father dislikes Signor Loredano – the Ambassador – very strongly for a slander spread about his Holiness when Loredano was at Rome. It might be thought I wished to curry favour with the Pope so that he doesn't seek to put another in my place.'

The name of Gatta, not spoken, was loud in the room. Ironic that both Rome and Venice, so opposed to each other, appeared to see him as a natural candidate for the princedom.

149

The Prince looked down at his hands, reddened with acid burns; at the heavy ring with its intaglio civet cat. He gave Sigismondo a desolate smile. 'Brother Ambrogio promises me all will be well if I renounce the works of the Devil. I am counselled that it would be advisable to let him think that I will. He's to preach before the Bishop in an hour's time and I must be there. Were I not to go, I would be thought to be against him and then the city will be against me.'

The simplicity of this was plainly no consolation to him. The lined face, turned to the light for a moment, had traces of tears. The reason for these and for the Prince's solitude became clear when he suddenly rose, half stumbled, and took hold of the breast of Sigimondo's jerkin, reminiscent of Gatta's gesture of the day before, and said urgently, '*She gave them to me*. Do you understand? He ate them. They were poisoned, I am sure.' The tears in the short-sighted hazel eyes welled and ran unheeded. 'The Princess gives me boxes of comfits as she gives me gloves. Does she want me dead?'

The voice was not raised, but it was full of pain.

'Your Highness, the gloves seem to have been put there by another. Why not the comfits? You must think that whoever has done it, whether they fail or succeed in their chief aim, also seeks to incriminate the Princess.'

The Prince dropped his hands and, becoming aware of the trickle of tears, brushed them away. His voice was low but perfectly audible. He looked straight ahead.

'Prove to me that she had no hand in this and you can name your reward.'

21. A White Powder?

To Benno, Sigismondo striding through the palace looked no more thoughtful than usual, but then he was not aware that any special cogitation was called for. He could not know of the delicacy of approaching a Princess for the second time in two days to inquire if she was trying to kill her husband. Trotting behind his master with Biondello concealed in his jerkin, Benno did not expect or receive any confidences and so was not apprehensive as he leant on the wall in the Princess's antechamber, gaping amiably at the beautifully painted ceiling and at an equally beautifully painted lady passing the time playing cup and ball while she waited to be called on for any minor service the Princess might require.

The Princess was choosing jewels to wear to Brother Ambrogio's sermon in the cathedral, from a jewel box held by one of her women. This did not seem to strike her as a mistake when sackcloth and ashes might have been more in tune with the occasion, but perhaps it was a deliberate act.

She raised her eyes as Sigismondo approached and made his obeisance. In her hand was a collar of pearls with a huge emerald pendant set in a triangle of gold. Holding it against her long neck she looked at Sigismondo as though studying herself in a glass.

'What do you think, sir? Does it become me?'

The strangely flirtatious question was delivered in her usual cool tones, and her glance roamed over the broad shoulders as though she were assessing him for some different kind of service from the one he was hired to give. His face gave no flicker of response, however. His voice was gravely respectful.

'You adorn it, Highness. Could it be otherwise?'

She laughed suddenly, and put the collar down beside the hand mirror of Venetian glass in a frame of gilt cherubs, a scent bottle of silver and lapis lazuli and an ivory comb, among several flasks and little bottles of paint and face and mouth washes.

'You're a courtier, sir, as well as all else we hear of you . . . Go!' This was to the lady with the jewel box, who withdrew, leaving Sigismondo and the Princess alone except for a cat on the windowsill.

Princess Isotta opened one of the small boxes and dabbed a finger in the scented paste inside. 'So, why are you here? His Highness sent for you after Signor Loredano was taken ill, I'm told. Does your trail lead you here once more?' Her face was serene, almost smiling, but there was a tension about her as though her air of calmness was only just maintained; as though she might perhaps not cry but scream.

'Your Highness, it is possible that the Ambassador was poisoned by a box of comfits which the Prince offered him.'

Her hands went flat down on the table and she stared at him. 'And you come straight here. You mean it was the box I gave him. Can the Prince really believe I would want to poison him?'

Sigismondo delicately combined a shrug and a bow, acquiescence tempered with incredulity. She was frowning, but her gaze left Sigismondo as she considered in her mind. When she spoke it was as if to herself. 'He would not dare. And what would it gain him?' She turned back to Sigismondo's unmoving attentiveness. 'Donato Landucci. He is the one who gave me those sweetmeats. He gives me presents all the time – poems, flowers, birds – but always sweetmeats. I don't care for them, but my husband does, and as I've no wish to hurt the boy's feelings, I take them and give

152

them where I know they'll be appreciated.' She bit her lip. 'I
believed that he thought himself in love with me; one of these
boys' passions. Can he in fact want to *kill* me? In revenge, say,
for his father's defeat? That would be reason enough. A short
time ago, sir – for I see I should tell what I had not thought to
speak of – Count Donato found me alone and made—' a
brief movement of her mouth and a gesture that almost
dismissed the event, '—what I took to be an attempt on my
honour.' She paused.

'Your Highness thinks it may have been an attempt on
your life?'

'It didn't seem so. I thought him only presumptuous, too
ridiculous even to be insulting, that he should suppose . . .
but if he has tried to poison me, it may be that he meant to kill
me – afterwards.'

She put a hand to her throat as if she pictured what form
her death might have taken.

Donato Landucci was drunk. This was not perhaps unusual,
but his page, who had grown fond of him although he was a
foreigner and technically an enemy, had not expected that he
would drink alone. Prince Francesco was his boon companion, but Prince Francesco had kept to his own apartment
since the visit of Brother Ambrogio. Surely if anyone needed
to get paralytic, it was Francesco after being robbed, beaten
and prayed for. However, his door stayed shut, and though
the Palace buzzed with the news about the Venetian
Ambassador, there was not a word between the two friends.
Count Donato's only visitor was the strange-looking mercenary with the shaven head, the man who had brought the
news of Gatta's victory at Mascia. The page's orders had been
to deny his master to everyone; he found himself genially set
aside by the shoulders and left to gape at the halfwit attendant
of the mercenary while the door he guarded was opened and
shut on him.

'What do you want? Get out.' Donato's courtly manners
were gone with the wine. He sprawled in the window

embrasure and looked up with strong resentment. No one could be trusted, not even his page . . . The poignancy of being so badly treated and far from home brought tears to his eyes. This man of Gatta's didn't obey, he was not getting out, but stood there with eyes that seemed to know what he was thinking, which was ridiculous but also dangerous.

'I am sent by the Princess Isotta, my lord.'

Donato's hand tightened on his winecup. 'The Princess . . .' He half rose, shook his head in an attempt at clearing it, and sat back sideways. 'She wants to see me?'

'She would like to know several things, my lord, which I am empowered to ask.'

Donato tried to get up, lost his balance and once more sat. His vision of a warmly penitent Princess begging for his return faded. He scowled at the brute before him. '*What* things? What have you to do with it?' If only he were at home in his father's castle he'd have had this creature flogged for walking in without leave. How dare he discuss a Landucci with the Princess? How could she let him near her? Donato poured himself more wine, managed to get the flagon back on the window sill, shook spillage off his hand, and drank.

'Her Highness wishes to know where you got the sweetmeats which you often gave her. Did they come from some special confectioner?'

Donato choked. He had to submit to being hit between the shoulder blades by the gross mercenary, who stood too close and now, before the humiliated Donato had recovered, went on insistently questioning .

'The confectioner, my lord. The Princess has instructed me to discover the name.'

Donato wiped the tears from his eyes and coughed again. He hoped that would account for the hoarse tremble in his voice. 'Why does she want to know? Does she not like them?'

Sigismondo leant an arm on the stone of the window embrasure and smiled down. Donato, not in the least reassured, was forced to wipe his eyes again but tried to stare back.

'The name, my lord?'

'I can't be expected to know that. It's my servant's business.' He meant to sound aristocratically condescending, and recognised with fury that it came out pettish. 'You must ask my servants.'

Sigismondo's smile did not change. 'I shall, my lord. And once the sweetmeats were in your hands, what did you put on them?'

For a shot in the dark, Sigismondo's aim was too good. Donato's wine flush faded dramatically. He pressed back against the stone to try to distance himself, if only by a few more inches, from the smiling face now leaning towards him.

'Put on them?' If only his head were clearer.

'You can't have heard.' The smile was encouraging, almost friendly. 'Your sweetmeats were offered to the Venetian Ambassador this afternoon. They must have been enticing. The Ambassador ate them all and is now dying of poison.'

'*Poison!*' Donato's voice cracked. 'Are you sure they were my sweetmeats? Was it the Princess who offered them to him?' His voice expressed in swift succession astonishment, regret and horror.

'Your presents of sweetmeats to the Princess always go to her husband. She does not care for sweet things.'

'The Prince? Always to the Prince? Didn't she eat *any* of them?' Donato put his hands to his brow. 'That *explains* it!'

'It explains the poison?' How horribly near the man was. He gave one's thoughts no room.

'I mean someone must have put poison on them before the Ambassador ate them. I never, ever, put poison on them.'

Still the man smiled. 'What did you put on them, my lord?'

'Nothing. It was harmless. It could never have done any harm. It was not—'

He was being pressed back by a hand on his chest. It was like the nightmare in which you dream you suffocate. The face was closer and no longer smiling.

'If you hold your life in any value, my lord, you will say

155

what you put on the sweetmeats. If you don't speak, it will be taken that it was poison.'

The man, after a final pressure, stepped back. The relief was amazing and Donato found himself pouring out words. 'To make her love me. She was kind but she never really saw me. I had to make her feel what I felt, you understand. Gian, that's my servant, Gian said he knew someone who sold spells and powders and things, a witch . . . outside the city, and he'd get me some, but then she sent him back saying I had to come myself, some mumbo jumbo about reading my hand and working out what stars to make her charms under—' Donato ungratefully ignored his reliance on this mumbo jumbo, '—so I went to this sordid little place and she did all these different things and ended up giving me a powder to put on something the Princess would eat.'

'A white powder?'

'Yes. She said it would taste of nothing and I must mix it with sugar and roll the sweetmeats in it. She said whoever I gave it to would burn for me before this next moon. I must give it myself into her hands.' He stopped abruptly. '*Was* it poison she gave me? Why? Why should she do that?'

'Did you tell her the love powder was for the Princess?'

Donato was the very picture of a young gentleman caught out in an act against a code of courtly love where secrecy rules. 'She said that to make it work she had to know the name of the one I loved and the sign under which she was born. I found that out from one of the Princess's ladies.' He looked briefly up at Sigismondo, embarrassed. 'The witch might not have known whom I meant.'

Sigismondo did not comment on the degree of rarity of the name Isotta, nor that a young man obviously of the court was most likely in love with the princess of that name. 'How long have you been using this powder on the comfits you give to the Princess?'

Donato tried to make himself think. 'Oh, a month. Two months. Perhaps more. I was in despair! She never seemed to change. I went back to the witch last week and she gave me more – told me to put it on thickly, and she did her spells and told me a thing to say when I was rolling the comfits in it, and she said my love would be in my arms by today, this very day.'

He stopped, reminded of the dreadful twist by which she had been in his arms and with what result. He had no intention whatever of telling this man *that* and it was, he profoundly hoped, not likely that she had already told him. The man's face did not show that she had and, a little heartened, he picked up his winecup again with a confused conviction that he needed to forget everything to do with that occasion and, particularly, everything he had said. As he drank, a thought that seemed straight from heaven came to him.

'It can't be poison she gave me. If the Prince has been eating all the comfits I've given the Princess he'd be dead long ago.'

Sigismondo did not reply. He bowed and made as if to withdraw. Another and infinitely less welcome thought came to Donato. He sat up. 'Are you going to tell the Prince what I did? He'll have me killed! He'll think my father put me up to it! He'll order Gatta to invade my father's land again!'

But Sigismondo was gone. Donato hurled the empty winecup at the closing door.

22. Repent!

All Viverra would have liked to attend Brother Ambrogio's sermon in the cathedral, but not all Viverra could manage to pack itself inside. Some had enough foresight and leisure – those whom his previous sermon had put out of business had had leisure thrust upon them – to arrive early and secure good places. The beadles at the doors were able to accept donations towards personal charity; consequently room was found for quite a few latecomers at the back; many were boosted on to windowsills or poised on a few inches of column base. The rest had to be content with standing on the steps crowding the beggars, which cost them almost as much, and forming a crowd in the square and streets outside where they hoped to hear at least a rumour of what was going on inside or to catch some scrap of the emanating grace.

One reason for the universal desire to be there was the general sense that much hung on the trend of the preacher's sermon. His first had been so uncompromising in its denunciation of everything most Viverrans had until now considered harmless or even desirable, and the effect had been so alarming, that many who waited during the restless hours were hoping he would now take a more forgiving view, and even praise the efforts they had made to purify their lives.

Those were the optimists.

The pessimists and all whom life had made cynical expected Brother Ambrogio to demand more of them and, in

159

some cases, complete their financial ruin. Oddly few of the latter had come in a state of true repentance for their former means of making a living. Their main hope was that after Brother Ambrogio had left the city – and it stood to reason that there were other cities in terrible states of turpitude for him to visit – normal life would eventually resume, although the cost to them of his visit might never be recovered.

Not a few citizens were mentally revising the amount they had intended to lay out on clothes or furnishings that year, and downgrading the dowries they had been going to offer with their daughters. Not a few were wondering when it would be safe to sell abroad the vanities they had hurriedly cached. One or two, such as the maker of playing cards who was now producing devotional pictures, showing a gilded cross against the towers of Viverra surrounded by an inscription declaring Christ the ruler of the city, were feeling smug. The young ones who had spent some exhilarating hours persecuting their elders and collecting for the bonfire felt confident of receiving further licence from Brother Ambrogio and looked forward to a continued reign of terror. They had quickly recovered from their encounter with Gatta's men and reminded one another that Gatta himself had brought his men to order and so must be on their side. Gatta would be there today to feel for himself the full influence of Brother Ambrogio's stirring words.

Gatta's presence was not the least thing that drew the citizens to the cathedral. Gatta would, after all, have been the hero of the hour for his victory over Mascia, had Brother Ambrogio not stolen his thunder; and his men's unregenerate requirements were sustaining a very lively substructure of the economy. Gatta would have made his entrance into Viverra in style, there would have been a public holiday, everyone dressed in their best, tapestries and embroidered banners draped over balconies and windowsills, street feasts, largesse and a thanksgiving Mass here in the cathedral. It was politic to stifle all regret at this. Had not Gatta forgone it? All the same, the women in particular yearned to see Gatta, and when he made his way to the cathedral in the late evening sunlight, dressed in suitably plain deep purple velvet, on a great black horse, the crowd roared for him and threw flowers, which he acknowledged by turning his handsome, battered face this way and that, like a cat hearing the mice applaud.

It was also politic not to be in one's best clothes, so the women in the cathedral, clad drably to be safe, gazed with mixed feelings when the Princess arrived. Nothing had inhibited her choice of clothes. Fawn watered silk might be demure in colour, but gold tissue over it was not, and the emeralds in her hair, at her ears and round her neck shone green fire in the candlelight.

Not everyone managed to get as far as the square, let alone the cathedral. There were the sick, and a few inconsiderately dying, whose attendants had also to miss the experience. One or two were frightened of crowds. There were servants with duties they had not managed to get excused from, guards who couldn't get out of guarding and, of course, those they guarded. Among these was Donato Landucci who, shortly after his interrogation by Sigismondo, found himself arrested and marched off to a definitively uncomfortable little room in the Old Castle across the palace gardens, where the walls were thicker than anywhere else and prisoners might be supposed to be safer. Donato, guilty of attempting to drug the Princess or, if he could be proved to know that she habitually passed his presents to her husband, of attempting to poison the Prince, did not feel safe at all.

The arrival of the Prince and Princess had been greeted with conflicting noises from the crowd, some cheering in the usual way while others, mindful that their ruler was, according to Brother Ambrogio, ruining their chances of salvation, produced a hoarse murmur like an angry sea. Neither Prince nor Princess took any notice, and they were received on the steps of the cathedral by Bishop Ugolino, at whose invitation Brother Ambrogio was giving the sermon. The Bishop was held in awe by the citizens more on account of his powerful voice and appalling temper than for saintly

161

virtues. There was keen curiosity to see how he would take the sermon. The Bishop had shown he was in confident command by his invitation to preach, but it was doubted that Brother Ambrogio would reciprocate with respect. The Viverrans were to have a first class chance of seeing in action the rivalry between Church potentates and the preaching orders.

Everyone thought the Bishop had dressed the part splendidly, in magnificent vestments of brocade embroidered thickly with gold, and with enough jewels on cope and mitre to support many poor families for generations under Brother Ambrogio's rules.

The preacher arrived at last, barefoot and in his coarse and threadbare robes. The contrast was widely appreciated.

He took a little time to get into the cathedral because of the number of people who tried to touch him and get his blessing despite the efforts of the Bishop's guard providing an escort. A blind beggar on the steps touched Brother Ambrogio's robe and sprang up declaring he could see, but as those familiar with him had long supposed as much, the miracle did not impress everyone. Flowers were thrown, as they had been at Gatta, and it was with red petals in his windblown white hair, like splashes of blood, that Brother Ambrogio entered the cathedral.

Leone Leconti, who had brought a sketchbook and a stick of charcoal, stood by a pillar in the shadows and added, to his rough drawing of the Princess sitting serenely waiting, a quick impression of the preacher's haggard profile as he made his way up the nave to the pulpit. There, he climbed the winding stair as the choir chanted the psalm: *I was glad when they said unto me, let us go into the house of the Lord*, and he came out under the sounding board and placed his hands on the cool stone sill, and looked down and round upon his audience. Prominent opposite him, in his episcopal throne beside the Prince and Princess and their children, sat Bishop Ugolino, the very picture of a brooding boarhound, the more awful for having the massive undershot jaw and mottled jowls

162

topped by a mitre. Brother Ambrogio waited for silence, and quite quickly the shifting, the coughs and whispers, the arranging of clothes and the fretting of a child, ceased. He crossed himself and began.

The people of Viverra found that they were not going to be praised for reformed ways. They were far, far short of the ideal which Brother Ambrogio had in mind, that true repentance and humility. How, he enquired, did they expect to get to Heaven with that most sinful of things, an army, outside their gates? A good many eyes sought Gatta at this but nobody could read the face tilted up towards the preacher. In fact, Gatta, after having incautiously strayed too near one of his cannon at Mascia, was still rather deaf, and felt himself well protected against impertinent exhortations. The Prince stirred uneasily. Gatta's army was his one shield. If Gatta retired, his enemies would at once reappear and multiply, and the Holy Father would as rapidly appoint a new prince for the Papal State of Viverra.

'Consider the words of our Lord, Who is above all earthly lords.' Brother Ambrogio extended his crucifix above his congregation and dropped his voice to a lower, more intense note that made some of his hearers shiver, inexplicably. 'Did He not tell us to forgive our enemies? Are we not to turn the other cheek? Give up, my children, the armies of Satan, men who stain their immortal souls with the sins of the world – with gambling, with whoring, with murder. Give up human armies, I say, and God will send armies of angels to fight on your behalf!'

Gatta's snort at this assertion might have been the result of his awaking abruptly from slumber. He had all the seasoned soldier's facility for taking a nap anywhere and the incense-heavy gloom of the cathedral was a peaceful change from the day's heat and the acclaim of the crowds. Brother Ambrogio gave him a smile of great sweetness.

'Fight for Christ! And your reward will not be on this earth where treasures rust—'

Some in the congregation were thinking painfully of their

particular treasures outside piled on the faggots of the new bonfire; treasures which were not going to get a chance to rust.

'—Look for your treasures in Heaven, incorruptible, where our loving Lord and all His saints will receive you, and where you shall have such treasure as your heart cannot imagine, treasures beyond the gift of earthly princes.' Brother Ambrogio's voice now became that thrilling whisper, audible nevertheless in every farthest corner. 'For I tell you, those that live by the shedding of blood must die without redemption. Dying with blood upon their hands, upon their souls, they will not be able to call upon the precious blood of the Lamb that died for them.

'REPENT!' This last word echoed electrifyingly at full volume. Brother Ambrogio flung his arms wide.

'Oh repent! I speak to you all of the judgement that is coming, of the Day of Wrath. Women that I see given up to the vanities of this world—' The crucifix faced towards the Princess. 'Every frippery, every finery, every plait and thread is a chain pulled on by a demon lusting for your soul. In the fires of Hell you shall be naked for evermore. What use your silks, your brocades then? Throw away your chains! The Judgement comes! The Judgement spares no man, no woman, peasant or prince. The peasant may plead before the Throne that he was ignorant, that he was oppressed, that he was driven by those above him, and God may extend His divine mercy. But what mercy can be hoped for by the oppressor, he who led other souls astray? What mercy for the prince who in his freedom uses the gifts of God, his wit and intellect, to destroy his soul? God will cast him down into the flames, there to learn what alchemy he will! There Satan shall fill his mouth with the molten gold he sought to make! There shall the brain he used to pervert God's holy Will boil within his skull!' As the Prince sat in the forefront of the congregation, his expression was hard to monitor; but nobody felt he could be smiling.

'Do not think, my children, that you are absolved of sin if

you plead *I did but as I was ordered to do*.' Brother Ambrogio now included the whole congregation in his compassionate regard. 'Soldiers believe that they must obey their commander, subjects that they must obey their prince. And truly a prince should be as a father set over you to lead you to God's ways. But I tell you there is only One whom you must obey, and if you neglect His commandments how can anything go well with you? Neglect not His commandments! The curse of the Lord of Hosts will descend upon you, as upon the Israelites who worshipped the god made of their own gold, and who came not to the land of promise. Turn from God and He will turn His loving face from you, your harvests will fail, your dealings cease to prosper, your sons will sicken, your daughters die. You will come not to the land of promise.'

When he went on, his words were spaced out, solemn, loud, portentous. 'But woe to him who, set in authority, turns to evil! Woe to him who seeks to pry into the secrets of God! Pray, pray, my children, that such a one turns from his ways. For by the grace given me by the most dear Lord I tell you that unless the works of the Devil are cast out from among you, that Devil will soon bring to an end your Prince's life; that without repentance, amendment and abjuration of such evil, your Prince will spend all eternity in Hell and you, his subjects who should have been his holy care, will be dragged down with him!'

That's torn it, thought Leone Leconti, sketching away under the shelter of his cloak. You can't threaten like that and get away with it. The city won't take that. Tell a prince he'll die soon? Tell a captain his army should disobey him? They're drinking it in, though! I wouldn't have believed it. Look at the young prince – he's riveted. What an angel's face! What beauty. It's got an austerity . . . but the Dowager! I nearly missed that sight; she's furious, and no wonder. The preacher can't do worse.

23. I Will Atone

But Brother Ambrogio had a target left. Turning his gaze from the stunned faces beneath him, he made a sweeping great gesture towards the east and the altar, in its frontal of cloth-of-gold, its cloth of exquisitely embroidered linen, the great bronze candlesticks either side with their candles fat as a man's wrist, the huge cross in the centre, set with rubies and sapphires – the Prince's gift – and the chalices and patens set with pearls and diamonds, the pride of the cathedral and of the Bishop.

'Be of pure life! Drive the vanities from your hearts and your worship. God is not glorified in these trumperies that defile your cathedral. He is not deceived by ornament and the display of trinkets. He requires – He asks only – the simple devotion of a pure heart. This abomination of vanity should not be on His altar; rather His altar should be in your hearts. Remember Lady Poverty, His dear servant. Let her lead you by the hand. Rid yourselves of these false treasures. Away with them!'

If Gatta had snorted before, now it was the Bishop's turn. He had listened intently, wanting to know what he was up against. He had received a horrified report in garbled gabble of yesterday's public sermon, and then had been mollified by the preacher's humility and obedience in the Prince's room. This had led the Bishop to believe that the fellow would respect him in his own cathedral. He had been grossly deceived. This arrogance – this disregard for doctrine – this flouting of the degrees of rank and the subservience proper in the poor! How dare he threaten Viverra's Prince with damnation! This could only lead to anarchy and the realms of chaos. The Holy Father would hear of this. A messenger to Rome would carry a condemnation of this dangerous rascal in the strongest terms. This meddling, halfwitted Franciscan knew nothing of how the world was run. Did he really believe an army of angels would protect Viverra if Gatta's men disbanded and the Prince's enemies marched against it? And the Church's treasures defamed now – works of beauty devoted to the glory of God . . .

'To the bonfire with these!' Brother Ambrogio pointed, and, popping up near the altar like a demon himself, Brother Columba advanced eagerly and seized the first chalice to hand.

'Stop! I command you in the name of—' A loud stertorous sound broke from the Bishop's lips instead of the Name he intended. He had propelled himself from the episcopal chair and still held on to one of the carved arms. His eyes turned upwards, his hand clawed the gilded wood, he staggered and crashed forward on to the marble floor.

There was a second of frightened hush, then outcry. A squad of clergy descended on the Bishop's sprawled form, which was lifted among them, with argument, and carried out by a door near the altar. One bold priest shook a fist at Brother Ambrogio as they went; but he, leaning from the pulpit, lost not a moment.

'See where God strikes down the covetous and the proud! Repent! Repent before it is too late.' And with a great shout of '*Misericordia!*' which rose triumphantly above the general hysteria and rang in the high painted roof overhead, Brother Ambrogio concluded his sermon.

He blessed the seething crowd, silently prayed for a second, and disappeared from view down the pulpit stairs. Brother Columba, now that all clerical attention had been removed with the Bishop, very rapidly swaddled all the altar furniture in the altar cloth and ducked and twisted his way through the crowd. God was gracious indeed. The second construction of his bonfire promised to be far more spectacular than the first.

Had a thunderbolt struck the square outside and decimated the assembled people, it would have had something of the same effect as the news hissing through the congregation as those inside the cathedral scrambled to be out. Bishop Ugolino had been felled at the altar by a simple word from Brother Ambrogio. A considerable number of people decided immediately to make disposition in their wills of substantial amounts to religious orders, with an eye to avoiding the wrath to come, this wrath so unpredictably illustrated upon the Bishop. If even the Church was not safe, what hope for the laity? They watched and made way with awe, falling on their knees as Brother Columba made his way among them to the pile of faggots on which the new scaffold of the bonfire had been erected, and added the cathedral treasures.

Someone had contributed an effigy of the Venetian Ambassador, whose sacrilegious offer the day before of a vast sum of money for the bonfire's precious objects had horrified the reformers. Look what had happened to him! There might be talk of poison, but anyone could see the hand of God in the matter, the first visitation. Now the Bishop had suffered. When would it be the Prince's turn? He had often fallen ill and then recovered, but it hadn't mended his ways; and in any case that was before Brother Ambrogio's word had been spoken against him. More dreadful by far than the prospect of his fate was that they, citizens of his city, were included in the curse.

The sermon had left its physical mark on more than the Bishop. He was carried tenderly to his lodging, but the Prince, tottering slightly at the shock and feeling far from well, was escorted with his family back to the palace between files of his guards. There were no cheers from the crowd this time, only the regard of hostile eyes and a hoarse growl, the sound of an uneasy, nervous and dangerous populace. The files of the guard, and Gatta stalking along with the regal party, prevented stones being thrown.

Gatta had been impressed by what he had heard of the sermon. Brother Ambrogio's voice when raised had penetrated his deafness, and Gatta was easily moved. At one point, tears had coursed freely down his face and he had responded to the preacher's '*Misericordia*!' with a broken bellow of his own.

There had been so much in his life for which he could legitimately feel remorse – so many villages destroyed; peasants raped and murdered, some by his hand but many more with his licence or command; cities put to the sword – that he had reason to feel personally the threat of death to people with blood on their hands. Gatta had a problem here, however. Blood was not only his medium, it was his métier. A man does not lightly give up his profession. The Prince depended upon him and, as importantly, his condotta depended upon him. Gatta was a practical man. He decided that in future he would wear chain mail under his doublet both in camp and in the city. If the Angel of the Lord was going to slay Ridolfo Ridolfi, he would have to get up very early in the morning indeed.

The one most impressed by Brother Ambrogio's sermon had yet to declare himself, but when the Prince and his family had reached the private apartments of the palace, he did. Prince Francesco had walked in a trance between the guards beside his father, seeing nothing nor hearing the grating murmur of the crowd. Now, his father was sending for his physician and his mother was engaged in icy argument with his grandmother which, to their surprise, ended in agreement that inviting Brother Ambrogio had been a mistake. The young prince began to strip.

His hat had been cast on the floor and retrieved by a hasty page. His cloak and doublet were flung after it before anyone took any notice. After all, it had been a very hot day,

September at its sultriest, and the young man was known to be impetuous. It was when a titter arose among the court ladies as the prince undid his points, and shirt and hose parted company that attention turned from the doomed Prince Scipione to his son.

'What are you about?' His grandmother, outraged, hurried forward. Too late. The young man had kicked aside the last garment and stood mother-naked before his fascinated audience.

'I abjure the world and all its vanities. I will come to God untainted by riches and rank.' He remembered, a bit late, to put a modest hand down to shield himself, but shaking back his long red hair he looked upward. 'I embrace the Lady Poverty. I will atone for the sins of my father.'

Thus did the heir and only son of Viverra's prince declare his intention of renouncing the world.

24. To Kill the Princess

Benno had met one witch already since he entered Sigismondo's service, It was true she had turned out to be merely a cantankerous old woman with no supernatural powers he could be sure of, but he found himself lacking in compulsion to meet another. This one might be really efficient. How did you know, with witches? It was a bit late to find out you were dealing with a real witch, by falling under her spell.

As their horses clopped over the narrow stone bridge crossing the river under Viverra's walls, Benno turned to look back at civilisation. Not that you couldn't get witches in cities, of course, but you felt a lot more vulnerable out in the open like this.

The sun was setting, too. Soon dark would come . . . Benno did not fancy going to visit a witch at night. There would be this old crone, whiskers growing out of warts, crouched muttering over a fire, watching them arrive. She probably knew they were coming right now. She would have a familiar, perhaps a hare, perhaps a black cat that would spring from the shadows and claw Biondello's eyes. Benno began to recite Hail Marys under his breath, nudging the sleeping Biondello curled up against his ribs under his cloak, to wake up and get the benefit. Perhaps, coming from Viverra where Brother Ambrogio's influence was so strong, they might carry a little of his power along with them. On the other hand, that might only make her cross.

He tried to distract himself in classic style by considering the misfortunes of others.

'D'you reckon they'll execute Donato Landucci for poisoning the Ambassador?'

Sigismondo, guiding his horse down a rocky bank in the dimming light, grunted. 'You've left out a few steps of the ladder. Whatever the young man meant to do, poisoning the Ambassador was not it.'

'Is the poor man dead yet, do you know?'

'His household and physician are not saying. But I am prepared to bet there is a horse waiting saddled and a messenger already with his boots on, ready to take news of his death back to Venice. Then, whoever was responsible, Prince Scipione will be in trouble.'

Benno's horse slithered on the stones in the wake of Sigismondo's great dun, nearly sitting. Benno, who had lived in stables for a large part of his life, put him right without thinking. The last lurid streaks of sunset lay on the horizon, bleeding into low purple cloud. A little wind, chill with the breath of autumn, got up from nowhere, and Benno shivered.

'I'd say the Prince is clean unlucky, anyway. He ought to give up the magic and stuff. Bet you something worse'll happen if he doesn't.'

Sigismondo's only response was a thoughtful humming. They rode on into the gathering dusk. The moon's pale disc began to strengthen in the sky among misty cloud. Benno made a decision not to ask his master what he intended to do when they confronted the witch, in case it turned out that Sigismondo didn't know. Besides, it was the sort of question his master most deplored.

Donato Landucci's servant, who had accompanied him to the witch to get the aphrodisiac for the Princess, had shown initial reluctance to betray his master's confidence. The reluctance had not survived Sigismondo's bribe and the threat Sigismondo seemed able to introduce with his very presence, and they were following his instructions in taking this path that led into the foothills. They had passed a collection of huts not far from the bridge, more like warts than a village, shut up for the night, from whose brushwood or reed roofs pale smoke had filtered, conjuring a pleasant picture of the fires within. Benno wished he were there, with a bowl of good soup in his hand. He wondered how much the people who lived there liked having a witch for neighbour.

The moon had come clear of the clouds by the time they found where the witch lived. Sigismondo had dismounted and signalled to Benno to do the same, as they arrived at the outskirts of a little wood. He put his finger to his lips and pointed.

Benno saw nothing at first. Then he thought he saw a pale thing flitting among trees in the distance. A ghost! He crossed himself and looked anxiously to Sigismondo who was quietly moving forward, choosing where to put his feet so that no twig cracked. Benno, praying furiously and with one hand on Biondello who had caught his fear and was shivering, tried to tread in his footsteps. Biondello thrust his head out but made no sound. He was a dog with a strong respect for danger. Benno lost sight of the pale shape moving between the trees until they were very close to it. Sigismondo had dropped suddenly to a crouching position and Benno instinctively copied him. Biondello, jolted, gave vent to a small alarmed snuffle, less loud than the stir of wind in the bush that shielded them. As the foliage parted further between Sigismondo's careful hands, Benno saw the pale shape clearly. If this were a ghost it had taken a wholly attractive form.

A young woman, dark hair flowing down her back, was lightly moving in a kind of dance in the clearing. As she turned, holding up some black object to the moon, it was clear that she was naked. The moonlight silvered her body, struck glints from her eyes and from the knife she held. She was murmuring something not distinct from where they listened. Then she stood still for a moment, eyes closed. Benno, suddenly terrified, thought she was sensing where they were; by now, although she was unexpectedly young, he

175

had worked out that she was certainly the witch, and whatever she was going to do with that odd little knife, like sacrifice something, he did not want to know. He strained his ears for, perhaps, a bleating somewhere or, worse, a baby crying. The night breeze brought only the rustle of leaves and a distant owl's screech.

She opened her eyes, held up her head, seemed to calculate, and turned. She crossed her arms on her breast, bowed three times, and spoke, as it seemed, to a group of tall plants growing there. Then she picked up a little pot from the ground beside her and poured something which ran slowly out at the foot of the plants. With her left hand she took hold of one tall stem, cut it with the black knife and then laid it in a white cloth she also picked up from the ground. She straightened up, bowed again, and walked off among the trees.

Benno, his mouth dry, became aware that Sigismondo had stood and was ready to follow. He had somehow thought that once they'd seen her making magic like that – because there was no mistaking magic when you saw it – his master would know the sensible thing to do would be to go away. They surely ought not to have seen it in the first place. If she knew, she would put a curse on them first thing. Biondello kicked his ribs and, though Benno was reluctant to put him down in this witch's wood, he knew the signs. Anxiety had gone straight to Biondello's bladder as it had to his own.

By the time he had stood against a tree himself, wondering if it was dangerous in this wood, and had retrieved Biondello, he had lost sight of Sigismondo and, momentarily, panicked. Suppose the witch had vanished him? Suppose he came on Sigismondo next minute, among these trees, turned to stone? He wished that either he'd never listened to servants' fireside tales or that he'd listened more carefully and knew what to avoid. He clutched the holy medals at his neck and tiptoed forward. He heard the owl again – nearer – and Sigismondo's voice.

Benno stumbled over a root among the fallen leaves and

came forward at a run. A hut materialised out of the gloom, and there was Sigismondo tapping on the door and speaking in his deep, quiet voice. A minute's silence, during which his master glanced back as if to make sure that Benno was there, and then the hut door opened on darkness. Benno gulped and Sigismondo stepped in.

The door remained open and Benno, clutching Biondello and muttering prayers, obeyed its silent summons and stepped into the darkness after Sigismondo. It was warmer inside and smelt of herbs. He brought himself to shut and latch the door. When his eyes had adjusted he saw a small fire on a patch of beaten earth, alleviating the darkness, its smoke rising lazily to the roof above. The witch was wearing a shapeless garment of thin grey stuff and Benno was conscious of disappointment along with his fear. She put some twigs on the fire and it flared up, illuminating her face. She was pretty! Why had he always been told that witches were old and ugly? But then of course her looks might not be real. Perhaps she thought that to be old and ugly would frighten people, but he found the idea of her being ugly *under* the prettiness much more frightening.

'What was it you wanted to consult me about?' She had a rustic accent and her question was put matter of factly. After a glance at Benno from which he shrank, she addressed herself to Sigismondo. 'Most people don't come at this hour.' One thing, her tone implied, that witches can count on during the hours of darkness is privacy. She was braiding her hair with quick fingers as she watched Sigismondo. Benno had just realised that he'd seen her naked and not felt the least flicker of desire. That was even more disconcerting.

'A matter of a love potion.' Benno heard the smile in Sigismondo's voice, inviting amusement, and the witch laughed.

'Not for you, I'll swear. Your voice alone would get you into most beds. It opened my door.' She threw the finished plait back over her shoulder. 'And now you're here, the light does you no harm either. If you want the potion for another,

177

it's not that simple. If it's to work, I have to know several things. I have to see the one who wants it.' She pointed to a little stool, and Sigismondo sat down.

'You've seen him already.'

She had begun to stir a little pot on a trivet over the fire and now she paused and looked slowly up. Sigismondo remained silent, hands on knees, returning her gaze.

'The young man who loves Isotta?' Sigismondo nodded and she went on stirring. 'I told him it would work if he did the right things. I suppose he forgot the words I gave him to say. Had he no luck?'

A long, disclaiming hum from Sigismondo. 'Very little luck indeed.'

'And yet I saw him in this Isotta's arms.' She shrugged again, took up a spoonful of what she was heating, delicately scenting the room with lemon and some herb Benno did not recognise, and sipped carefully at it. 'Perhaps it wasn't the one he wanted that I saw. We can all make mistakes.'

'A mistake was made. Someone has died from it.'

'*Died*?' Her hand tightened on the spoon, which dripped on her gown unheeded. 'That's not to do with me. I don't deal in poisons. There are those that do; I don't.' She was on her feet, the grey gown for a moment clinging to her, and her eyes glittered. 'Are you here to accuse me?'

'To question, not to accuse. If there have been mistakes, I don't say you made them. The young man to whom you gave the potion is in prison, his servant has talked. Others may come here. It would be better to tell me everything first.'

She looked at him intently. 'Who are you? What is your authority to question me?'

'My name is Sigismondo. The Prince has given me authority.'

She stepped back among the shadows as if preparing to vanish. Benno thought she might go up with the smoke through the roof. Then from out of the dark behind her a little cat came, fur softly shining in the firelight, and walked confidently with raised tail to where Sigismondo sat. It nosed his knee, and then in one jump it was on his thigh and pressing its cheek against his hand. Its purr was louder than the fire's noises.

'Tell me what you want to know.' She had come back into the light and stood, looking down at the cat and extending a finger to reach the top of its head, a finger that brushed Sigismondo's hand. 'I am shown I can trust you. Who has been poisoned?'

The straight question got no straight answer but another question. 'What did you give the young man to put on the comfits? The powder?'

She crouched, caressing the cat on his lap as it arched against her hand and Sigismondo without discrimination. The watching Benno thought they might just as well be beginning to make love to each other. Trust his master to cuddle up to a witch!

'Do you know herbs, Sigismondo? You have the eyes and the mouth of a man who knows things that few know. Vervain and southernwood I prepared. Most country wives would know to do as much, although they might not gather them at the right hour, the right time of the moon and with the right ceremony; they would not know to choose the times and the words according to the stars under which lover and beloved were born. That is my mystery.'

Sigismondo, smiling, took hold of her hand that stroked the cat. 'That is your mystery; I don't pry into it. *The powder*.'

She left her hand in his. 'The powder is Spanish fly. No doubt you've heard of it.'

'I have. And you must have heard that it can kill.'

'Only in great doses, recklessly used. I gave him only enough to rouse desire.'

'He could have saved it and given it all together.'

She laughed. 'Not he. He was too anxious to see its effects day by day.'

'Where did you get this Spanish fly? It doesn't grow in a wood.' He let go of her hand, and the cat suddenly jumped down, leaving her crouched at Sigismondo's knee.

'There's an apothecary in Viverra. I pay him with herbs

179

he doesn't know where to find. Is that an end to your questions?'

'There is only one more. Why did you want to kill the Princess?'

25. THE DOVE OF GOD

She was quite still, her lips parted. A flare of the fire showed her gaze fixed on him.

'The *Princess* is dead?'

There was a silence, then she sprang away from him. 'I did nothing, *nothing* that could have killed her. I gave the young man nothing but what I said. It couldn't kill. I don't sell poisons. Ever.'

There was a pause, another little silence while he looked at her. Then he rose. 'And the apothecary? Did he know for whom the drug was meant?'

She shook her head. 'Whatever killed her did not come from me. I swear it.'

'It may have come from him. Where does he live?'

'In St Thomas' Street, at the Silver Pestle, next the bakehouse.' She came a step nearer. 'The poor Princess – dead?'

'No. Another ate the sweetmeats.'

'I couldn't see her dead.'

The little cat had reappeared, and sat on its haunches beside the fire. The witch shivered. Sigismondo felt in the purse at his belt, and then bent to put a silver piece beside the cat. 'For your help,' he said. 'The sweetmeats are believed to have killed the one who died. The apothecary – had he any cause to wish you ill?'

'I don't know him well. I bring him herbs, we talk about

181

them, he tell me what he needs. I can think of nothing that would make him hate me.'

'Perhaps he harbours feelings for you that you've not responded to. Hatred can grow from that.' Sigismondo turned towards the door.

'Wait a little,' she said. 'I can help you more.'

'What can you tell me?'

She looked at him gravely. 'I can tell you, sir, that you're hurt; and *that* I can help with.'

Benno had been uneasy enough when the witch referred to her power to see things beyond her sight. Now that she had divined Sigismondo's wound he began to pray silently. He had nearly crossed himself but thought it might draw her attention, and stopped. Perhaps she would be angry at a Christian sign in her house.

Sigismondo was smiling. 'Hey, I should have asked your help. The wound's irking me enough.'

Benno was given a leather bucket. When she came with him to the door to point out the path to the stream, he caught the smell of her hair – rosemary – and of her skin. He sighed as he set off in the moonlight, wondering why a clothed witch should cause desire when a naked one hadn't.

There were steps dug out unevenly in the stream bank, and Biondello lolloped down them to drink. The stony bed had been dammed to make a small pool, overhung with ferns. Benno filled the bucket, looking upstream where the moon made the water bright between the dark overhanging banks. Back at the door he picked up Biondello who, although he did not chase cats and was a prudent little dog, might decide to investigate the witch's familiar if he were free to do so. Benno was taking no chances with an affronted familiar's powers.

She had lit a small lamp, adding the scent of warm oil to the woodsmoke and herbs, and Sigismondo sat half stripped while she examined his back. Apparently she had not heard of the bonfire, for he was telling her about the skirmish around it, and what it was built of.

182

'They sound like an odd pair of priests,' she said. 'I'm going to clean this with vinegar of garlic.'

It seemed to Benno, crosslegged on the other side of the fire, that his master was getting on very well with the witch.

'Why do they want to burn the pretty things?' she asked, picking over the ingredients of Sigismondo's former poultice. 'I thought priests had churches full of paintings and gold things.'

'I don't argue with priests,' said Sigismondo. 'They come in all sizes and of all natures. These two, a priest and a plain friar, tell us that the pretty things are graven images that take people's hearts from true worship. Other priests say that the riches of the Church stand for the riches of heaven.'

'I don't argue with priests either,' said the witch. 'You've not put burnet in this.'

'I had none,' said Sigismondo, his voice smiling.

'And you a fighting man?'

'That's why I had none.'

'Here. Put this in your scrip.' She handed some burnet over his shoulder.

Benno was holding Biondello by the ribs in a grip of iron, letting him extend a working nose towards the cat. It had proved impossible to hold him still, and Benno thought that a whiff of the sulphur the cat must surely carry about its person would daunt Biondello into docility. The little cat swung its head to look at Biondello, caught his smell with fastidious nostrils, then turned away, flung up a leg and started to wash. Benno hoisted the little dog on to his lap and held him; and as if profiting from a good example, Biondello dived at his own flank and began to chew and rootle there.

Benno looked about. Small as the hut was, it had a little half-loft under the roof, reached by a ladder made of a notched tree trunk polished with use. Herbs and roots, some tied in bundles, others in parcels of cloth, hung round the walls, and there were earthenware jars in a row on an uneven ledge.

The witch was busy mashing her mixture of herbs on to

183

the linen pad, rinsed out, she had peeled from Sigismondo. 'This will take out the heat of it,' she said. 'It had grown angry.' She held the poultice, whispering quietly for a moment, and then put it on, and she and Sigismondo got the bandages replaced.

He put his shirt on, and laced his doublet while she cleared away the things she had been using. Benno noticed that she had spells to murmur to each one, and although he thought that he ought not to listen to her words in case they were dangerous, he found he could not understand a single one.

She put out the lamp, and brought goat cheese on a plate made of bark, and some dried fruit, and a little bread, and salt in a jar. Sigismondo took a little of everything, no more than a taste, saying he had already eaten. Benno, battling with misgivings born of fear, did the same. The witch ate the rest as if she had been fasting; without greed, but down to the crumbs of cheese and bread, and Benno wished he hadn't touched any of it. Then he thought it might have offended her if he'd refused, and gave it up as a question of etiquette, of which he was aware he knew nothing.

'Thank you for your hospitality.' Sigismondo's voice had much in common with the cat's purr. They were all sitting on the beaten, clean-swept earth round the fire by now. The witch put her hands on the floor behind her and leant back, straight armed. The cloth of the loose garment lay on her body.

'You're not going?' she said.

Benno had slept in more uncomfortable places than the floor of the witch's hut. He hoped his master's bed was at least softer in the half-loft, but did not suppose that was of first importance to him. Biondello slept in the curve of Benno's body, next to the covered fire. Benno woke because Biondello sat up, suddenly, and uttered a short whimper. It was early day, from the faint light round the door and filtering through some window up in the loft.

184

Sigismondo's voice said, without any particular emphasis, 'There are people coming.'

After a moment Benno could feel the approaching tramp of feet. Then, alarmingly, they stopped. There was silence. Biondello turned and clambered inside Benno's jerkin. Benno, hefting the dog's rear end more securely inside, stood up.

There was a crash against the door and the whole place shook.

Sigismondo landed on the floor beside Benno, falchion in hand. He said, 'Get her out of that window. There's a bank outside. Hide her. Stay with her.'

Benno clambered up the ladder. Outside the door a voice chanted, triumphant, aggressive. Again came the crash against the door. Sigismondo kicked the bar from its socket, and at the next effort the door swung wide, precipitating a young man on to all fours. Outdoors flared a torch in the early light, and as the young man began to get up Sigismondo's boot caught him in the neck; he fell along the base of the wall and lay still, while the others crammed the doorway, shouting. They expected a frightened woman and they found an armed man. The torch set fire to a bundle of herbs that flared, illuminating everything more brilliantly for a second and then falling in sparks on the torchbearer, who yelled, brushing at the sparks and retreating under more bundles of herbs. Light gleamed on Sigismondo's chest and shoulders, on the linen bands, on his head and on the weapon in his hand. One of the men crowded himself out of the door again, shouting of devils, and his place was taken instantly by Brother Columba, robe kilted up, flaring light showing the wide eyes in his eager face.

At this moment the witch, her garment looped over one arm so that it left her legs bare, scrambled halfway down the ladder, grabbed a jar from the shelf and darted back into the loft; Brother Columba, pointing, howled Latin at her. The only man who seemed to have come armed had a staff and he struck at her, caught the ladder and jarred his arms. The pommel of Sigismondo's falchion jabbed his upper arm and the blade feinted at his face. He raised the staff and was punched in the belly.

Brother Columba, the dove of God, came towards Sigismondo with his hands now tucked into his sleeves. By now the roof was alight and flaming upwards, the torchbearer with his hair full of sparks was blindly brushing at his head and his shoulders and got himself to the door. Brother Columba stood for an instant facing Sigismondo. Then his hands flashed from his sleeves and one came flailing at Sigismondo's head with a weapon that could hardly be seen. It was parried with a swift arm; but it was a seven-tailed whip, whose weighted hooks flew out, some wrapping themselves round his wrist and others slashing his head and shoulder. The friar jerked the whip clear and stepped back with it ready.

Sigismondo could no doubt have killed him. Instead he leapt up to the half-loft; and Brother Columba, with a howl of Latin invective, seized the torch and flung it after him. The dry bedding flared.

The friar got his cohorts out of the place and stood chanting as it burnt, his arms raised on high, triumphant. In the light of the flames the men round the hut did not resemble the instruments of God, unless devils can be called so, shouting and prancing – except for one who still lay incapable – grinning, howling. When the little building collapsed they extended their dance all round the flaming ruin, and did not leave until, in broad daylight, the embers were dying.

26. OUR QUEST IS OVER

At dawn, when Brother Columba had led his little band of enthusiasts out of the river-bridge gate of Viverra, he was followed quite soon by someone else in humble brown robes, like those of the Franciscans. This inspired in the gatekeeper, a man attached to drinking and games of chance, a hope that Brother Ambrogio might be the next to leave. In fact the departing figure was not wearing proper robes but a sacking gown with a hood, which he had got from a beggar to whom he had handed a purse of gold. The beggar was first rendered speechless with astonishment and then, as soon as he could find a wineshop that dared sell what he wanted, speechless with intoxication, unable to comment about, or even to know, the moment when the purse of gold left him for another.

The young prince, treading barefoot and exultant out of his father's city, reflected on the ease with which he had achieved his aims. He thought he was saying his beads but he was not yet familiar with the mental concentration needed in solitary prayer and was holding one bead without noticing how long it had been in his fingers.

After the initial horror of his announcement that he intended to lead a life devoted to God, it was his mother, strangely, who had come to his support. While his grandmother raged and wept, his mother, cool as always, had taken a cloak from a nearby courtier and put it gently round him.

Then she had held his hand – released from the need to preserve his modesty – in both hers.

'My son, it is a noble thing you aspire to. I shall write to my cousin, the Abbot of Montesacra, who I am sure will accept you as a novice. He is a man of the sternest ideals and will be the guide you need in a holy life.'

Francesco had at first agreed, although he was a little disconcerted that his mother had not made objections. When St Francis had thrown down *his* clothes and abandoned his family, surely his family had been loud in resistance? True, Prince Scipione was stunned and staring; true, his grandmother had fallen on her knees, begging him to change his mind; and there was a good deal of horrified comment and tears among the courtiers, and protests from his father's councillors, but he felt that his mother's acceptance detracted from his sacrifice. On the other hand, it would enable him to submit himself to the strict discipline which he had heard was the rule at Montesacra, which was surely what he wanted.

The Princess knew her son very well; far better than he, deceived by her habitual air of detachment, could guess. She knew that a letter to her cousin the Abbot would ensure Francesco's vocation being tested by such rigours of the monastic life as would completely and very quickly change his mind.

After a bit of time spent praying in the chapel, Francesco came to the conclusion that Montesacra was not what he wanted. Brother Ambrogio, after all, had inspired him to embrace a holy life, and Brother Ambrogio was not a monk, anonymous and confined within monastery walls, obeying the strictures of an abbot: he was a friar, free to live his life in the open, in contact with the laity, setting them the example of his unworldly life. That Brother Ambrogio as a friar would be under orders to go out and preach, that he would have had to ask permission of his superiors before he could come to Viverra at the Dowager Princess's call, were matters never considered by the young prince. Above all, he sought freedom, not just from the ties of the world but also from family and obligations. He believed that Brother Ambrogio had said that he acknowledged only the authority of God Himself.

He, Francesco, would become a friar like his blessed name-saint of Assisi; or better still, he would first become a hermit and lead a life so renowned for its purity and selflessness that people would come to him for his wisdom and beg him to intercede for them at the throne of Heaven. Possibly abbots would come. Not everybody gave up a princedom at seventeen.

He had acted at once on this vision. Gold he was going to renounce but he was practical enough to bring a purse with him, to wear his plainest clothes and to take a rosary. He needed coins to make servants and guards look the other way when he slipped out of the palace before dawn. If they had heard talk of his decision they may have supposed he had thought better of it, or was off to an early Mass.

Meeting the beggar, who wore a dirty robe so like a friar's, so soon, was another sign that God favoured his intent. Perhaps it was a further favour that he was beginning to discover; the robe not only chafed a skin not used to anything but silk and linen, but that the itching it provoked might be due to something, or things, else as well. Moreover, it smelt. He told himself that saints lived with lice as well as poverty and that he was saved the trouble of acquiring a hair shirt. He was also finding that the stony streets were remarkably – well, stony.

Once outside the city he paused, hugging his arms in the sacking sleeves, surprised at how cold the morning mists of autumn could be without a fur-lined hunting cloak. Then he had set forward, with his beads, and no very clear idea of which way to go. God would surely guide him. He had been told often enough, as a child, that hermits inhabited caves, and whether there were any caves in the neighbourhood he had no idea. Still, he had better not linger. He was still close to the city, and he should get as far as possible from it before the search for him, bound to ensue the moment they

189

discovered he was gone, got under way. A suitable cave would be the thing, and in the paintings of hermits the caves had seemed to be among hills, so he took the hill road. Who would think of looking for a prince in a cave? He thought with pity of his family mourning his loss. One day, when his prayers and his holy life had earned remission from Purgatory for his poor benighted father, they would understand. They would be grateful then. He hoped they would not send that shaven-headed man out after him, the one who had brought him home so shamefully in the onion cart. He was the sort of man who might think of looking in caves.

Back at the palace his poor benighted father was suffering as much as Brother Ambrogio could have wished for his attachment to sinful pursuits. One terrible thing after another! On his return from a sermon in which he had been publicly rebuked in his own cathedral, and his subjects encouraged before his face to think he would shortly be dead and justly damned, he had witnessed his only son, his heir, renouncing the world.

He had never felt particularly close to his son, who seemed interested only in hunting and drinking with his friends, pursuing ladies of the court romantically and women of the town practically; and he could not recognise in the boy that impetuous energy which drove him to his own pursuit of knowledge. He had wished, frequently, that Francesco would show some sign of thinking of less trivial pursuits. Now an ironic Fate had granted the wish.

With no son to inherit, he was at everyone's mercy. His position had inevitably weakened. He wondered if he ought, as his wife said, to have ordered Brother Ambrogio arrested, or even assassinated, for treasonous incitement. A Sforza, a Visconti, would have done so. He was left with a wild hope that the Church would not accept an only son, an heir.

And his enemies were trying to poison him. The Landucci boy seemed to have tried to poison the Princess, who herself might be her husband's enemy. Gatta, too, might be not his supporter but his foe.

Prince Scipione stood in his chamber wondering whether it was worth going on. Why not swallow poison voluntarily and have done with all his troubles?

It was at this moment that a messenger arrived from Doctor Virgilio. Now the Prince had been debating whether, for the good of his soul and of his people, he should dismiss the alchemist. It would solve some of his problems at least, and it would placate Brother Ambrogio, who seemed to be ruling the city. He took the folded paper from the messenger very doubtfully, and broke the seal.

A short message; one that changed his mind completely.

Come quickly. Our quest is over.

That could mean one thing only: Doctor Virgilio had made gold.

27. ALL IS VANITY

The apothecary took them for two mercenaries from Gatta's army, here for salve for wounds received at Mascia. The big one, in black and with a shaven head, had got a nasty slash over the eye just lately. The blood was not long dried, and it made the strong face beneath look more dangerous. His companion's only obvious disability was a patent shortage of wits. Both of them wore clothes recently acquainted with mud and weeds. He had heard there was discontent in the camp and perhaps these men had been brawling. Soldiers, however, paid well and he came forward from the back of the shop, where Mario was pounding Pieta Casati's ointment for her child's sore eyes; and he prepared to be obliging.

'Oh, Master Buselli, you *must* help me!' The girl, appearing from nowhere, was extremely pretty; one glance told him that, giving him time to whip the spectacles off his nose and push them behind him on a shelf. Now he couldn't see her so well, which was a pity, but at least he didn't look so old. The girl had turned to the two men, all flutters and apologies for rushing in front of them, pushing back the tendrils of blonde hair that escaped so charmingly from under her cap. 'Forgive me, sirs, I'm desperate. My mistress is dying from toothache. If I don't get back with remedies in an instant, she'll beat me – the tooth's driving her mad!'

'I'll give her mullein in clove oil; you'll make her a poultice of it. But she'd best have that tooth drawn.'

193

Such remedies were already made up. He had only to hand over the packet and take the money, unfortunately. He smiled at her and tried to retain for an instant the hand that took the packet. With any luck, of course, she'd be back; it took courage to have a tooth drawn, and if the girl's mistress possessed it she would have had the tooth out before this. He watched, still unconsciously smiling, as she again thanked the mercenaries and, blurred though his sight was, he did not miss the swing of her hips as she left the shop.

He turned to the two men with less interest than before.

'Some salve for you, sir. That's a nasty cut you have there. What manner of weapon gave a blow like that?' He was pulling out little drawers, his back to the men, selecting his ingredients, when the deep voice replied, unhurried, amused.

'No weapon so terrible as a flail in the hand of a jealous man—'

The apothecary turned, with a vision of this man, naked as his head, tangled with some slut in the straw stacks, and an angry peasant coming on them, threshing the face raised to him over his wife's. This man must have moved smartly to avoid the full force of it.

'—And all for nothing, alas! I've not won her fancy yet, for all his fears.' The man became confidential, leaning his arms on the scored wood of the counter, pushing the scales askew, so physically overpowering that the apothecary wondered if the woman shrank from him in fear of being crushed in his embrace. 'What have you to persuade a girl? You know—' He tapped the side of that Roman nose with his forefinger. 'Something to put in a cup of wine that'll make her hot for me. What d'you recommend?'

It was the crucial question. Benno, gaping behind Sigismondo's shoulder, saw the little man respond. The call for love potions must be as frequent as the call of love itself. People just could not be counted on to love those who desired them. Donato Landucci wouldn't be the only one wanting some help, and the wonder was that he hadn't sent straight to

194

an apothecary instead of fooling around with spells from a witch; cut out the middleman.

'Undoubtedly this, sir.' The apothecary had half turned his head and tapped one of the jars ranged on the shelf, labelled in painted script which of course meant nothing to Benno. 'This will make her hot enough, though I cannot guarantee it would be for you.' He snickered. 'Get there before her husband comes, or your money will be wasted.'

Sigismondo was still looking at the jar the little man had tapped. He spelled out the letters, 'C.A.N.T.A. . . . What does that stand for?'

'*Canta?*' The apothecary started, and turned his head again. He brought his face closer to the pottery jar and then shook his head. 'Oh no, sir. You mistake. *This* is the one I indicated.' He tapped the next jar along and spelled out 'C.A.N.T.H., Cantharides, sir. The Spanish fly. Expensive! But your honour will not care about the cost.' Grotesquely, he copied Sigismondo's gesture of tapping the nose. 'But, as I say, you must be there or the heat will go to warm another. Now, as to dosage—'

'That *Canta*.' Sigismondo had produced a coin that the apothecary blinked at, leant closer to see, and then blinked at again. 'What would that *Canta* have done if you had given me that by mistake?' He spun the coin on the marble slab and his tone was of idle curiosity. The apothecary replied in the same offhand way.

'Why, you'd have made her cold instead of hot, sir; Cantarella is a poison.'

'She'd know by the taste, then.'

'Sir, it is tasteless. White, like refined sugar.' He paused, and looked at them sharply. 'You understand, this isn't common knowledge.' He showed a set of teeth like an old weasel's. 'But you gentlemen of the sword realise that not everyone chooses a clean way to kill.' An ingratiating smile reflected the value of the coin over which his fingers closed. 'Here's the salve, sir. And how much would you be wanting of this other?' Once more, he tapped with his knuckles backward on the jar behind him, and Sigismondo laughed.

'Hey, you're trying to make me *kill* her. If her husband finds us out, he'll do it without the aid of your Cantarella.'

The apothecary had turned, as before, tutting at his mistake and now a little disturbed as well as surprised. He felt along the shelf, recovered his spectacles and fixed them firmly on his nose.

Sigismondo had opened the box of salve and was anointing the wound on his brow and cheekbone, memento from Brother Columba. He smiled widely at the apothecary.

'This is doing me good already! Hey, say I'd put a pinch of that Cantarella in my drink, how would I know I'd done the wrong thing?'

'Well, sir, you'd sweat and get the gripes, shake like the palsy and soon purge and vomit.' He had warmed to his description, a professional show of knowledge. 'Then you'd die, and no one any the wiser.' The weasel teeth briefly appeared again, and Benno wondered how many wives had paid this man to become widows. Sigismondo listened with respectful attention, and so, unobserved by the apothecary, did a boy in furred blue velvet and feathered cap who had just come in at the shop door and stood there in the shadows. Now he stepped forward and nodded cheerfully at the apothecary.

'Well done, Master Buselli. You described exactly what happened to the Venetian Ambassador. They're all talking about it in the streets. Fell down at the Prince's feet yesterday, dead at dawn today. And no one the wiser, just as you say. No one bought any of that stuff from you recently?' He nudged Sigismondo, too young and confident to believe his gesture might be taken amiss by this large and dangerous-looking man. He was rich, of good family and from the palace. No harm had ever come to him and the death of another in the throes of poison was cause for entertainment rather than sorrow. 'I've come for her Highness's face wash.' He grinned and settled his brimless cap more firmly on his curls. 'To hear the town talk after that sermon you'd think every girl in the place owed her complexion to nothing but morning dew. Her Highness is not such a fool; and she's not a girl any more either, but—' He rolled big brown eyes towards the rafters, 'is she a beauty!' Sigismondo had turned round to look at him, and the boy pointed in recognition. '*You* should know. You're the man who brought the news from Mascia. I was in attendance. The Prince wants to see you, I hear. There's more news than I can tell you here.' He nodded at the apothecary who stood, the package in his hand, looking anxious. Taking the package, the boy said, 'Good day, Master Buselli. Keep a stopper on your poison bottle while the Venetians are looking for someone to strangle.'

He went out, tossing the package from one hand to another and laughing gaily at his joke. The apothecary had sunk on a stool behind the counter and was barely visible and certainly not audible as Sigismondo and Benno followed the page out. Benno wondered if this apothecary, purveyor to the palace, also supplied the alchemist with his extraordinary materials. By the shop steps, a barber had set up his stall and Benno had to dodge as he whipped the cloth from a customer's shoulders and shook out the clippings. Another man, his face yellow in the light of the awning spread over the stall, waited patiently with bared arm to be cupped and bled; a dog, as yellow as he was, waited just as patiently at his side. Benno felt his shirt stir with the alert Biondello as he hurried up the street in Sigismondo's wake.

In the street of the vegetable sellers, poising a melon in his hands and sniffing at it to test its ripeness, his master spoke.

'Vanity, Benno. Never forget, all is vanity, as the preacher says. If Master Buselli hadn't wanted to impress a pretty girl, he might have saved Viverra a peck of trouble.'

28. Set Off at Once

'Your Highness, I am convinced that a mistake led to the poisoning of the comfits. I have questioned those concerned.' Sigismondo stood, tall, relaxed, hands clasped before him. Prince Scipione, hunched in his armchair, held one hand over his eyes as if to shield himself from unwelcome revelations.

'What makes you think they are not lying?' Gatta, arms folded, leant against the painted wall behind the Prince, more in command of Viverra's fortunes than was the Prince himself. In one of the niches over his head, a muscular bronze Hercules, asserting his triumph over the Nemean lion under his feet, appeared to mimic Gatta's pose. 'Have them brought in and put to the question properly and we'll see if they told truth or not.' For a man who knew the effect of pain better than most, Gatta showed a touching faith in the extraction of truth by torture. To be suspected, after all, was as a rule halfway to being dead, therefore torture was only a means of hurrying the inevitable. The Prince looked up at Sigismondo under his screening hand on which the great ring with the Viverra arms hung loose.

'But Donato Landucci meant to seduce her Highness?'

Sigismondo scarcely shrugged. 'A boy's passion for the most beautiful woman in Viverra.' His tone implied that the boy could not really be blamed; the Prince, however, was not likely to accept the secret doctoring of his wife with aphrodisiacs as a compliment – even though the attempt had miserably failed. Something in the Princess's manner when she had discussed Donato with Sigismondo could well suggest more had happened than she was saying, but she was not likely to have confided in her husband if it had. Gatta started again.

'This wise woman—' Sigismondo had deliberately avoided the word *witch* throughout his story, '—where is she now? Let Brother Ambrogio get his hands on her and she'll be cinders in an instant.' Gatta laughed, showing his crooked teeth. 'But it's not that boy who's to blame.' He pushed himself off the wall, took a step forward and crashed a fist on the table, making the Prince start and his mouth twitch violently. 'Landucci! Landucci himself. Can't your Highness see it's the old fox plotting again? Perhaps the boy really thought he was putting Spanish fly on her Highness's sweetmeats, perhaps the old crone of a wise woman he went to see is in his father's pay. Perhaps he never went to any such being at all.' Leaning on his knuckles on the table, beside the seated Prince, he stared at Sigismondo with the golden eyes that had helped to get him called The Cat, and he smiled again, less pleasantly. 'Perhaps there are others in the pay of Landucci.'

It was a glove thrown down, almost as dangerous to ignore as to pick up. Before Sigismondo could reply, another stepped forward, someone who had been standing, arms akimbo, head on one side as if critical audience at a play, far enough from the Prince to seem beyond his immediate authority, near enough to Gatta to show whose man he was. Michelotto was smiling as usual.

'Why not send for Landucci and confront him with his son and his . . . spy?'

'No, no . . .' The Prince seemed embarrassed, most likely because he was conscious that Sigismondo was his own spy, and on the very man whose captain was making this suggestion. He flinched as Gatta turned on him, and looked unwillingly up into his eyes.

'Why not, indeed, Highness? If Landucci's the spider at

the centre of this web, pull him out of it and let's see what he says. Michelotto shall fetch him to Viverra, and if he's obdurate we'll tear his son to pieces before his eyes and get the truth that way about this poison.'

The Prince did not brighten at this inviting prospect, on the face of it so sensible. He cast a miserable glance at Sigismondo who still stood silent before him. Michelotto came past the table and threw a loving arm round Sigismondo's shoulders. The Prince, even in his distress, wondered that two men without hair could have such different skulls. Michelotto's pointed ears gave his the look of a faun, while Sigismondo's majestic breadth hinted at his greater strength. If only minds could be as naked to sight . . .

'Highness, if Ridolfo Ridolfi agrees—' Michelotto affected a solemn pronunciation of his commander's full name, '—I would propose Master Sigismondo ride with me to seize Landucci.'

Sigismondo's arm hooped Michelotto's waist with steel. 'I could ask for nothing better, your Highness. If I'm accused of working for your enemies, then let me serve you by bringing them to your justice.' He turned a genial face on Michelotto, whose smile had become as constricted as his waist. 'You, sir, shall observe me in all things, and report to his Highness whether Landucci shows knowledge of me or no.'

'But we need you here – my son is missing and you found him before.' The Prince was agitated. Impossible to keep track of all that was happening: his joy at the success of his quest for gold, a joy that remained as a bass note to all this; his sleepless night of excitement as he and Doctor Virgilio caressed the small shining knob of gold and attempted to duplicate the lucky experiment; his anxiety at the news that his son, his heir, had not only renounced the world but then promptly vanished; and his own life in danger, as the poisoned gloves had proved and perhaps the poisoned sweetmeats too . . . He felt far from safe, and far from well. His protector should be the man at his side, who had signed contracts to fight for him, who had conquered the traitors

201

Carlotti and Landucci, but the man he felt safer with was the mysterious man facing him.

On the other hand, if this man were true to him, accompanying Michelotto would give him the chance to discover Gatta's purposes more easily than if he stayed with Gatta himself. Michelotto was privy to his commander's plans, and Sigismondo might be able to get the man to talk of them, to gauge Gatta's intentions.

The Prince cleared his throat and placed his hands before him on the table in an attitude of authority. 'Nevertheless, although we need you here, we agree. You both shall go and bring Count Landucci here to answer charges against himself and his son. You have our leave to set off at once.'

29. THE CAVE

Just about the time that Sigismondo was setting off on a journey that should fetch Landucci back by the same hour tomorrow, and Prince Scipione retired to his daybed to make up the sleep he had lost, a search party of the Prince's guard were refused admittance, or even parley, at a Dominican priory a mile out of the city. They took the abrupt and laconic refusal for evidence of guilt – these people must certainly be sheltering Prince Francesco – and they hurried back to Viverra for further orders.

At about this time, too, Prince Francesco found his cave.

It had been a long, frustrating search. Dawn, when he had set out in such an exhilarated state, seemed a long time ago by late afternoon. He had had nothing to eat. He had pictured that Franciscan friars – and in his newly acquired gown he looked very like one – had only to appear, holding out begging hands, to be showered with blessings of which the material manifestation was food. Unfortunately there was a shortage of people on the road to the hills, so there had been little chance for any display of such charity. He had been offended when, at last entering a village, he had been confronted by a burly peasant with a mattock over his shoulder, who had shaken a fist under his nose and ordered him to stay away from his wife. Impossible to explain to such a brute that he was not at all the kind of friar who figured so amusingly in after-dinner court stories of cuckolded husbands and lustful nuns; that instead he was one who had abandoned impure thoughts as he had abandoned his rights to Viverra. In the village he met no better welcome. A cur tried to bite his ankle and succeeded in tearing a piece off his unsavoury robe. The village children had been overcome with laughter, even to rolling in the dust, at his efforts to fend off the dog. He had gone on his way with a growing belief that human beings were not to be trusted and man's only refuge was in God. He was not to know that only respect for his apparent cloth had prevented them from pelting him with stones.

Not far from the village was a little wood with a stream running through it. He sat on a mossy bank and put his feet in the blessedly chill water. They were very sore, dusty, and bleeding from scores of tiny cuts acquired on stones and twigs. He could not recollect seeing barefoot friars limping as he had been doing for the last mile or two, but then he supposed they had had time to work up protective calluses. They were denied the mortification he had undergone. He said a thanksgiving, for both the suffering and the water, and he drank from his cupped hands, unaware how lucky he was to be upstream from the village as he did so. He dried his feet on the end of the robe, smearing them with as much dirt as they had before, and as he did so his eye was caught by the gleam of purple berries shining in a shaft of sunlight on a bush not far away. He jumped up and hurried to it, reaching for the berries, pulling them off and cramming them into his mouth with more enthusiasm than he had shown for many a court subtlety in all its glory of spun sugar. The taste was bitter, but he took this also for a mortification. There was no one to point out to him that berries, in a wood close to a village, were likely to have been left on their bush for a good reason. Before he left the wood, he was down on all fours and vomiting on to the moss; reminded, in his pangs, of his father's seizures and feeling for the first time some genuine sympathy with him.

He lay, weak and panting, wondering if he was safe now or

if he would die. There came into his mind a memory of what the palace had been gabbling about before he left, the poisoning of the Venetian Ambassador, and he wondered if Signor Loredano had suffered as he had just done. His whole midriff ached. There had been a first, terrifying rumour that the Ambassador had collapsed with the plague, which had been creeping mile by mile from the East towards Viverra. Then came the whispers, reassuring in the circumstances, that it was only poison, such as had killed pretty, silly Ginevra Matarazza only a few days ago. Who was the poisoner, though?

He lay letting his thoughts drift, forgetting to repeat prayers, waiting hopefully to feel better. Whoever wanted to kill Ginevra could hardly have been driven to kill Signor Loredano from the same motive, although one page had put up an ingenious theory that posited a lover jealous of the Ambassador's success with Ginevra; whereupon all the other pages had pointed out that Signor Loredano was really only interested in boys as they could all testify; and that even if that theory had been tenable, this mysterious lover should have poisoned Gatta as well.

Francesco knew what no one was saying: that the death might be a complicated revenge of his father's. Venice, in the past, before its most recent quarrel with the Pope, had suggested to the Holy Father that Viverra as a Papal state required a more forceful personality than Prince Scipione at its head. Perhaps all his father's troubles stemmed from that moment.

Then, when he had wanted to go and talk things out with his dear friend Donato, he heard, incredibly, that he had been thrown into prison, in the Old Castle, for putting the poison on the sweetmeats. Had Donato been lying all the time? Was he an enemy as traitorous as his father Landucci? Had he meant to poison the Princess whom he professed to adore?

Francesco's stomach heaved again. He rolled over and groaned. After Donato had poisoned Prince and Princess, no doubt he himself was to have been the next victim. Brother

Ambrogio was right; put no trust in any creature, not even your dearest friend. Seek God. Francesco became aware now that he had not been praying. *Pray constantly.* So Brother Ambrogio had urged him. Seek out solitude, where live the birds and the animals, innocent creatures of God.

A bird, flying through the wood about its own purposes, muted as it passed and the prince felt something land on his head. Realising what it was, he wondered if he should take it as a comment on his thoughts or if it was, as his old nurse used to say, a lucky omen.

If the passing bird had been on its way to shelter, it knew something about the weather. It was no lucky omen in that respect. As Francesco recovered from parting with the berries, and sat there on the moss, his stomach feeling even emptier than before he had found them, waiting to gain strength enough for his search for a cave, the wood darkened swiftly as if a giant bird had flown over. The trees began to lift and toss their branches as if in concern, leaves eddied down to join those scuttering like small brown animals beneath. A low penetrating mutter in the sky made him look up. He knew what that meant.

Should he seek refuge under the trees or make another effort to find the safety and shelter of a cave? The scuttering of the leaves brought to mind that it was in woods like these he was accustomed to hunt, and though wild boar are always dangerous they appear far less so when viewed from a tall horse or, if on the ground, when armed with a stout spear and surrounded by other men so armed. Francesco stumbled to his feet. God have mercy, he prayed. Have mercy on all those suffering, and let me find a cave.

God was dilatory, no doubt having His reasons. The rain met Francesco in torrents as he came out of the wood. He stumbled unsteadily on, unable to see more than a step or two ahead, where water ran among stones, the rain dripping from his hood providing a private waterfall. So lost in his misery that he hardly knew if he were going uphill or across, rubbing water off his nose and chin, his feet so cold that they hardly hurt him, he all but missed what a sudden flash of lightning, God's finger, showed him.

Through the curtain of rain, darker than the gleaming rock surface among the boulders strewn on the hill, was a hole. No path led to it that he could distinguish, and a scrubby bush growing in the crack above it half veiled the opening, but without doubt he had found his cave. He battled his way up to it, slipping on scree, and pushed aside the dripping twigs to enter. The dark inside was almost warm after the rain's chill, and he remembered to fall on his knees straight away and give thanks. What was hunger or sickness compared to this sign that God watched over him and therefore blessed his intentions? In this cave he would live and die, though probably not until after many years devoting himself to contemplation and earning the love of all – a vision of the peasant with the mattock came to mind – by his exemplary life.

He rose from his knees, put back the hood and started to explore. At once he discovered yet another sign of God's intentions for him. Food had been provided! No ravens came to feed him, but then he was not yet of the calibre of Elijah; here was a small store of apples and nuts placed in a high niche of rock a little way inside the cave. He did not stop to consider whether any agency other than spiritual could be responsible for this bounty. He simply ate, cracking nut-shells with a stone, pausing only when it occurred to him that he might be glad of an apple later on, supposing God should not send him breakfast tomorrow early.

Now that he was less hungry – although apples were not as filling as one might think and his stomach was still turbulent – his next need was to be warm and dry his clothes. God had not provided a fire but – and Francesco gave thanks again – here were all the materials for one, stacked where the wall made a sharp angle with the sloping floor so that he had to grovel for them: dry sticks, some billets of wood, even twigs for kindling. Francesco had seen fires made in the open, and he was beginning to take this wood to the opening of the cave, pleased that he had thought to consider where such a fire should go so as not to suffocate him, when it came to him that he had no means of lighting a fire.

He searched again. The cave, an enlarged fissure in the rock rather than the domed shape he had envisaged, offered nothing that could light a fire, even if he knew what it should be. In his life up to this point, fires were things he saw already lit. He had witnessed flint and tinder being used and he wondered God had not provided these also, since the bush outside was dripping rather than burning.

There was no means of starting a fire but, where the cave curved at the back, he found something immediately as attractive: a bed. Dry grass had been piled on pine branches, and clean heavy sacking spread over it; there were even scented herbs scattered over, for he smelt rosemary and thyme. Aware all at once how bone-weary he was, how many miles he had walked barefoot today, he pulled off the stinking wet robe and cast himself down, rolling the sacking round him; with the smell of herbs, and the sound of the rain outside lulling him, he plunged into sleep. Palace beds had never, never offered such comfort.

The rain was still falling heavily when he woke up. Another sound, familiar but different from that of the rain, made him stir, turn and blink his eyes at what he saw. A fire was crackling. The wood had been shifted and now burnt with bright flowers of flame and, by its light, he saw something far stranger. A woman was standing by the fire, a girl with long unbound dark hair. As he stared, she now began, with sinuous grace, to undress. Francesco raised himself on one elbow, peering round the rock.

This was recognition by the Devil indeed. St Anthony had been visited in the desert by demons in the shape of lovely women. The pictures Francesco had seen showed demons clad in furred dresses, immodestly bared at breast and thigh. This demon had abandoned everything and, spreading the garments about, crouched completely naked by the flames, holding out her long dark hair towards them.

He should act. He should rush out and accost her, holding up his rosary, send her back to her abode in Hell. Two reasons at least held him back. Firstly, she was so very pretty for a demon. There could be only advantage in extracting the maximum from a temptation. Secondly, he was not feeling at all able for action and drama; in fact, he was weak and feverish, the soaking of the day before had thoroughly chilled him and he was not sure he might not be suffering a hallucination. Besides, he was naked.

He must remember: this was the Devil trying to frustrate his holy intent. Francesco knew nothing about spiritual pride – he had too recently started to listen to sermons – so that he could not recognise spiritual pride in believing that Satan might be especially inclined to fight for the soul of a future prince, at least one who would have been a prince if he had not sacrificed all earthly things. No, he would show the Devil that he was equal to the event. He would rise to it.

Rise he did, imperfectly clad in the sacking bed-cover, and came forward from the shadows, rosary in his out-stretched hand.

He had not really pictured what might happen. The demons who afflicted St Anthony so sorely with their luscious flesh were painted flying off suddenly, showing horns and tails when the good saint routed them. This creature evidently had no idea how to behave. She started up as he appeared, snatching clothes to her, and now as suddenly she crouched again, her eyes glittering in the firelight. What else glittered in the firelight stopped his advance abruptly. Her hand grasped a long, curved knife and it looked as if one spring would drive it through his heart.

30. The Rescue

Benno was impressed with the Landucci castle. It looked old, about the age of the Old Castle at Viverra that Prince Scipione used both for his laboratory and as prison. Unlike Viverra's, it was not partly in ruins. It did a good job of squatting on its mound like a huge stone toad, menacing them as they rode up the track towards it. Benno saw how Landucci could have felt impregnable in such a place, ready to challenge his overlord Prince Scipione. As Michelotto's troop clattered through the great gate, Benno, close behind Sigismondo, wondered how on earth Gatta had managed to bring Landucci to heel. Mascia had been a messy, frightening business and, if Sigismondo had not killed Scala so soon in the final attack, might have been a lot messier. Benno, gawping absently round the soldiers' fires at night, had gathered it was unusual for a condottiere to engage in actions that could prove punishing. A condottiere preferred to be paid not to fight, and certainly objected to losing too many men, his stock in trade. Those wasteful of men could not hope to attract much of a following, either. It had been a personal enmity between Scala and Gatta that had made the siege at Mascia remarkable.

'A favour, my friend.' Michelotto had urged his horse forward to come alongside Sigismondo in the van, and Benno watched his master turn with a smile. 'When we take

211

Landucci back tonight, will you ride by him and keep him safe? As long as we're in Landucci's county we can't be sure his people won't be stupid enough to try a rescue. With the slayer of Scala at his side, who could succeed?'

'You honour me.' Benno detected an answering sarcasm in his master's voice. Sigismondo had told him of Michelotto's request for him to be of this party, and that it was to enable Michelotto to observe his behaviour to the traitor. Benno made no sense of this. What was Sigismondo supposed to have had to do with Landucci?

When they came into his chamber, Landucci certainly showed no sign of recognition. He had been playing chess. The board still lay on the broad dais platform of the bed, the pieces askew. Landucci's hat was askew also, as if he had thrust it on in a hurry, just as he had moved to sit on the bed as more dignified. Under the hat his face, swarthy and deeply lined, showed his disturbance as he glanced from Michelotto to Sigismondo, two shaven heads come to confront him in bizarre unity. 'Why does Prince Scipione send to me?'

Michelotto gave the most exaggerated and fanciful of bows.

'Prince Scipione, my lord, sends not *to* you but *for* you.'

Landucci rose to his feet. 'For what reason? What is it supposed that I have done?'

'It is to answer for what your son has done.'

This brought a small scream from a woman in a silver-netted headdress sitting beside the bed. Her face was handsome enough to make it likely she was Donato's mother; that she remained seated when Landucci stood up made it plain that she was his wife.

'My son?' Landucci demanded. 'What is he supposed to have done?'

'Poisoned the Prince Scipione.' Michelotto spoke with relish. Landucci's wife put her hands over her mouth as if to stifle further outcry. Her husband professed confusion rather than alarm.

'The Prince sends for me, yet, you say, he is poisoned?'

212

Obviously, this was a man hoping to arrive too late for the deathbed.

Michelotto, smiling, enjoyed the mystery. 'Your son has been so active, Lord Landucci. Unimaginably! First, the Lady Ginevra Matarazza dies from putting on poisoned gloves—'

'We had heard that! Who says my son had anything to do with that? Anyone in the world could have put the gloves in the coffer. The lady was stupid enough to put them on.' Clearly he had no sympathy for poor Ginevra, unluckily stepping between Prince Scipione and death.

'Anyone in the world, indeed.' Michelotto's face assumed grief, watched in terror by Landucci's wife. 'But you see, when your son is proved to have given poisoned sweetmeats to the Princess knowing she would give them to her husband, it is naturally thought—' a brilliant smile succeeded the false grief '—that he provided the gloves as well.'

Landucci stepped forward, his face contorted with a sudden, violent rage. 'Who blames *me* then? Why should *I* be sent for? I gave my son as hostage for *my* behaviour, not for his. He has been in the Prince's hands. The Prince cannot touch me.'

'Alas!' The false grief was back. 'He can, he will. You are to return with me to Viverra at once.'

'What will happen to my son? Where is he now?' Donato's mother was on her feet and came up to Sigismondo, who had stood silent by Michelotto during all this. She had been studying the two men and she had decided who had the kinder face although there might not have been universal agreement on the point. 'They haven't killed him?' She could hardly say it for tears. Sigismondo bowed and let her draw him aside to the window embrasure where they talked for a few moments. His deep voice could be heard assuring her that her son was alive, and well, even though he was in a cell in the Old Castle. While he was speaking, Benno by the door with a couple of Michelotto's men, watched Michelotto speak to Landucci, no doubt advising him of the need for acquiescence, for

Landucci's face changed as he listened, and he offered no more angry protests but looked thoughtful.

They had a bite of bread with oil, and wine, before starting back to Viverra. It was already dark but the moon, though behind clouds, made it possible to ride. The castle was full of activity. Landucci chose an ugly old grey to ride, and said a curt goodbye to his still tearful wife. His household muttered and shifted, but his acceptance of the situation kept them from making trouble.

Biondello had trotted alongside the party some of the way there, and was now very willing to be tucked into his usual cradle in Benno's jerkin. As they reached the road at the foot of the castle hill, Sigismondo called Benno up from the rearguard to his accustomed place, and Benno noticed how close the party kept. He had been unable to work his way forward until, at Sigismondo's summons, they let him through. There was a difference in their bearing, too. He had not ridden with soldiers on duty before. They had chatted and even sung on the way here, but now, because they were escorting a prisoner it seemed, they were silent.

Michelotto commented affably on the night. Landucci did not reply, but his grey, sidling, betrayed its rider's nervousness. It was luminous in the pale light. Sigismondo said, 'I can smell rain.' He had put up his hood, but Michelotto did not appear to feel any chill in the night air. The path, a horse road not spoiled by any wagons, took a straight line across country, up and down steep rocky hills among pine woods and scrub. Landucci had his horse on such a tight rein that it kept tossing its head to get more freedom, and sidled so that Benno dropped behind a little to keep clear of its quarters.

'Benno.' Sigismondo's voice was quiet but unexpectedly curt. 'I've told you: always follow me.'

He put his hood back and as he turned to speak his eyes scanned the countryside. Benno could smell rain now, beyond where Viverra lay the skies were black, and there was a glimmer or two of lightning. Round the riders stretched the dim patchwork made by a full moon behind cloud: the pallid

214

grey of boulders; black, impenetrable shadows under trees. As the group climbed a hillside into a little wood, there came distant thunder as if the far hills grumbled.

Suddenly, with a roar of shouting, men burst from both sides out of the woods, swords dully gleaming. The attack focused on the centre, on Sigismondo beside Landucci's very obvious mount. Michelotto forced his way past Benno to Landucci's other side, while the vanguard wheeled and closed in on the attackers. Sigismondo's sword swept and fell, whirled, rose and fell. Benno, pushed aside by the rearguard, crouched in the saddle and made his frightened horse keep as close to Sigismondo as he could manage, which meant pushing across behind Landucci's grey. It seemed to him in the shifting mêlée that he saw Michelotto's arm swing back with a falchion and plunge it, under Landucci's short cloak, into his back below the ribs. Benno wondered in confusion what he had really seen, but had all he could do to keep behind Sigismondo. Landucci seemed to crouch, like Benno, over the high pommel of his saddle. Michelotto had a sword in his hand – definitely a sword – and fought furiously. Then the rain came. In an instant all was dark, and everyone was blinded doubly by the sluicing wet as well, but in the second before, Sigismondo had spurred his horse forward and, seizing Landucci's rein, swept uphill through some gap in the crush only he had seen; with Benno at their heels. They did not go far. Benno's horse stopped when theirs did; in the wet darkness hooves trampled. Sigismondo grunted, and spoke to Landucci.

'My lord, you're hurt?'

'He's dead,' said Benno.

Prince Scipione woke from a sleep in which he had held gold in his hand and his son had taken it and thrown it away. He patted sweat from his face with a napkin, feeling the embroidery rough on his skin and wishing linen could be plain, and handed the cloth back to the alert page, who, listening from his post outside the curtain, had distinguished

215

between the muffled sounds made by a man suffering nightmare and the soft groan of a man facing the world of reality. His pages were fond of their Prince who, although absentminded and at times irritable, was kind and considerate when he was feeling well. Now, once again, despite having slept, he did not look well at all.

'Some wine, your Highness?' Since the incident of the comfits and the death of the Venetian Ambassador, a taster had been hastily summoned. This unlucky man had already sampled what the page now offered, without noticeable effect. There were stories of poisons designed to kill after the passage of days and without previous symptoms, but there were also people who thought to touch a toad was fatal. There had to be risks.

Nevertheless, the Prince waved the cup away. 'No, no. Where is her Highness?'

'Her Highness is with her ladies. They prevailed on her to go into the garden, to take the evening air.'

The Prince pondered this, and then issued an irrelevant command. 'Fetch Signor Leconti . . . No! I'll go to his studio.' Artists, like scientists, resented interruption and, if they were any good, became absorbed when they were working. Experts of all kinds fascinated the Prince. After visiting Leone Leconti he would go and see Doctor Virgilio again. It might be that the miraculous conditions had been duplicated and he had succeeded in making more gold. The thought of this was like the gold itself, warm, enticing. First, however, he must make amends to his wife for having suspected her.

Leconti had been finding some difficulty in settling to work. On the way back from the sermon, his book full of satisfactory sketches of the cathedral audience and of the preacher, he had been enjoying in retrospect the theatrical entertainment of the sermon. Then he had recognised an item pushed cockeyed among the objects on the bonfire. It was a portrait done two years ago, on his former visit to Viverra, of the pretty wife of a rich burgher. The man had been pleased enough to reward him with a tidy sum and had fortunately remained ignorant that the painter had also spent time cuckolding him. The painting had been one of Leconti's best, one of those in which eye and hand had been in peculiar accord. He had caught, too, exactly that look of arch self-congratulation on the pretty face, the glow of light on the skin . . . superbly executed; and now it lay to be burnt.

After this disturbing sight he found it hard to care about the spiritual expression on St Francis's face; he did not resent the invasion of his studio by his patron as much as he usually did. Nor did he mind being told to abandon the triptych for the moment and bend all his energies to finishing the illuminations for the Book of Hours destined as a present for the Princess. It would be a pleasure. He rather enjoyed the fiddling care and detail that went into each picture. Most had already been roughed out and drawn, some had been filled with base colour, some coloured wholly, others awaited the brilliant addition of blue, green or gold . . . He got out the pages, unwrapped them and gave orders to his assistants on preparation and grinding of the pigment. The Prince also ordered that the precious box of lapis lazuli, so carefully listed in his accounts, should be fetched and some be weighed out for Leconti. For the Princess, skies should be magnificently blue.

The Prince now felt better about what he had done. He was deeply troubled still by thoughts of his missing son. Surely the boy would soon come to his senses? If he were indeed in that Dominican priory which had refused entry to or even speech with his searchers, the Bishop might say a word which should be effective; and if that failed, it would be time to apply, as a last resort, to Rome. He was halfway to the Old Castle, hurrying through the cypress walk almost at a trot to reach the laboratory, when he remembered that Bishop Ugolino was out of action since his fit after that sermon. As for Brother Ambrogio, the Prince comprehensively regretted that his mother had been so misguided as to bring down on them that vulture in friar's form. Had he listened to Brother Ambrogio, he would have dismissed Doctor Virgilio already instead of being poised to become richer than the Pope himself.

He was a little surprised to find no page on duty and the castle door ajar. Nor was there the sound of the pump forcing the chemical smells, so familiar, so exciting, down the stone passages. Was Doctor Virgilio trying something new and unorthodox? The Prince once more broke into almost a run. He thought again of the treatise he intended – should it after all be in Greek, or should he stick to Latin? – in which he would discourse on the Philosopher's Stone. He would have the inestimable advantage over all the scholars he had read: *he* had found it!

No one pulled aside the leather curtain. No one stood there to pull it. There was silence beyond. He pictured them all dumbfounded, gathered about Doctor Virgilio as he displayed the second piece of gold. He jerked aside the curtain and stood in anticipation.

No one was there.

No assistants, no Doctor Virgilio. The vessels, retorts, instruments, mortars, lay pushed about. The fires were out, the silent pump's great handle yawned to the vaulted ceiling. Books were in a pile, all shut. The Prince stared round, unable to take in, to credit what he was seeing. At one whirlwind stroke, all his hopes were gone, like dew as the sun rose high.

What had happened? *Where* was Doctor Virgilio? The Prince wandered, disbelieving, picking up a pair of compasses here, a pestle there, touching the cover of a book, peering into a vessel at still-glowing violet sediment. Had he gone? Left? But why? Surely no one would leave a patron so anxious to reward him?

The Prince sank on to a battered, acid-scarred stool; after a long minute he got to his feet and, not unlike a sleepwalker, one hand on the wall, made his way to his study. He sat down before the desk, fingered the draft beginnings of his treatise, and then raising his eyes stared hopelessly into his future.

31. Beg from Me

Prince Francesco did as the knife told him. Normally a courageous young man, he was at more than one disadvantage: half naked, having to hold up the sacking with one hand, he was standing with swollen bare feet on cold uneven sloping rock. He had eaten several apples on an empty stomach, which was now loudly convulsing. When the apparition with the long knife told him to stop waving that rosary and turn his back, he did so.

'Now,' she said, 'turn round.' She had put on a shift and a dress, both damp, and she sat down by the fire, knife in hand. 'You sit there. You'd best tell me what you're doing in my place here, if you're not as simple as you look.'

'*Your* place?' Not a shelter offered by God, then.

'*My* place,' she said. The glitter of her eyes in the firelight gave him a sudden conviction he had found an abode of demons; or of one demon at least. 'That's my blanket you're wearing. Have you no clothes? Did you walk in here naked?'

'Oh no. I've got – I've got my friar's habit.' He had better let her know what she was dealing with. In a sense, he was throwing down the gauntlet.

'You're a *friar*?' She stared, and looked him over; then, suddenly, she grimaced, showing her teeth, white and sharp. 'Well, you're an odd one then. I've seen a good few. One of them burnt down my house yesterday morning. Believe me,

219

I've no time for friars. They've taught you well already, taking other people's goods—'

'I was soaked—' But his excuses died on his tongue. Her cloak, or some garment that lay by the fire, was moving, moving of itself, first into a little mound and then a longer shape. It shifted again, and a cat, small and striped, emerged with dreadful deliberation and looked at her as if for orders. He had no dislike of cats, but could he be sure this Thing really was a cat? It now regarded him with narrowed pupils through the flames.

'What are you going to do for me?' she demanded suddenly. Her hand went out to touch the cat under the ear, and he thought the question was directed at the beast, but she turned to him, repeating: 'What are you going to do for me? Your brother burnt my house down, you've taken my blanket and slept on my bed, and I think you and not squirrels ate my apples.'

'I'm not going to do anything for you,' he said, gripping his rosary so hard that it bit into his hand. 'I serve only God. You can't get me into your service.' He sounded, he thought with disgust, like a child. 'You cannot inveigle me into the service of your master.' That sounded better.

'My master?' She leant forward, and all at once made that grimace again. This time, more used to her face, he identified the grimace correctly. She was grinning. 'Did God tell you to thieve food and a bed?'

'I had no intention of stealing. I thought—' Before this young woman's sharp and dangerous eyes he found himself quite unable to say what he had thought. To his feverish mind she had appeared as a demon but, if no demon, she was no ordinary peasant girl either and her cat looked suspiciously like a familiar. It would be as well to make his own position plain. 'I have left my home,' he went on more firmly, 'to lead a holy life. You shall have your blanket back. I will put my – my habit on. Although it is wet.'

'I've heard friars believe in mortification of the flesh,' she said. 'You're covered in fleabites. No! Stay where you are.'

She had got the knife again, and at her tone the young prince stopped his efforts to get up, and the cat stopped its quiet washing and looked at her. She rose and went to the back of the cave, picked up his robe and shook it; then, she looked in the bedding. 'No knife,' she said. 'You *are* simple after all. How did you expect to live?'

He looked at the garment she held out to him and could not summon up the holy joy with which he had first put it on. However, he laid her sacking blanket aside and got into the horrible robe, and at least felt modestly covered. He answered her question. 'I shall live as a mendicant as St Francis did,' he explained. 'By begging.'

She could not, he felt, appreciate what it meant to a son of a princely house to beg for food. She did not appreciate it, but sat down unimpressed as before.

'All right,' she said. 'Let's hear you. Beg from me.'

He did not at all see his way to doing this. To begin with, it was totally different from his imagined picture. People would bring him food in respect for his holy life, for which he had not had time yet. But living on roots and berries had not so far been a success.

'You're going to starve pretty soon if that's all you can do. Nobody's going to give you anything for gaping like a stockfish. You're hungry, aren't you? And you're a friar? Then beg.'

Prince Francesco put out his hands, took, as it were, his courage in them and said, 'In the name of God, give me food.'

He felt, in conflict, another flash of that holy joy. She reached behind her, picked up a bundle of cloth, undid it, and produced a flat loaf of bread. She broke it and handed a piece across the fire. 'In the name of God, then. Eat.'

She could not be a demon. Francesco managed not to cram the bread into his mouth. He even managed to say grace. Nothing had ever tasted so good.

'Have you,' he asked, 'anything to drink?'

'Plenty outside.' She stood up, and he followed her to the entrance. To his surprise, the sky was beginning to go pale

221

with morning. The rain had ceased. She picked up an earthenware bowl that had been standing in the rain, and he drank. He was giving it back to her when a white glare illumined them both. He turned, bewildered, to see a huge red flare miles away in the valley, topped by a swelling cloud of smoke. Then it was gone. He could see nothing when he turned back to the woman.

'That's in the city,' she said.

Their ears cracked as the great sound came and a muffled boom rebounded from the hills.

32. Brother Columba Is Raised Up

Brother Columba felt virtuously exhausted. He had started the day brilliantly by burning a witch alive. Although his original intention had been to bring the creature, bound and whipped, all the way into the city to decorate his bonfire in the great square, it was a good second best – if not so public a demonstration of his industry – to see her hut go up in flames and know she was cooking inside along with that demon whom she had summoned to protect her. Brother Columba smiled at the memory of blood starting from brow and cheek as he wielded his discipline. The evil brute had known the pain of earthly chastisement before he went to his master in Hell. It had been an auspicious, a splendid, start to the day.

In fact coming back to Viverra had been an anticlimax. He could not find Brother Ambrogio to report his success, and the palace people were surly and unresponsive to his questions. The truth was, Brother Ambrogio frightened them, but Brother Columba they wholly disliked. He had no idea it was his staring eyes that often made them turn away as he asked his questions or even before.

Unable to display his worth to his superior, Brother Columba was forced by his own energy out to the streets again. Viverra must be kept up to the mark. He must drive home the effects of Brother Ambrogio's sermon yesterday. By the time they left this city and travelled on to bring God's message to another, Viverra must be thoroughly purged and in a state of grace.

He spent a busy and happy day with his corps of ardent youths, organising the closure of several wineshops that had had the temerity to reopen; the stoning of an old woman, denounced by her neighbours, who should know, as a witch, and she had proved she was by shaking her fist and cursing at Brother Columba. The stoning of a painted trollop went off less well, partly because the crowd he had collected was very dilatory at finding stones, and partly because the flaunting trollop was more agile than the old woman and had hared off down a narrow alley hung with washing that impeded their pursuit. Then, his planned descent with his teenage gang on a couple of brothels that had dared to open after dusk had been ruined by the storm. All day the autumn sun had shone through an ominous haze, tempers had risen and found satisfying vent in the prosecution of sin; and now the heavens themselves spoke. Pale flashes beyond the hills had made Brother Columba speak with pleasant anticipation of the Day of Judgement, when the moon will turn to blood and fall into the sea; for he was confident that when the sheep were sorted from the goats he would be a prominent sheep.

This belief sustained him, as he sheltered in a doorway beneath a lantern and watched the rain sluice the cobbles. His faithful gang had scattered to their homes, hoods pulled up, jerkins or overskirts held over cropped heads. Vice would have to await its punishment till morning; there was no problem about its vanishing overnight. Brother Columba, waiting until he could make his way to his lodging without being drenched, used the time for prayer, warmed by the memory of the morning's fire.

He woke, aching, still on his knees but propped against the stone arch of the doorway, his head sunk on his chest, his rosary dangling from his fingers. A pig was sniffing him suspiciously; although at ground level and in the street, he did not appear to be useful garbage. Struck on the snout by a

224

rosary, it galloped off down the street, indignant, as Brother Columba rubbed his legs and yawned. The rain had stopped. He felt restless, anxious to be about God's work again.

On his way to the palace, through streets empty of all but the occasional scavenger in this lessening of darkness before dawn, Brother Columba was blessed with inspiration. It felt like a breath, which must come from God: he had burnt the witch *in situ* as it were, at yesterday's dawn; why not the alchemist today? He had not forgotten Doctor Virgilio's contemptuous dismissal of him. The man should be shown the anger of the Lord. It was a continual surprise that Brother Ambrogio had not yet flushed this devil from his den; but then, he had been occupied in wrestling for the soul of Prince Scipione.

So he, Brother Columba, would do it. If the Prince were still lured from God by Doctor Virgilio and his accursed works, there was a tried and sure method of removing both.

The guard let him into the palace yard, and he skirted the building under the shuttered windows of the long façade, crossed the formal gardens and came to the gate. It was not difficult for an agile, skinny man to climb the crumbling wall beside the gate and soon, in the grey light, he was approaching the Old Castle through damp grass and the scent of bushes diffused by rain. His heart was hammering at the thought of this final showdown. Doctor Virgilio worked by night, as was proper to his vile trade; his assistants might be asleep. In the bosom of his habit Brother Columba carried tinder and flint. He could scarcely wait to see again the glory of cleansing fire blossom as it had when devouring the witch's hut.

The emptiness of the laboratory puzzled him sadly, as it had puzzled the Prince some hours before. He had seen a light as he approached the castle, in a window, but there was none here. In fact the light burnt in the Prince's study, where he had fallen asleep over the treatise he would now never finish. Here there was only the smouldering glow of a fire through

225

the ashes heaped to smother it; and there was the increasing faint light of dawn. Brother Columba stared round in a dismay as profound as the Prince's. However, unlike the Prince, he knew what action to take. The Devil had withdrawn; there should be no chance of his return. Brother Columba began to make his bonfire.

Methodically at first he used the fuel from its stack as the basis, piled up in the middle of the floor, with stools and wooden clamps and bookstands, and then books, the devilish books. He knew books could take time to burn. He tore the pages from their covers, hurting his hands and spurred by the intransigence of the paper and the cuts on his fingers to increasing rage. He flung the pages down, and the covers, working more wildly, building the pyre. The furnace embers, coaxed to life by the convenient bellows, could be shovelled under the paper and he watched as they ate into the pages of blasphemy, flowered, and the fire took hold. Now he could work from a little distance – he could pick up the jars and vessels from the shelves, from the benches, and fling them into the flames. How good the smash of glass and pottery, the flare as a liquid or powder turned the flames violet or green! The fire was so fierce now the containers spread it as they shattered . . .

Really it was a pity that Brother Columba, although he saw the last vivid white flash as he hurled the jar full of magnesium into the fire, never lived to hear the magnificent explosion that followed. By the time the noise bounced off the hills Brother Columba was well on the way to discovering God's opinion of the way His work had been carried out.

The Old Castle's age had not had much effect on its strength. The explosion lifted the two upper floors and the decayed leads of that tower, fragmenting them as they went high into the dawn air. The blast sent tremors through the ancient walls, shaking out mortar, but chiefly it snaked through the passages and halls, took stairs at a leap, jumped an object here and shattered one there, wrapped the curtain rod of the leather curtain round a pillar of the crypt, shifting the great column a fraction of an inch, and raising every atom of dust in the whole place.

Any explosion which so affects the structure of a building is going to have a profound effect on life in the vicinity. Animals often display awareness of impending disaster which human beings do not feel. The little cat who usually favoured Prince Scipione with her presence when he sat in his study, had got up and left him dozing at his desk shortly before Brother Columba picked up the fatal jar, as if the destructive activity of humankind disturbed her with its potential. The Prince was quite alone when the three doors of his study variously blew in, the desk's high shelving caught the blast and went over; cupboards flew open, books, boxes and bottles crashed from the shelves, the lamp on the hinged arm broke on the floor and luckily went out. Not so lucky, the Prince himself, underneath the weighty structure, passed almost without intermission from sleep to unconsciousness. His spectacles, knocked from their hook on the side of the desk, lay convenient to his outflung hand, in pieces.

Other people quite unknown to the Prince, not far either from him or the laboratory that night, also experienced some of the interesting effects. Three men, one extremely tall, one with long, greasy hair obscuring his face and a sword that rode his back from shoulder to knee, and one with an air of manic menace, had for the past few days been haunting a corridor of the Old Castle where lay the cells for important prisoners of State. In adjoining cells, Donato Landucci awaited the arrival of his father to stand trial for poisoning the Prince, and Antonio Carlotti of Mascia awaited a punishment not yet determined by the Prince but certain to satisfy the appetite of the Viverrans for spectacle. Both had been aware, in the last few days, of what each hoped was an effort at rescue. Shortly after their gaoler and his guard had left their twice daily food and drink, they could hear a gouging, ferreting, scrabbling sound like a giant mole outside. Both had put ears to the oaken iron-bound doors that shut them in, trying to locate the sound. Both had become bored, tonight, and gone back to bed.

Both had been awake again at the time the explosion interrupted the work and subsumed it. Both doors were blown in. Donato was in luck, still lying on the pallet to the side of his cell. He was bundled to the floor after the door struck the end wall and he lay in a cloud of brick, mortar and stone dust, perfectly deaf and wondering if he had been executed without warning. Antonio Carlotti's bad luck did not change. He had been woken by the usual sound of stealthy chiselling, and getting up to listen more closely, he had met his door on its way in.

The three men who had been mistakenly working at this door might have thought God Himself had taken a helping hand, but their minds at the time were otherwise occupied. Aldo and Fracassa, working in unison on the lower hinge, were heaved by the blast and tumbled head over each other's heels along the passage and halfway up the spiral stairs at the end. Pio had been dealing with the top hinge and the force of the explosion elevated him after the door that had met Carlotti and posted him through the high cell window from which it had just stripped the bars. It was quite a distance down to the river but it may be doubted that Pio had the detachment to consider this.

Across the gardens in the palace itself, the sound and shock waves spread with all the unpredictability laid down by the laws of physics. The damage, less extensive of course than in the castle, yet offered effects of interest. The Princess Dowager started awake from troubled dreams when her bed canopy of figured brocade took off from its hooks in the ceiling to descend on her in smothering folds. The maid on the trundle bed in her room woke at the same moment and screamed to see the labouring monster on the bed.

A great wind blew out every candle in the palace chapel where Brother Ambrogio was keeping vigil. He had been doing penance for feeling personal triumph at his success in putting the fear of God into Doctor Virgilio that afternoon.

Here came the Devil's reply in a roar of Satanic rage. He gripped the top of the prie-dieu and prayed on in the darkness, as ten yards of badly keyed fresco detached itself and smashed round him.

The Princess Isotta escaped the indignity suffered by her mother-in-law; her bed canopy, ballooning, held to its hooks; but she herself was hurled out of her bed on to the floor while the lunettes of her windows broke from their lead framework to strew the sheets with splinters of blue and red glass. The Princess was shielded from further injury by the burly form of Gatta which landed on top of her and received several flesh wounds from slivers of glass lodged in his shoulders. His first thought, that someone had scored a hit with a cannon, was followed at once by a swift review of which of his enemies might have been so lucky.

Sigismondo and Benno, returning from their mission to escort Landucci, with a corpse to show for their pains, had been told by a sleepy palace guard that the Prince was at the Old Castle. They were crossing the palace garden when the laboratory left its moorings. The wind of its passing blew them off their feet. Benno landed on his back on a low box hedge, winded and deafened while the huge blaze of light spread momentarily above him in the sky. The next thing he knew was Sigismondo plucking him off the hedge, much of which seemed to be trying to grow inside his doublet. He staggered when set on his feet, and gazed round. Biondello, fired from his shirt like a rocket, now dropped among fragments of the tree he had lodged in. He too staggered, and shook his one ear, before he picked himself up enough to pelt after Benno who was pelting after Sigismondo, even though it went clean against the nature of either of them to run towards trouble.

Sigismondo did not waste time going to search the wreck of the laboratory, open now to the strengthening light in the sky, bleak as a battlefield but without corpses: Brother Columba's relics being unevenly distributed over the land-scape outside. Benno stumbled coughing in the dust after

229

Sigismondo, trying not to lose sight of him. He had never been to the Prince's study but supposed this was it when Sigismondo, his back arched with the effort, struggled to raise a massy wooden structure from the floor. As Benno, crouching, put his shoulder also to the shape, it rose, creaking, with pieces falling from it, and Sigismondo overturned it away from them before kneeling over the slight body it had hidden. Benno, fingering grit from his eyes, saw Prince Scipione, his face a mask of white dust, blink as Sigismondo put a hand to the pulse in his neck.

'Highness, can you move your feet?'

Stone me, thought Benno, does he want him to start dancing? He peered through the settling dust to see the Prince's toes in their velvet slippers wriggle experimentally. Sigismondo grunted his satisfaction.

'Now, Highness, tell me if I hurt you.' He felt under the Prince's shoulders, along his spine, slid an arm beneath and helped him to sit up. The Prince, looking decidedly puzzled, cooperated.

The confusion in the Prince's mind, increased by the blow to the skull he had received from the floor, suddenly crystallised on his last vivid memory: the empty laboratory.

'Doctor Virgilio! He must be found – brought back!' He looked round urgently into Sigismondo's face. Benno read from his master's expression that any bringing back of Doctor Virgilio would have to be accomplished in several baskets.

'Your Highness – there has been—'

'He's gone! Left! Taken everything that was his! Taken the priceless secret to who knows whom!' Tears made dark streaks down his mask of dust. Sigismondo now was thoughtful.

'Did he tell your Highness this?'

'Gone!' The Prince wailed like a bereft child. Benno wondered why they both spoke so faintly and why his ears were ringing like Sunday bells in Rocca. He did not hear the arrival of the crowd who burst into the study, but Sigismondo directed a look over his shoulder, and the foremost spoke.

230

'Your Highness! Thanks be to God! What happened?'

Benno could hear the questions shrieked over his head though the sound made his ears bubble uncomfortably. The Prince was unhelpful, surrounded now by courtiers and pages anxious to relieve Sigismondo of his burden.

'Send for Doctor Virgilio! *He must start again*!'

33. Gatta's Daughter

'I can never thank you enough for saving his Highness. What a saviour you have proved to us!' The Princess, wrapped in a loose robe of indigo velvet over which her hair flowed free, was almost tearful. She offered both hands to Sigismondo and, as he knelt to kiss them, Lord Ridolfo Ridolfi was announced and Gatta came in. He was fully dressed and furious. 'Who's done this? What caused that explosion? Who threatens the Prince's life while I am here?'

Clearly it was a professional insult to Gatta, commander of the armies of Viverra, to have his employer blown up on the premises. He glared at Sigismondo, who was rising to his feet. 'Where is Landucci? Where's Michelotto?'

'Michelotto is gone to report to you at your house, lord. 'As for Landucci—' Sigismondo shrugged.' I was on my way to tell his Highness about Landucci when the laboratory blew up.'

'Did you see who did it?'

'No. It may be that they did not survive. It may be that some experiment destroyed the laboratory by accident.'

'Where's his Highness now?'

The Princess spoke. 'In his bed, and the doctor attends him. Thanks to Master Sigismondo here, he seems likely to recover soon, with no more than bruises.' She did not mention the blow on the head which made him ramble in such agitation, calling for Doctor Virgilio. Her husband's fantasies had been a permanent feature of her life, and this was not a new one.

Gatta's glare transmuted itself into a beaming smile. He came to embrace Sigismondo and left an arm across his shoulders. 'You shall have your reward! And Landucci? Has he confessed?'

Sigismondo's dark face had no smile. 'If he has, lord, it is at the Judgement Seat. He is dead. There was a rescue attempt – an ambush – and he paid for it with his life.'

Gatta had begun a question when a page asked the Princess's permission to admit Michelotto della Casa. She gestured her permission and Michelotto was ushered in. He advanced and flourished an elaborate bow, smiling and alert. Gatta redirected his question with energy.

'What's this of Landucci? How did he come by his death?'

Michelotto cast eyes and hands towards the painted ceiling. 'Dear God, his people were no friends to him. In the scuffle, it seems that one of them killed him by mistake.'

'Why was he not better guarded?'

Michelotto laid an admiring hand on Sigismondo's sleeve. 'If the hero of Mascia could not defend him against such an attempt, had I a chance?'

Gatta all but scowled at the term *hero of Mascia* applied to Sigismondo, but the Princess, listening intently, prevented further argument.

'It is one enemy the less. God is protecting us. You have heard that Antonio Carlotti died in the explosion?'

Gatta gave his fanged grin. 'Who is left, Highness? Now, if Venice and the Holy Father—' He paused, his glance giving significance and reminding everyone that against opponents of such weight, beside whom the Carlottis and Landuccis were nothing, he, Ridolfo Ridolfi, was the only shield the state possessed.

'My lord—' The Princess extended an elegant hand and drew him to her side, where he stood and raised the hand to press his lips to it almost lingeringly. 'We do depend on you.

When news comes from Venice of how the Republic takes the death of Signor Loredano, you must be here.'

'I will not fail you. I will stay in Viverra, but I was to have set out today to meet and bring to Viverra my daughter, of whom I have spoken to your Highness. She is on her way from her convent, with an escort provided by the Abbess who dared wait no longer to send her. There is word of plague in two outlying villages.'

There was a flutter of busy hands, everyone present crossing themselves as if to ward off both the fear and its dreadful cause. The Princess looked at Sigismondo. 'Send him in your place. If my son is not at Pontenova Priory – and I have sent today to force enquiry – then Master Sigismondo may have the luck he had before, and find him on the way.'

'Your Highness's wish is law to me. Master Sigismondo shall go to bring my daughter to Viverra.' Gatta's look was fond, but it was directed at the Princess and he quite missed the glance Michelotto gave him. The one delegated to fetch Gatta's daughter should have been Michelotto.

Benno was enjoying the rural expedition, a pleasant change from that which had left them with Landucci's body. There had been no chance for talk with his master since he had carried the Prince to his room – getting quite a habit, that – and in the bustle of leading a small troop of men out of Viverra, Sigismondo had told him only that they were to meet and escort Gatta's daughter. Benno, his face lifted to the autumn sunlight, was busy speculating on her probable looks: Gatta's tawny hair, now, lots of it, and the green-golden eyes . . . Benno hesitated when he envisaged the mouth . . . Perhaps she wouldn't be pretty at all. It wouldn't matter, for now that her father had become so important she could be married off to almost anyone Gatta pleased to choose. And no good wondering about her looks, because as an unmarried girl she'd be swathed in a veil before strangers and there'd be no chance to check if he was right.

He did get to see one face he recognised.

235

They stopped at a village to buy olives and raisins, and just beyond it dismounted by the wayside to drink their wine and make a breakfast. Sigismondo had stayed to round up one of the men who had got into an argument in the village, and he was about to dismount when a girl came up to his stirrup.

'Salad for your bread, sir?' She held up a basket of basil, wild garlic, tarragon and fennel. Her dark hair was bound back today, in a rope twisted with green ribbon, but there was no mistaking the witch.

Benno came to take the reins, and Sigismondo swung from his horse and, watched by the soldiers, stood turning over the herbs in the basket, smiling, sniffing them or chewing a leaf here and there in sample. The listening Benno alone knew that the talk was nothing to do with salad.

'You've found somewhere to live?'

'So did someone else.' She laughed, and the soldiers nudged one another and commented. This Sigismondo was no slouch with the girls, see him getting off with this one. Maybe she liked them hairless. She looked hot stuff. 'I went to a cave I use, and found someone before me, making bold – a young madman with a cracked idea of being a hermit and no more idea of looking after himself than a puppy.'

'Young? And wanting to throw the world away? What was he like?'

'Beautiful as the day, with dark red hair it'd be a shame to cut off. I left him tinder and flint up there—' She jerked her head towards their right, where a long grassy slope corrugated with gullies and scattered with boulders led up to a scarp of huge rock, protruding as though some great animal lurking beneath had shouldered its way through the soil. Above this, in shadows and cloud, rose the bulk of the hill, indistinct, a ridge leading back to the range beyond. 'I'm not playing nursemaid to him, pretty though he may be; I'm on my way north and I'm not coming back until I hear the preacher has left. If that boy doesn't learn fast, I'll find his bones cluttering up my cave when I get back.' She handed

236

Sigismondo a bundle of greenstuff in return for the coin in his hand. 'It's not my business if such a crackpot dies.'

'It's surely his own affair,' Sigismondo agreed, folding his bread round the garlic and biting. Benno, chewing at his own meal, was puzzled. She had seen the young prince! Was Sigismondo leaving him to starve? Wouldn't the Princess give a fortune to get her son back to Viverra? Here was Sigismondo talking as if it was nothing, while up the hill a gold mine was waiting. Suppose someone else found him? Yet, of course there must be some plan in his master's mind, as always; he only wished he had any idea what it was. He'd have liked to nip up the hill and give the poor young man his own bread and wine. He knew so well what hunger was like but then he'd known since childhood – it would be much worse for a prince who'd never been short before.

Benno was pondering this with sympathy when Sigismondo's great horse became restless and needed all his attention. By the time he had it soothed and under control the witch was gone and Sigismondo with a summoning wave brought the soldiers to their feet. Holding the stirrup for his master's foot, Benno gave a discreet jerk of the head at the hill with its unseen cave.

'You going to leave him, then?'

Sigismondo hummed and turned the horse's head. The soldiers were getting into double files, ready to set off once more. Gatta's daughter, it seemed, was more important than the young prince.

Benno turned out to be, as is usual in this world of uncertainties, both right and wrong about Gatta's daughter. He was wrong, to start with, about the veil. She had one, it was true, but wore it thrown back; and as it was almost transparent, and green, it was obviously intended to frame her face and set off her hair, which was indeed tawny and abundant. Her eyes, also, were that curious colour like her father's, but her mouth, while generously full-lipped, had the advantage of regular teeth. The impression was of a young lady of immense confidence and tearing spirits, delighted to be out of the convent where she was being educated, determined to enjoy herself. She spurred her horse forward to meet them, leaving the elderly nun at her side tutting and shaking her head.

'You're *not* Michelotto! In the distance I thought you were!' She smiled and gave Sigismondo her hand, which he bent his head over. 'Where's my father? His letter said he would meet me.' Looking past Sigismondo at Gatta's men watching with acute curiosity, she went on with exaggerated alarm, 'You're not *brigands*? Don't count on my father paying any ransom . . . What a shame, I can see his badge on your men.' She was still laughing when the nun, head of the escort, caught up, and with frigid correctness, demanded Sigismondo's credentials. He handed over a letter with the Ridolfi seal and introduced himself while the girl stared frankly round, taking in the landscape, clicking her fingers at Biondello, and pulling her collar away from her neck. Bet the convent's pleased to get rid of her, thought Benno, as her glance skimmed his face and returned to rest with more approval on Sigismondo's; she's likely to lead even Gatta a dance till he's got her married off, and her husband a dance after that. She's not exactly pretty. It's just that something about her makes men turn their heads and want to follow.

He noticed, behind the nun, an elderly woman whose glossy black braids contradicted her wrinkles, and whose small black eyes never left the girl. Perhaps an old nurse who'd kill for her nurseling, he thought; let's hope she never needs to.

Now the escort provided by the convent was turning back, the old nun giving her blessing to the girl in the clear conviction that it was well needed. With a last suspicious stare at Sigismondo she wheeled her mule for the journey back to the convent, where they were probably still celebrating their boarder's departure. The girl waved a joyous good-bye to restraints and boredom, and turned expectantly to Sigismondo.

'What's Viverra like? At least it won't be prayers all day!'

34. A Man Is a Man

Sigismondo called a halt on the way back, at the very spot where they had halted a couple of hours before. He unpacked from the baggage mule a painted linen cloth which he spread on the grass, and he led the young lady to sit down there. For her and the duenna he produced cakebread, and a flask of wine which Benno supposed must be far superior to that which he was swigging. Sigismondo sat on the ground and pointed out where Viverra was, and the spur of hill that hid Mascia, and told of Gatta waking Carlotti from his bed when the town was taken. Then to Benno's astonishment he told the young lady about a hermit who had come to live on the hill where they now sat.

'—a saintly man, it is said, who mortifies the flesh and sees visions of the future.'

'The future?' Caterina Ridolfi had been ready to be bored at the visions of saints, but the future! That was totally different, that captured the imagination of a girl whose main interest was whom she might have to marry. 'Is he a horrid old man, like St Jerome in pictures with his skin hanging on his bones?'

Sigismondo appeared to give thought to this, and returned a doubtful answer. 'They say he's young to be so holy, and blessed with angelic beauty; but I've not been up to the cave myself. In any case, my lady, I am sure your father would forbid your going to see him.'

239

Caterina's chin went up. She bit determinedly into her bread, frowning, and then said, 'Monna Maria will go with me, so my father can't possibly object. You shall show us the way.' She turned to the elderly duenna, who had been dozing, and jogged her awake, saying, 'Maria, we are going to find out what's to happen to us. Isn't that fun?'

While Benno thought it might be a lot else besides fun, he hoped he would get to go with them to this cave, and was delighted when Sigismondo sent him a glance and the faintest of nods.

Caterina enjoyed the climb and scramble up the hillside. She needed Sigismondo's hand in assistance more often than a duenna strict with the proprieties should have allowed – Benno had been groom to a young lady with such a duenna – but Monna Maria was fully occupied with avoiding loose stones, catching her foot on roots and her skirt on brambles, and panting with the exertion.

As they neared the cave a noise from within made Caterina stop and peer ahead with redoubled curiosity. 'What's that? Is he having visions?'

The sound died away, Sigismondo stepped ahead of them. It broke out again.

'Is it a wild beast?'

If it is, thought Benno, and he's dined off that poor young prince, then it's given him awful indigestion.

'Wait here, my lady. I'll see.' Sigismondo bent his head and shoulders under the bush that masked the cave and vanished into the dark cleft. Monna Maria clutched Benno's arm and endeavoured to thrust him in front of Caterina, who was pushing ahead. Only a minute went by before Sigismondo appeared again with the young man in his arms. He laid him with gentle care on the ground outside the cave, while the others crowded to look. Benno was amazed to see how thin the young prince had got in so short a time. He was not pale, however, but flushed with fever and moaning. As he lay there in his coarse robe, he tossed his head to one side and the cowl slipped off his dark red hair. An

240

identical expression mellowed the faces of both women, young and old.

'Poor, *poor* young man. He'll die if he's left here – won't he?' Caterina demanded fiercely of Sigismondo, who shrugged. 'But how can you be so callous? We can't let him die! He's a holy man! He needs nursing and proper food. He'll never get looked after in a village as he should be. But I know! I know, we'll take him with us to my father's house. You and I, Maria, will nurse him hack to health.'

'An unmarried girl nurse a man! Fie! Your father would certainly never permit—'

'A *holy* man, Maria.'

'A man is a man.'

'And my father need never know if we don't tell him. Think of all the things he doesn't know.' She gripped the old woman's arm and nodded significantly. 'You can arrange things. You can arrange anything. I know you can.'

This knowledge was based very clearly on experience; it could only be wondered what Monna Maria had arranged in the past. A calculating look now came into her face. 'There's your father's men down there. They'll talk for sure.'

'*You* won't tell, will you?' Caterina did not actually lay her hand on Sigismondo's, but her eyes did her pleading for her. 'And you'll think of a way to carry him there?'

A loud groan from the sick young man here made her peer anxiously downhill, where the soldiers were out of sight beyond boulders and bushes. The jink of harness, and men's voices, came up to them. Sigismondo was silent, waiting as if doubtful. I'd never've had the cunning, Benno thought, to leave it to her.

'I know!' Caterina skipped at her idea, and began to laugh. 'My litter. You saw the awful thing. The Abbess wanted me to ride in it and keep the curtains drawn in front of the soldiers. Well, I had to, she was like that, but once the convent was out of sight I was out of it, old Mother Simplicita couldn't stop me. The litter's perfect. You shall say you're feeling tired, Maria, and we'll pop him in with you.' She looked down at Francesco, whose groans had subsided and who lay with his eyes closed, the image of a suffering angel.

'All very well, but how do we get him down there and into the litter without them seeing?' Monna Maria twitched at her headdress and smoothed a dyed braid. She turned to the silent Sigismondo. 'You could carry him, sir?'

'Certainly.' His voice, after their feminine ones, was surprisingly deep. 'If the Lady Caterina were to give orders for the litter to be put in the shade down there,' he pointed to a small copse by the side of the road beneath the hill, 'so that you may rest your aching head; then she could draw the men's attention by some means.' His eyes gravely enquired of the young lady, and Benno envisaged her undoing her bodice to find some wayward insect, as he had seen a conjurer's assistant do in Rouen. 'I shall stay up here to consult the hermit alone, and in fact bring him to the litter.'

'Perfect. Come, fellow, help me down.' So it was that Benno found himself guiding Gatta's daughter over the stones and down the slope while Monna Maria slithered and gasped behind them. By the time she reaches the bottom, he thought, she's going to need that litter. As for Gatta's daughter, she had her father's grasp of strategy. Once she reached the men, she gave orders for the placing of the litter, showing exactly where it was to be put under the trees, half shielded by an immense boulder long ago shed by the hill. Then she tenderly helped the limping Maria towards it and turned her attention to the captain in charge of the troop, a stocky, swarthy fellow with a short bow slung on his shoulder.

'Let me try that, sir.' He reluctantly unshipped it and strung it for her. She deftly plucked an arrow from the quiver at his back. 'I can hit a deer at forty paces. I'll wager you a gold piece I can hit that tree – there, with the twisted trunk – and split the branch that's hanging.'

Without her duenna, Caterina had become a little dictatorial, but subtly charming; a feminine challenge. The men clustered round, laying bets on their commander's daughter; those betting against her giving gallant excuses.

Their attention was all for her and the tree. Only Benno, crouching to talk to Biondello, peeked in the opposite direction and caught a glimpse of Sigismondo passing with his burden to the hidden litter. He reflected on the luck that had provided Caterina Ridolfi with a featherweight duenna. He'd seen some in the past that would have foundered a mule-litter like this one all on their own even before sharing it with however thin a young man.

Sigismondo now joined them, interrupting the surprised applause for the young lady's archery, to order them to the road again. As the mules were being put to the litter, a particularly loud groan issued from within, and the curtain was opened a crack to show Monna Maria's face with eyes half shut in anguish, emitting the doleful cry, 'Oh take care there! My head, my head!'

She may well say that, reflected Benno as he followed Sigismondo in the cavalcade. It'll be the first thing to roll if Gatta finds out about this.

35. Benno's Stomach Tells the Truth

Caterina Ridolfi was prudent enough, as they approached the city, to lower the pretty green veil over her face and ride demurely beside the litter. A man of Gatta's was at the gate, with a message from Gatta that Sigismondo was to go straight to the palace, so Benno did not get to see how the young lady and her duenna managed to convey their captured hermit still in secret into hiding in Gatta's house; he felt sure they would do it, and the more easily as Gatta was not there to welcome his daughter.

Benno could not fathom why Sigismondo had contrived a situation so full of danger for everyone. Perhaps his master, living a life of risks himself, was entitled to put other people in the way of them. Since he began service with Sigismondo he had felt the wind of Death's scythe himself more than once.

Gatta was descending the great stair towards the marble hall where Prince Francesco had made his horse caracole so short a time ago. His manner was preoccupied. The abrupt urgency of the summons was not consonant with what he had to say.

'Her Highness wishes you to look for her son again.' The matter so occupied him that he did not ask after his daughter, unless he took for granted that Sigismondo's presence meant she had arrived safely. 'News has come from the Priory that Prince Francesco is not there and she fears very strongly for his life. Her men have found no trace of him round Viverra

245

and she believes in your luck: you are to set off as soon as you can be ready. You,' he turned to Benno, 'get provisions and be at the gate within the hour.'

With the yellow eyes on him, Benno scrambled. First here, now there, no peace for the lucky. And Sigismondo had only to say, *Look under your own roof.* That battered face was intimidating; Sigismondo must be very sure of what he was doing. His slight nod had been enough – they would go on this useless journey.

Benno had not been in the city since the disintegration of the laboratory. He wandered from shop to shop, buying some of the things he knew Sigismondo liked and treating himself to a favourite or two of his own, for this expedition was surely almost a holiday. As he listened to the talk in the shops and round the stalls in the great square, he thought there was a general change of mood. He passed wineshops that had been closed when he and Sigismondo sought the apothecary, but which were open now. People sat on their benches as if challenging any objectors. Benno began to believe that if any of the youthful gangs who had roamed the streets looking for sin to chastise, were to appear now, the chastising might surprise them. He learnt of lecturing adolescents who had had their hides tanned for them by their infuriated elders; one, who had righteously staved in the casks in his father's cellar, had been locked in there and only let out, very sick from the fumes and abject, for a severe beating. Where was Brother Columba, the inspiration of the gangs? Brother Ambrogio had given a remarkable sermon, true, but how had his predictions been fulfilled?

Everyone remembered that the Prince had been threatened with death. What had happened? He had *escaped* death, and by a miracle. God is the performer of miracles. What better sign of God's forgiveness, even His favour, than this sparing of the Prince's life? God had blown up the alchemist and his evil works, leaving Prince Scipione purged of sin and almost unhurt.

What of those who had been killed, beside the

alchemist? Who were they but the Prince's enemies? God had made a point of destroying Antonio Carlotti of Mascia in a very conspicuous manner. It was a shame He had pre-empted the execution, promised for later in the autumn, a special occasion for the whole family . . . There was more excited talk about the fate of Count Landucci, summoned to answer about the attempt to poison the Prince. Set his son to do it, the wretch, and now struck by lightning, it was said, and God couldn't put it plainer than that: the Prince was protected, his enemies could expect Divine punishment even in this world.

Therefore, Brother Ambrogio could be wrong. Wasn't it a sign from heaven that the storm raging over the hills and over Viverra only a day ago, the storm that had killed Landucci, had also destroyed the bonfire waiting to be lit here in the square? It had been tumbled to the ground and no Brother Columba had turned up to rebuild it; and it was remarkable how the objects piled on it had vanished before morning as though spirited away. God did not mean these little harmless things to be burnt, for He could have sent a lightning bolt from the skies to ignite them on the spot.

Brother Ambrogio had not only been demonstrably wrong about the Prince, but had also incited the snatching of cathedral treasures that had struck Bishop Ugolino down; though the Bishop was now said to be recovering by the special favour of God. No one was particularly fond of Bishop Ugolino, as good a hand, or voice, at denunciation in his own line as any Brother Ambrogio, but after all a Bishop has every right to thunder anathemas in his own cathedral and nobody was obliged to take it badly. Repentance was a business between a man's confessor and his own soul, not to be forced on him by jumped-up juveniles and foreign friars. What about the disappearance of poor young Prince Francesco? Whose fault was *that*, one may ask? Stuffing his head with talk of spiritual kingdoms – all very well in the next world, by God's mercy – but the prince's duty lay here in Viverra supporting his father against the state's enemies and learning how to rule justly.

The original reason that had made Viverra listen with such attention to Brother Ambrogio, was not forgotten either. The skull that had ridden into the city ahead of him had spoken to all Viverra without a tongue. Plague had been crawling towards them across the countryside for months, and brought the idea of imminent death before their eyes too clearly. The latest news now, which had filled the churches with thankful prayers, was that it had veered to the east, away from Viverra, like an evil mist rolling from the hills to reveal sunlight. And who had attacked that hideous skull but the young prince?

People also began to count up the cost to trade of the preacher's visit. There was even talk of his being responsible for damage to the vines done by the late storm; God had manifested His will with unmistakable force to break the influence of the friar.

Benno was listening to this bold theory with his mouth open and a drink poised to put in it when the cathedral clock sonorously spoke the hour.

Sigismondo would be waiting.

Benno arrived at the palace gate out of breath, Biondello panting behind him. He had arranged with a palace groom to have horses waiting, and he was there although there was, Benno saw thankfully, no sign of Sigismondo. He tipped the man, tied the horses to a ring in the wall and sat on his heels to pass the time in dozing until his master came. Biondello flopped down beside him and lay, head between paws, the picture of philosophical resignation.

One of the horses stamped and Benno jerked awake. Biondello was yawning, and scratching behind where his left ear ought to be. Over the square came the sound of the cathedral clock again. Benno felt a stir of fear in his stomach. Was he at the wrong gate? What had kept Sigismondo? Could he have decided to tell the Princess after all that her son was found?

If so, he would have sent a message or come himself to tell Benno.

The feeling was worse than the gripes. Biondello whimpered at him as if he sensed it too. What was to be done? Try the other palace gates, or the city gates, though he was sure Gatta had meant this gate, leading from the great court. Should he ask at the palace, to see if someone had forgotten to bring him a message?

As he untied the horses he decided on this last course. It wouldn't do to go haring off to other gates and miss Sigismondo on the way. As he crossed the paving stones of the great court a horrible idea occurred to him. He remembered the peculiar three who had tried to kill Sigismondo twice in the belief that he was Michelotto. Suppose they had caught him unaware and been successful? But catching Sigismondo unaware would be a feat in itself and Benno did not estimate the three as capable of it. That last time, his master had known what they were up to even with his back to them. Yet everyone did make mistakes, and that long sword one of them carried might well compound a final, fatal mistake.

Benno had to wipe away a cold sweat by the time he reached the doorman.

He got news of his master at once.

'Gone. Off to find Prince Francesco. He's left. You'd best hurry.'

Benno stopped thinking and began to panic. He had spent too long in the city and Sigismondo had set off without him.

'When did he go?'

The man turned, and spat into the yard. 'Oh, an hour ago, I'd say. I've been here about that long and I was told he'd just gone.'

Benno stared. He had been at the gate for over an hour. He tipped the fellow to take the horses back to the stables for now and, scooping up Biondello, made his way through the winding stairs and passages of the palace to the tiny room allotted them, where they stored their few belongings.

His stomach hadn't lied. There, still rolled up on the

pallet, was Sigismondo's big wool cloak and, beside it, the leather scrip that held the herbs and ointments he always carried on their journeys.

Benno sank on his heels, with a hand on the scrip for comfort, and stared into the distance. He had never felt more afraid in his life.

36. WHO WANTED HIM DEAD?

'A word in your ear.' Gatta had been so close, his breath was indeed warm in Sigismondo's ear, his arm about his shoulders. 'Her Highness is concerned about more than her son. There is someone I want you to see.' He clicked his fingers; a palace page, evidently awaiting the signal, ran off, and Gatta led Sigismondo to a small anteroom at the foot of the stairs. They were followed almost at once by the page with a girl. He all but pushed her in, and shut the door.

She was a plain girl, with brown eyes beneath swollen lids. She had been crying and was twisting her apron in her hands. She shot a glance of terror at Sigismondo while she bobbed her curtsey.

Gatta spoke in a voice intended to soothe. 'Tell again what you saw in the Prince's room.'

She hesitated, crumpling her apron. Gatta let an edge slide into his voice. '*Tell.*'

She started at a gabble, glancing from Gatta to Sigismondo as if uncertain which was the more frightening. She made many excuses and her account was broken, but it emerged that she had been finishing her work in the Prince's bedchamber by cleaning the little oriel off the room when she heard someone enter. Fearful of being surprised by the Prince himself or his chamberlain, when she should have finished her cleaning – Gatta cut into her reasons for not having managed to do so – she had hidden behind the curtain, hoping for a chance to slip out. Peeping through (she mimed the little shifting of the curtain with her finger) she had seen not the Prince but someone else whom she knew.

'And who was that?' Gatta pressed Sigismondo's shoulder, emphasising the importance of the answer.

She mangled her apron. 'Young Lord Landucci.'

'You saw what he was doing?' Gatta would have made a good lawyer.

'He was putting a pair of gloves in the little coffer by the door.'

Gatta's slap on Sigismondo's shoulder was triumphant. Sigismondo hummed thoughtfully and the girl started as he spoke. 'By your leave, another question. Why did you wait so long to say this?'

A low bawl answered him. Tears seemed to spurt rather than flow. Gatta made an impatient gesture and she fled from the room. He turned with a shrug to Sigismondo.

'I asked that, of course. She was simply frightened. After Ginevra died,' he crossed himself, 'she heard of the poison on the gloves. No secrets in palaces. And you see what a fool she is. She got the idea she would be poisoned too. Or have her throat cut.' He grinned, as one who knew about cutting throats. 'And who's to say she's wrong?'

'What does the Princess think?'

'Ah, that's the point. She doesn't want the boy tortured. Now, you and I are practical but . . . women! No, she wants you to go and see him, question him and get the truth from him by any other means you can. My belief is, she thinks his father's to blame, that he put the boy up to it. I don't know. There's talk among the waiting women of the boy's devotion to her, that he was always bringing her presents, so perhaps he had his own reasons for wishing his Highness dead. As to all that, we'll see what the Prince thinks when he's well enough to give an opinion. *Mine* is: send Donato Landucci to go and tell his father about it. That way, the Prince gets rid of a family of traitors. But meantime, we humour her Highness, eh?'

Sigismondo bowed. It might take a little time but Benno was good at waiting. He gave a message for him to the page at the door and, looking back from the courtyard steps, saw Gatta tousle the boy's head and set off up the stairs.

He crossed the park once more. Workmen were mending the timber of the castle doors, and a big black-bearded man stood in the entrance watching them. The civet cat was embroidered on his doublet and he had a ring of keys hanging from one fist.

'Master Sigismondo? I'd word to attend you.' He turned and led the way, through an arch and along a pathway cleared through the debris in the inner courtyard. The curtain walls and the towers enclosed it oppressively. 'We had to move the young lord after the accident. Door of his cell was blown in. He was still there – said he'd given the Prince his parole and prison made no difference – but he'd have known well enough he wouldn't get far. No harm in trying to make a good impression, though.'

Sigismondo stooped to pick something up, a friar's sandal with the fastening torn away. He tossed it aside on a heap of rubble and followed the gaoler in at a narrow tower door and up spiral stairs.

'This place is a warren,' the man said cheerfully. 'To think the court used to live in it! But it's still strong for all it's been through,' and he patted the stone newel. They went up two flights before turning off on a landing where several doors attested the stoutness of the fabric by their solid, iron-bound strength. The gaoler sorted among his keys, found one, and unlocked a door. There was a bar to lift too as though, parole or no, they were taking no chances with young Lord Landucci. He pushed the door and stood aside, saying, 'Here's one to see you, young sir.' Sigismondo approached. The gaoler, saying, 'Mind the step,' took his arm a moment as if to assist him, and suddenly thrust him forward.

There was no step, only a drop of some five feet. The door clanged, as Sigismondo landed and rolled over to break his fall. The lock went home with a grunt and the bar slammed into place.

The cell was empty but for dust, which had covered Sigismondo as he rolled. He stood up, and looked levelly round. A high window, deep in a worn embrasure, cast the shadow of its bars across his head.

He looked up at the stone vault above, and at the door. Locked, barred and flush with the wall, it offered little hope. There was no hand or foothold to sustain anyone working on the lock, or on the bolts that fixed the bar-socket to the outside. At some time the foot of the door had been damaged, by rats, damp or some desperate prisoner, and a metal plate had been nailed across. This had slightly sprung, by a quarter-inch perhaps, and he went to look at it.

Then he examined the wall beneath the window.

Brother Columba's misuse of chemical properties had not disrupted the fabric of the castle anywhere but in the laboratory tower, but it had disturbed it. The stones, vibrating to absorb the shock, had shed a considerable amount of old mortar. Inserting fingertips and boot-toes, Sigismondo made his way up to the embrasure. The sill slanted upward to the bars, indeed all four reveals of the window opened outward to the room, on the excellent principle of allowing the maximum light while presenting the minimum area for enemy attack, or that more ancient enemy, weather, to get in. Sigismondo now inched his way up the sill to examine the bars. He picked rust off them with a finger. He grasped one, then the other, and shook them. He let himself down again to the floor.

He cast about among the dead leaves and dust in the corners, and found a flake or two of stone. Then he searched the walls for broken surfaces and, with the hilt of his poniard, knocked some more sizeable flakes free. He carried those to the door and set to work on the iron plate, hammering the pieces of stone into the gap behind it until he could get hold of the end and, again with the hilt of his poniard, prise it further.

He had been left with his weapons, as if in casual certainty that he could have no possibility of using them again unless, in the ultimate pitch of despair and hunger, to take his own life. A man who is to be fed is not left with weapons he might use on his gaoler. He was there to starve. By the same token, no one would take notice of any noise he made, for it would be supposed he was uselessly beating on the door.

He had taken off his leather jerkin and sliced pieces to wrap his hands in as he pulled the iron strip from the door. The stone wedges dropped and were hammered in further along. The nails at the far end, with their heads bent over, took a long time to shift from their hold, but came away with a grating screech at last.

Sigismondo tucked the new tool in his belt and climbed once more to the window.

Quite the most difficult part of the next operation was maintaining himself in the embrasure. Only the decrepit state of its surface enabled him to wedge a foot against a remnant of concrete facing and get an arm through the bars. Braced between these two holds, he dug with his strip of iron, and rasped at the rusty base. Every so often he was forced to stop, to climb down and stretch, to rub his arm, to wrap the end of the iron in another piece of leather.

Once he almost lost the metal strip out into the air. He got down, threaded a jerkin-lace through a nail hole and tied it to his wrist. Then he climbed up again. His face never lost its intent calm except for that moment, when he grimaced as if in retrospect and set to work once more.

By early morning, after some hours of steady labour by moonlight, he knotted his belt to the bar, climbed down, and exerting all the strength of his shoulders and back, one foot braced on the wall, gave a series of wrenching pulls. The bar came free.

He sat down on the floor, flexing his hands; he stretched, and contemplated the second bar. If he had been Benno he might have got out past it, but as it was he had still the task of at least bending it. Perhaps the thought came into his mind

255

that he was fortunate in having bars and not a grating to deal with.

Morning was definitely showing as he again stood up, stretched, and climbed to the window and set to work on the second bar.

This one was more firmly embedded. It was many hours later that he succeeded in loosening the base. Every so often he had to climb down and rest. He had a few sling-pebbles in his pocket, and he sucked one of them. When dark came he still worked on. He had got the bar sufficiently free by early the second morning. He tied the metal strip to his belt as an extra weapon, and climbed through.

Weather, and the explosion, had rusticated the surface of the outer wall, as he had observed on his way across the park. There was a long moment of extreme jeopardy when, holding on by fractional gaps between stones above the window, he had to manoeuvre his body out and climb upward while he got his feet to the sill. Once out, he paused for a moment and then began the descent. He owed much to the age of the castle, to the negligence of anyone who might have maintained it; and to Brother Columba.

He could only feel for footholds, but he looked closely in the early light for handholds. He moved slowly down the wall, not vertically but at a slight diagonal. Every so often he paused, when he found a reasonable foothold, and leant against the stone, flexing first one hand, then the other.

A rotten stone crumbled under his foot once and he hung there while the fragments trickled down the wall below with an ominous whisper. After that he was more cautious still in transferring his weight.

He came to the bottom. His foot touched grass and for the first time he looked down. He lowered himself onto the slope, turned, and sat there, elbows on knees, hands drooping, among the juniper bushes. A small rain had begun to fall.

The light was growing. He moved to the foot of the slope, and briefly knelt, and rose crossing himself. He stopped only to contrive, from the last of his jerkin, a rough hood, tied round the neck with a thong. He drank water from the juniper leaves. Covered with dirt, his hose and shirt torn, his fine boots battered at the toes and grey, he was not immediately recognisable. He climbed the park wall and dropped into the street at sunup, just as the city gates were opening. He slouched along looking like almost anybody, setting off to find who it was that wanted him dead.

37. IT WAS HIS LUCKY DAY

Benno must have sat for some time in the growing dusk before he came out of his daze enough to wonder what he ought to do. His master might be dead. He might be lying somewhere wounded and in need of help. Where? For a start, there was the whole of Viverra to choose from. He might be slumped in some dark alley with a knife in him. He might be already thrown into the river. Benno shook his head. No point, and no sense, in that line of thinking – Sigismondo wouldn't be easily got rid of and if he went into the river there'd be a few bodies ahead of him. If he'd been attacked in the city street there'd be mementoes lying about.

Did that mean it would be a good idea to go round Viverra asking who'd seen a man with a shaven head fighting a lot of others? There'd be bound to be a *lot* of others or Sigismondo would be here now.

Who was the last person seen with his master? Gatta. Ask Gatta where Sigismondo was when he left him? Gatta's yellow eyes seemed to look at Benno in the dusk and he rejected that course of action. He, a servant and apparently a half-wit, approach Ridolfo Ridolfi, the great condottiere, and ask questions? Even if he was allowed near him he'd never be listened to.

And then, suppose Gatta was *why* Sigismondo had disappeared?

259

Gatta was suspicious by nature. You didn't get from being nobody to being as important as he was by trusting people. Sigismondo had been sent to fetch Landucci, so he'd told Benno, just so that Michelotto could judge if he and Landucci were in league. A silly idea, Benno thought. There'd been no chance even of contact between them, let alone a motive; but such ideas weren't far-fetched to those who lived, or died, by intrigue. Could it be Gatta?

Yet Gatta had been cordial, smiling, his arm round Sigismondo. Was he a Judas?

The servant here said Sigismondo had left on the orders of the Princess. Could she have summoned Sigismondo and kept him talking till this hour? Had the Prince recovered and sent for him? Still it didn't account for Benno being left so long, as now literally he was, in the dark.

He got up, rubbed his cramped legs and went to the window. From here, a few nights back, he and Sigismondo had seen the lamp burning in the Prince's study. No light now. Against the soft glow of the night sky in which the moon was just beginning to show, the silhouette of the Old Castle was denser black, and jagged where the explosion had ripped the top out of one tower. Benno brought up his hands under his chin and prayed. God, who had spared them both that night as they had walked unknowingly towards danger, surely God would protect his master now?

He thought of adding to his prayer the plea that his master was a good man, but left it out. Good men didn't necessarily get protected. All the stories of the saints told you that the more good you were the worse you incurred suffering.

The scratch of claws on the floor reminded him and he bent and picked Biondello up. 'We'll go and find him,' he said into the little dog's wool. 'We'll try the camp. Gatta's men may have heard something. We'll go there and listen about.'

Benno tucked Biondello into his doublet, picked up Sigismondo's cloak and leather scrip, and his own pack of food, and was gone.

* * *

Gatta, like any seasoned campaigner, disliked any parade at his comings and goings; not for him the trumpet that announced the arrival of the great, nor the reception committee lined up on the steps. A lifetime of surprise attacks had made him believe that more interesting things can be discovered from arrivals out of the blue.

He was far from expecting anything interesting when he paid a surprise visit to his daughter. He had been with the Prince discussing what should be done with Donato Landucci. Fate, however, had made her own arrangements as to what he should find here at home.

Gatta had been delighted that day to see his daughter looking so well and so pretty, and he felt confident that, with the dowry he could now offer with her, he could set his sights higher than a man born a peasant could reasonably have hoped for. A year ago he had considered Michelotto's suggestion that he should be Caterina's bridegroom, but the idea now seemed absurd. He had given her a purse of gold to spend as she should please, a necklace of topaz from Mascia to match her eyes, Ginevra's parrot to amuse her, and carte blanche to have dresses made for her wedding chest. The chest itself was now being carved and painted with rustic scenes by the best craftsmen in Viverra. Caterina had pressed him to say whom he had in mind for a husband; he had said only that the man would be worthy of her – he did not add, when he had found him.

So he went to her bedchamber, brushing aside maids anxious to be of assistance and to fetch their lady to her father. A glance round told him she was not there, and hearing voices in the adjoining little room where, Caterina had mentioned, Monna Maria lay ill, he strode to the door and pushed it wide.

His daughter, it seemed, had found a man for herself.

Unless Monna Maria had undergone some miraculous change, it was not her duenna in the bed on which Caterina

261

sat with her back to him. She was in the embrace of a naked young man.

The sound that alerted them to his presence was the hiss of his sword out of its scabbard. He had its point at the young man's throat as he drew back speedily up the piled pillows and Caterina cried out and sprang to her feet.

Gatta's surprise at finding his daughter in the embrace of a strange young man was nothing to his surprise that the young man was not strange at all; that eyes he knew quite well were staring horrified at him above his sword's point.

'Don't! Don't! He's a holy man—' Caterina became aware that her defence did not suit the situation. Gatta shot a look at her. Although her hair was tossed about over her shoulders, her bodice was laced, her dress not even crumpled. It was possible, he thought, that he had arrived in time. The parakeet strode lurching to the end of its perch and flapped.

Gatta lowered the point of the blade.

'A holy man indeed. Was he thinking of making a saint of you? Taking you to heaven with him?' His jagged teeth gave a certain quality to Gatta's grimace.

'*Nothing* has happened!' She bared her own teeth in a defiant assertion. 'What do you think I am?'

'Whore!' The parakeet, never at a loss, offered its entire vocabulary; and Caterina stamped.

'*Do you know who this is*?' Gatta's sword specified the prince, who flinched.

'I've told you. He's a holy man from the hills, a hermit. He was ill – very ill. . .'

'She saved my life.' The prince found his courage and his tongue. Having a sword at the throat is unnerving even to those who have been in battle, and his conscience had him at a disadvantage too. However, he was not ashamed of his intentions. 'I want to marry her, sir.'

At this point Monna Maria, who took her duties as duenna quite seriously, returned from the privy, furled in a bedgown to give colour to the general word that she was ill. Seeing her employer, her charge and her secret all together made her stop dead on the threshold and imprudently squeal, drawing all eyes. Gatta's attention, which she most dreaded, returned at once to the young man.

'Marry? Do you know what you are saying?' Princes ally themselves to princely families; people born in huts rarely qualify as their fathers-in-law.

'He can get the Bishop to free him from his vows,' Caterina declared, her eyes shining. Gatta waved this aside with an impatient hand.

'This is Prince Francesco, girl; son to the Prince of Viverra. His marriage is a matter for a Council of State.'

As he spoke, his face changed. His own position, as commander of a victorious condotta at the gates of the city, might somewhat influence that council's deliberations. What a man had become could outweigh his birth.

He sheathed his sword and sat down on the bed.

'Come. You were dying, were you, Highness? How strong is your Highness now?'

'I have recovered, sir,' said the prince, with a touch of bravado.

'So it would appear. No one must know you have been here. If you seek to marry my daughter, her honour must be untouched by scandal.

'*You.*' He turned with sudden ferocity to Monna Maria who, hoping he had forgotten her, had begun to tiptoe away. 'Send for my confessor.'

He was going to kill her for failing her trust! Weeping, she ran into Caterina's room and, opening the door to the antechamber, gave the message to a waiting-woman, who rushed away, startled that Monna Maria was so very ill that a confession was in order.

When the priest arrived, he was met in the doorway of the antechamber by Gatta, who demanded that he should bring a Franciscan's robe like the one he wore. The confessor, who had been enjoying a slight respite in Gatta's house from the life he tried to lead with good grace in camp, hurried to fetch his old, campaign-tattered habit. He wondered if his patron intended to perform penance for the sins his confessor had good reason to know he was still committing. Perhaps a night on his knees, or prone, in Franciscan dress on the cold marble of the chapel?

He was not to know. When he rapped on the door, Gatta took the bundle from him abruptly and he was dismissed. He went away confused, wondering when he was to give the last rites to Monna Maria who, the waiting-woman had told him, was dying.

Gatta sent his daughter to her own room when he presented the young prince with the Franciscan gear. 'Put that on.

'Now, come.' Prince Francesco found himself being escorted quite unceremoniously out of the room, the cowl pulled well forward, putting his face in shadow, helped down some twisting backstairs – his legs did not feel strong – and to a door to the street, which was opened by an old man who staggered up from dozing on a bench. Gatta looked out and, after a moment, said two words in the young man's ear that sounded like, 'Wait outside', ducked his head at him, and saying aloud 'Farewell, Father,' thrust him into the street and shut the door.

Francesco, dazed, feeling far less well by daylight and in the life of the street, stood by the back door, waiting, wondering what strategy Gatta had in mind. There was a commotion behind him.

'You thieving rascal.' Gatta had apparently come round the corner from the street and was aiming a kick at a man on crutches, who lost what was left of his footing and stumbled against the prince. Francesco, by nature courteous, tried to stop the man from falling and lost the concealment of his cowl, a garment never designed to stay on luxurious and slippery long hair.

'Your Highness!' Gatta struck a hand dramatically to his brow. 'Your Highness is found, thanks be to God! Let us go to your mother and father. She will be rejoiced to see you, and it will be better than any medicine to his Highness.'

The beggar who had been the innocent cause of the discovery had his crutches retrieved and restored to him by a fascinated crowd, and found himself the richer for Gatta's kick by a number of donations. It was his lucky day.

38. A Lovers' Quarrel

Benno had to wait till dawn to get out of the city, but he had luck at the camp, the sentry he came across remembering him from Mascia. Benno had gone shares in a bottle of wine with him after the siege, and had accepted congratulations on his master's slaying of Scala. As a result, Benno was forgiven his total lack of idea on passwords; halfwits are not supposed to have memories.

'Looking for your master? He hasn't come in this way, not since I've been on watch. Not a man you'd miss, eh? You should have stayed in Viverra, there's some of us haven't had a chance to go in yet.'

From the grumbles of the sentry's partner on duty, Benno gathered that the mood in the camp was of active discontent. They had been cheated of their triumphant entry after the victory of Mascia; even cheated of a proper welcome in the city because of a certain obnoxious friar who was even said to have preached against them in the cathedral. Certainly no one would turn down a chance to be properly received in the next world, and they had all been busy getting absolution for any little outrages committed at Mascia, but there was a general sense that soldiers should be allowed latitude. 'Risk our lives every day, we do. Try asking Michelotto for leave if he's not feeling generous. You can get hanged in camp quicker nor killed in battle, you can.'

It was clear that asking Michelotto anything was a risky

action. To ask after Sigismondo's whereabouts could be very dangerous indeed. If Gatta were the cause of Sigismondo's vanishing, Michelotto was Gatta's man and, in his own flamboyant way, as frightening. All the same, he was the one likely to know all that went on. Benno decided on stealth.

He did his own disappearing act into the life of the camp. No one took much notice of him as all day he hung about on the periphery of groups of talkers, of gamblers, of those cleaning weapons, bringing rations, or cooking what they had managed to get hold of. The gossip everywhere confirmed the sentries' opinion, but the only word of Sigismondo was an ominous remark from a man eating a thrush he had just roasted: that the man who had killed Scala had best watch his back – by rights there should be only one hero, the leader of the condotta.

By nightfall Benno had decided on a desperate course. He would see, in the dark, how near he could get to Michelotto's tent. With luck on his side he might overhear talk between Michelotto and his captains, perhaps, or even with Gatta himself, who visited the camp each day at un-heralded times. If Gatta had done something to Sigismondo, it would be important enough for mention. Benno defiantly refused the idea that Sigismondo might be dead. He was somehow convinced that if Sigismondo were dead he would have made Benno aware of it.

Benno had been taught during his time with Sigismondo that if you wished to move unsuspected you must not creep. He walked casually among the tents without the furtive glances he longed to give, yet taking advantage of shadows cast by the moon, the same moon that was lighting Sigismondo in his slow work on the bar. He was troubled by fears, not of the supernatural, but of the entirely natural, that he might trip on a tent peg or snag a guy rope and fall headlong at Michelotto's feet. To anyone who knew of Sigismondo's disappearance, Benno was a suspicious charac-ter. He hoped he would not sneeze. It didn't cross his mind that Biondello might bark, because he was a dog that acknowledged the presence of danger by complete silence, and he was dumb now, shivering with tension as Benno picked out Michelotto's tent and at last dropped on all fours close to the canvas. The tent was marginally less gaudy than Gatta's with its scalloped top and red silk lining, but it was a spacious-enough affair in blue and white stripes. There were voices inside. Suppose one were Gatta's?

It was not Gatta. One voice was a woman's, the other he thought to be Michelotto's. The woman raised her voice, the man spoke in soft, affable tones. Benno pressed close to the canvas, hoping anybody carrying a torch would keep to the main alleyway. If he was discovered here, where he could only be a spy, it would mean hanging.

Disappointingly, it seemed to be a lovers' quarrel. The woman at least was quarrelling. She must be a camp follower – Michelotto would certainly have the pick – and surely it was rash of her to shout at him hysterically? There was a slight commotion inside the tent as though they struggled together, the girl crying out sharply in pain. Benno thought if it was going to be a rape he wouldn't listen.

It was not. The canvas fly at the entrance slapped back, rather nearer to Benno than he had realised, and a man appeared in the shadows, hauling a girl along by the wrists. She was incoherent with weeping, but Michelotto was being reproached. It was the old story: he never sent for her now . . . she still loved him, she did as she was told . . . she'd done everything for him, was it her fault if the wrong person had got the gloves . . . ?

She stumbled. Michelotto had pulled her close and then flung her from him. She made a clogged sound as though she was going to vomit, and landed on her back within a foot of where Benno crouched, his heart beating to deafen him, so loud in his ears that he thought Michelotto would hear it. The girl lay there. She must be despairing, knowing herself hopelessly rejected. She made no sound. Michelotto had gone back into the tent, dropping the flap, and there was the splash of pouring wine. Somewhere a dog started others barking, and Benno felt Biondello put out his nose, sniffing warily.

After a minute, Benno realised that the warm wetness reaching his shin was blood. The moon had shifted and a cloud cleared. Benno was still in shadow but the girl was not. She lay looking up at the night sky, sightless, her throat gaping like a second mouth.

39. The Ruin of Viverra

Prince Francesco was surprised to find himself popular in Viverra. News that he had been found spread fast. The people knew that he had been lost to them in renouncing the world, and that the palace had been sending out search parties since then. His absence, short as it was, had caused a sense of insecurity, and the sight of him now reassured them. They were pleased to have him back, hopeful that he meant to stay – pleading with him to remain their prince – and there was tacit hope too that Brother Ambrogio was losing authority at the palace. It took all four of the men Gatta had with him, and Gatta's own awe-inspiring presence, to keep the prince from being mobbed before he reached the palace gates. It really was gratifying.

His welcome in the family would have been appropriate to the Prodigal Son, and Francesco could not help remembering as this came to mind that, during his brief attempt at being a hermit, he would have tackled swine's food without hesitation. Now wine and a collation were sent for, his mother embraced him with tears in her eyes, a marvel to him, and his grandmother had to be supported by her waiting-women in a half swoon. He had scarcely drunk a cup, which he needed after the recent debilitating excitement, when his father arrived.

'My child!' Prince Scipione presented an odd sight, as a black eye given him by some flying object from the desk after

Brother Columba's bonfire had by now attained a mixture of burgundy and ochre that went well with his robes. 'My dear boy, you are back!'

He clasped his son fervently, surprising both of them. As a father the Prince had always been absentminded to the point of neglect, but his accident had imbued him with a strong sense of his mortality, intenser by far than from any former illness. Now the future of Viverra was restored to him. As he held him at arms' length after the embrace, he took in that his son wore the robes of a Franciscan, and he demanded in dismay, 'Have you taken vows?'

For answer, Francesco, with the sense of theatre he had displayed before, tore off his cape and cowl, and shrugged out of the habit so that it hung from his waist held only by the rope belt. 'I've taken no vows, Father. I have returned to carry out my duty to you and to Viverra.'

There were more embraces and more tears. The Princess Isotta was beginning to regain her calm but she touched her son's face with tenderness. Onlooking courtiers were also in tears. Courtiers, after all, need a court; there had been fears as to what might happen if the Prince – as so often seemed likely – were to die suddenly with no one now to succeed him. Not a few had wondered whether they must adapt to the thought of a condottiere as prince. It wouldn't be the first time such a thing had happened in the city-states about them. As they applauded and wiped their eyes, they covertly studied Gatta's face to see how he was taking this restoration of Viverra's heir.

The extraordinary thing was, Gatta had brought the prince back himself. There were those present who would have wagered that, if Gatta were to find Prince Francesco, he would ensure the young man was in no condition to return except in a box; they now had to think again. No doubt Gatta had other, more devious plans. At the moment he was being embraced by Prince Scipione as the agent of his son's return, while Francesco explained why he had been where he was found.

272

'I was in pursuit of a vision.'

Faces fell. Visions, fine for a friar, were less advisable for princes. Francesco, his face glowing, turned towards Gatta who waited with folded arms for the revelation.

'I saw this vision outside the city, on the hillside. A creature of surpassing loveliness.' He paused and added more hastily, 'Her veil blew aside for a moment in the breeze. It was a revelation to me. I followed this vision into the city, to the house of Ridolfi.'

'To my house? *My daughter*?' Gatta seemed smitten with astonishment. The whole room was stunned to silence.

'Whoever she is,' Francesco turned to his father, 'I can marry no other. I swear by the saints, I swear by my patron St Francis, that I will marry none but she.'

As an explosion, it was as effective as that in the Old Castle; the Princess Dowager required the support of her women all over again, and the Prince himself could not prevent a look of acute dismay, not flattering to his commander. Large in his mind was the question of Francesco's almost-agreed betrothal to the Duke of Scioggia's daughter. Presents had been exchanged . . . he found he had spoken some of these thoughts aloud. Princess Isotta hardly altered her expression of detachment, and Gatta himself shrugged and spread his hands as if to disclaim any ardour to become so intimately related to royalty. The Prince smothered his incoherency, with the acute realisation that he was inevitably on the brink of alienating either his commander or a prospective ally in Scioggia just when he needed them both.

'Impossible. It is *impossible*!' The Princess Dowager had recovered her senses, and with them the energy that made her a power to be reckoned with at court. She marched forward. 'You cannot marry *his* daughter.' She glared at Gatta as though some offensive peasant had stamped in straight from the pigsty. 'Think of your family! It would make you the laughing stock of the world! You will be the ruin of us!'

Gatta took one step and thrust his face forward almost into hers. He resembled a cat ready to tear its prey to pieces.

'And you, madam, *you* will be the ruin of Viverra!'

He turned and, without a bow or leavetaking, strode from the room. His footsteps could be heard retreating in the appalled silence that followed.

40. YOU?

Sigismondo had an uncanny ability to sense where Benno had got to, even when Benno thought himself well concealed, and he had also an appreciation of Benno's shrewdness which would have surprised anyone who took Benno at face value; but it was neither of these things which brought him to the camp. It does not take a sophisticated logic (which Sigismondo also undoubtedly possessed) to work out that if you are sent somewhere by someone only to land up in prison, that someone is likely to be the reason why you do. Sigismondo was in Gatta's camp to observe Gatta. Anyone who arranges for you to starve to death is worth watching; and Prince Scipione's original requirement had been to see if Gatta's loyalty still held.

Moreover, he had a good chance of encountering Benno there. Once Benno found his master had vanished, he was not going to advertise his identity; to do so could attract quite deleterious attention. A camp is as good a place to be anonymous as anywhere in the world, and an apparent lack of wits perhaps less noticeable among soldiers.

Sigismondo surmounted the password problem by helping a man struggling to secure a wine cask that threatened to fall from a wagon. To the sentry who passed them through, the man who sat astride the casks and looked down broodingly at him as the wagon trundled by, the man with the saturnine face and the hat like a dead bird over a worn leather hood, did not at all bring to mind the hero of Mascia.

The soldiers by the commissary, as the cart's driver and Sigismondo trundled the casks down planks from the wagon, were ready with offers of help and with gossip. The predominant subject was that their commander had stormed in only half an hour ago – mortally insulted by the Prince, said those who had been with him – and was even now in his tent debating his revenge with Michelotto.

The man who delivered the casks was ready to tip Sigismondo and offer him a ride back into the city, but he had unaccountably disappeared, the first man who'd ever done him a good deed without hanging round for a reward.

This angel in disguise was proceeding through the camp, along one of the orderly alleys, past ammunition stores and bivouacs, and among the tents, with that air of knowing where he was going and what he was about which dissuaded even the zealous from checking on him. No one really gave the tall stoop-shouldered man in the shabby clothes and altogether disreputable hat a second glance; nevertheless he was recognised.

There are creatures who do not rely solely on their eyes and are therefore not deceived by clothes and bearing. A small, dirty, one-eared dog came racing through the straggling knots of soldiers, levitating over obstacles, and flung himself at Sigismondo, his tail a blur. Sigismondo bent to caress him, expecting to see the pair of scruffy boots that hurried to plant themselves eloquently before him.

'I'm sorry, comrade. He's mad after garlic sausage. You had some lately?' Benno's eyes spoke more volumes than his boots: they swam with tears and his voice was gruff. Sigismondo picked up Biondello in both hands and surveyed him, and strolled on, Benno trotting alongside. As some men nearby turned their heads, Sigismondo replied in an accent so rustic you'd have hesitated to cut it with a knife in case it bit you.

'Sausage? My guts're bursting with sausage. I thought you was offering your cur for dessert. I see you've had his ear already. Let me buy you a drink to go with the rest of him.'

Benno had scarcely time for a checked snuffle in agreement when a commotion started up in the main alley behind them, shouting and warnings to make way. As they stepped aside, a horse was led past them, steaming and lathered, its rider bent over the pommel in hardly better state; a small crowd of Gatta's men followed, full of curiosity. Sigismondo, and therefore Benno, joined the crowd and they were drawn at its tail to the very flaps of Gatta's tent. Benno wondered if he had rightly heard Sigismondo's murmur of 'I smell canals', when all he could smell was horse's sweat. His mind was confused, by anxiety and now by relief, and it took him a minute or two, watching the exhausted messenger being helped from his horse and then held upright, before he realised from the Venetian saddle where the horse came from. The news carried was not to the Prince of Viverra but to the leader of the army outside its gates. Benno didn't suppose the Most Serene Republic had sent a replacement for the Ambassador to the Prince yet, either.

The red silk tent flaps shone in the sun as their poles were lifted back to admit the Venetian messenger with dignity. The small crowd outside, gathered at a respectful distance, could see Gatta on his feet extending his hands in welcome, Michelotto at his side, pages hurrying to offer wine.

'Scala's head was a success.' This time Benno heard the murmur clearly. Sigismondo, turning his head aside from Biondello's frantic licking, smiled at Benno whose heart rejoiced that his master, whatever dangers he had surmounted, was back and in control.

They had a first-class view of what was going on in the tent, as if at a puppet show, where the man who had most likely tried to murder Sigismondo was receiving the Venetian. Gatta saw no reason to keep the interview private, any more than would a prince receiving an envoy before his court. More men, getting news of something going on, came to watch.

Hearing was harder. No one in the tent raised a voice and spectators had to make what they could of the dumbshow. A letter was offered by the bowing messenger, and accepted. The man was invited to sit and take wine – he sat awkwardly after so long in the saddle – while Michelotto read the letter to Gatta. It was then time for deliberation. Gatta stared at the letter, asked questions, gestured to have bits read to him again, and sat and brooded while Michelotto talked with animation, seeming to offer the main points of the letter once more. He appeared to be triumphant, which made Benno sure that the letter meant no good. Still in his mind was the poor girl's pleading before she was killed.

Some sort of decision seemed to be reached. Gatta's secretary was sent for and came in haste, his boy carrying his desk. More significant still, his astrologer arrived in a hurry with his portfolio of charts, the Zodiac tooled in gold on the cover. Michelotto advanced as though to usher him in, when a commotion rose again in the main alley, and Michelotto stepped out to see what it was. Benno shrank down in case Gatta's eyes lighted on him, and he turned his head as everyone did, to see what certainly no one had expected.

Young Prince Francesco was riding towards them, preceded by a running sergeant anxious to warn his commander of this uncalled-for visit. Gatta could have used the warning no doubt, had it been in time, but his own eyes made it redundant. Staring, he rose and came from the tent as the young man dismounted.

'Your Highness honours me – honours us all.'

Spider greets fly, thought Benno. It's true the prince doesn't know Michelotto had the gloves put to poison his father, but at seventeen he should know better than to put himself in Gatta's hand like this.

The pages emerged, and closed the door-flaps of the tent. What might be planned for the young man was to happen in private.

There was not long to wait, watching the blank green front. A page swung one fly back and Michelotto emerged. So far as anything could be judged from his strange lively face he seemed exhilarated. No matter what was going on in that tent, he was stimulated by it. He glanced round at the crowd a little distance in front of him and Benno, fading behind a man- at-arms, saw that Sigismondo, under his dismal hat, was looking stolidly down and had reduced himself in height by giving at the knees.

'Every man fully armed and in light marching order. At once.'

That's it. Gatta's going to march on Viverra. With the young prince in his hands he'll find Prince Scipione easy meat. Not much point my master going to warn him, I suppose – not much he could do to stop this lot. And that burning village on the way to Mascia . . . would they burn the palace? Loot it? What would become of the Princess?

The crowd was dispersing swiftly at the wave of Michelotto's arm, and Sigismondo at a slouching trot went with them. Through the din of men running, shouting and arming, and the neighing of surprised horses, a man cupped his hands and roared, 'You there!'

Sigismondo swung his head, surly but obedient.

'Get that cart, fellow. Hurry.'

To disobey or protest would draw attention. Sigismondo pulled down the shafts of the indicated cart, and meekly taking one, indicated the other to Benno with a jerk of the head. They dragged it, Benno aware of Sigismondo doing most of the work, after the man who had summoned them.

He was now walking along with Michelotto. Benno felt cold. They were recognised after all, had been singled out, brought to their doom . . .

The cart was certainly an instrument of doom. Michelotto and the man in charge stopped in a clearing among tents, where a great beam had been set up, nailed to supports nine feet high. A ladder leant against it, and a man manoeuvring astride the beam was adjusting a knot on one of four nooses spaced along, to his satisfaction but hardly to that of the four men standing below the beam, their hands tied at their backs.

Nearby a man, stripped and cursing, was being hitched at the tail of a horse that fidgeted and stamped as if it knew what to expect in the way of noise from this appendage. Another horse waited patiently, head hanging, harnessed for a cart. Benno bit his lips and blinked, expecting any minute to be seized and tied just as soon as Michelotto looked round and saw them. Biondello shivered in the hammock of Benno's jerkin.

Michelotto was busy, luckily. With his back to them, he moved down the line of those condemned, saying what appeared to be some cheerful words to each, testing the firmness of the cords on the wrists as he went. It was clear that he ran the camp on perfectionist lines and liked to check things for himself. The man on the ladder had descended in a hurry and was attending him respectfully, while Sigismondo and Benno busied themselves, heads bowed and faces hidden, in hitching the horse in the shafts. Then Sigismondo, without being told, went round and took the tailboard off the cart, and drew back, carrying it before him. This brought him behind the thick upright that carried the beam, with a full view from there of Michelotto who was finding fault at the end of the line, where a man's wrists were apparently not securely tied. Michelotto whipped off the binding, waving away the hangman. He retied the man's arms, talking to him in a low and, it seemed, an encouraging voice. Benno imagined Michelotto quite capable of running through the main features of the afternoon's attractions for him; he remembered, and wished he hadn't, Sigismondo's remark that it took a long time to die from hanging unless the hangman could be bribed to pull on your feet as you swung and break your neck for you, or to let your friends do it. Perhaps Michelotto was pointing this out to the victim, or mentioning that this hangman didn't take bribes, for he finished his monologue with a comforting hug of the man's shoulders. As he turned, Sigismondo bent to put down the cart's tailboard against the upright, but Michelotto's attention was elsewhere, on the men gathering, some on foot with weapons burnished and ready, others in brilliant colours on horses groomed into glossiness. The condotta was in its Sunday clothes, and Benno wondered why it was necessary to wear your best to march on Viverra. No one had bothered to dress up like this before Mascia.

The reason was not at all far to seek. Trumpets blared, shrill, triumphant, and riding slowly into view along an alley lined with his men came Gatta, splendid in a cloak of violet-lined brocade on his great black horse in its trappings of gilded leather and silver. Beside him rode Prince Francesco, not at all like a prisoner, in tawny-brown and green, a scarlet curled plume fluttering on his velvet cap. Gatta bent towards him deferentially, gesturing this way and that to what he had to show. This was not after all a preparation for an attack, this was a parade.

'No victory without discipline, Highness,' Gatta was saying as he pointed to the beam and the men standing, forlorn or defiant, beneath it. 'A man who breaks the condotta's laws is as much our enemy as any met in battle. A man with light fingers here is called upon to prove he's got light toes too as he dances on air.' He laughed, and the prince joined in. It was a laugh social rather than hearty, as if the prince did not really count a hanging as a welcome entertainment. Michelotto, now alongside the horse that was to walk the cart under the beam, just as clearly did.

The hanging did not start at once although the priest had been helped up into the cart. A sergeant had arrived with two prisoners under guard, and begged Gatta's pardon for asking his attention with his report of a find. Gatta had taken over the security of the Old Castle after the explosion, and it was his men who patrolled the corridors and monitored the safety of the state prisoners kept in the cells that were still viable. They had discovered two men, this very hour, trying to force the lock on young Count Landucci's new cell. The implications were important enough for the men to be brought at once to the commander.

As the two were pushed forward, stumbling, Benno only just managed not to gasp. One, unnaturally tall and angular, glared with frenzied hatred up at Gatta. The other tossed back a mane of blond greasy waves to grimace. Where was the third? Benno would not have wondered, if he had seen Pio soaring out of the castle window during the explosion. Michelotto had come to stand by Gatta.

'That servant girl, Michelotto, told us that Donato Landucci provided the poisoned gloves meant for the Prince, that destroyed poor Ginevra. These men, if they were breaking open his cell door, must be his friends.'

As Gatta addressed Michelotto by name, the two prisoners had sharply turned their heads to look at each other. Well, at last they know, thought Benno. Gatta was grinning down at the two. Questioning them would be a pleasure; punishing them, a delight.

'And that?' Gatta pointed to a weapon carried by one of the guard, who brought it forward and handed it up to him. It was the very long old-fashioned sword Fracassa carried at his back, and he looked quite mutilated without it, as if he had lost a limb. He might lose a few more as Gatta's prisoner.

'We'll see these thieves hanged first, your Highness, then we'll take time for these traitors. I've been told it was young Landucci who tried to poison your father with the gloves and your mother with sweetmeats. He deserves to be burnt alive. You must want to put the torch to him yourself, pretending to be your friend as he did.'

The prince gave a faint smile, passing this over; he might not be entirely convinced, or in this case less anxious for revenge than Gatta assumed.

Gatta nodded to Michelotto, who moved back to supervise the hanging. The man at the end, first to go, was hoisted up into the cart in a clumsy scramble, helped by the priest, and the noose put round his neck.

'Your Highness!'

'No mercy, you dog,' Gatta growled, showing his fangs, and the man, desperate, raised his voice.

'A secret, your Highness. For your ears alone. I must tell you before I die. I beseech your Highness . . .'

The prince frowned, his horse sidling under him. Michelotto called out cheerfully, 'He's been babbling about a secret all morning. About your Highness's father. Doesn't want to take it to the grave.'

'Let the rogue tell it to the Devil—' Gatta was raising his hand when Prince Francesco urged his horse forward.

'I'll hear him.'

Gatta bowed and watched indulgently as the prince brought his horse alongside the cart, leaning to hear the man in it, close enough for the secret to be said into his ear.

What happened next was too swift for understanding. Sigismondo had appeared behind the cart and struck the prince's horse a swinging blow on the neck. At the same moment as the horse reared and turned, the cart started forward as Michelotto smacked the shaft horse on the rump. Sigismondo gripped the condemned man round the thighs with one arm as he came off the tail of it, and took his weight – or was he pulling to break the man's neck? The victim's arms were free. He hit down and backward at Sigismondo, who caught his wrist. The prince circled. calming his horse, his doublet ripped at the side. Now it could be seen that the condemned man had a knife.

A roar came from the crowd, an animal noise of shock. Gatta spurred forward, and he had Fracassa's great sword in his hand. Whom would he kill? The condemned man pushed the noose off over his head and Sigismondo lowered him to the ground, kicking and struggling.

'Michelotto promised me my life! I was not to hang, if I killed the prince!'

Michelotto had come, swift as a snake striking, dagger in hand, 'Liar! Traitor! You dare to say—'

The dagger rose, the condemned man cowered back, but Gatta brought the great sword between them with a jar of steel that knocked the blade from Michelotto's hand.

'I am the justice in this place. I'll hear more.'

Michelotto stepped back with a shrug, his face mirroring his scorn for anything the man might say. Sigismondo too had stepped back the moment Gatta intervened and had been swallowed by the crowd that pressed forward eager to see and hear this confrontation between their general and his second in command. Two of them had seized the man who accused Michelotto, and held him while the great sword pointed at his heart.

'Your name?'

'Enzo Scappi.'

'How did you get your hands free?'

'*He* tied them that way. And gave me the knife.' The jerk of the head at Michelotto produced only an incredulous smile.

'Did anyone see this?' Gatta demanded of the crowd.

There was an awkward mutter, then the hangman on the ladder offered, 'He did retie Scappi's hands. I didn't see no knife. '

It was patently unlikely that Michelotto would be clumsy enough to let the transferral of the knife be seen. The retying of the hands was significant. So was the shift of the sword-point to Michelotto's chest, a move that caused an intake of breath among the crowd.

'Your answer?'

Michelotto had kept his smile. Now he raised his eyebrows. 'A man will do his utmost to escape death by any means he can. Why should I wish his Highness killed?'

'You tried to kill his father!'

Benno, horrified at hearing his own voice, looked round in all directions, as everyone did, to see who had spoken.

'Bring that man out.'

Benno's little ruse had failed. A man beside him knew he had called out and now gripped his arm and used him as a weapon to force a way to Gatta's stirrup. The sword left Michelotto's chest and lifted Benno's face until he had to look up into those fearful yellow eyes.

'Why do you say that, rascal?'

284

'The poisoned gloves.' Benno spoke with rigid unmoving jaw, feeling the sword fray his beard. 'He got a girl to put them in the coffer in the Prince's room.'

'How do you know this?'

'I heard her say. Last night.'

'Where is this girl?' Michelotto stood, contemptuous, with hands on hips. 'This is a halfwit. He doesn't know what he is saying.'

'Where is this girl?' Gatta reinforced the question with a twitch of the sword that made blood run with the sweat down Benno's neck,

'He cut her throat. She said she'd tell and he killed her.'

Michelotto laughed. 'I killed a girl? And in front of you?'

'You didn't see me. I was in the shadows. You threw her down on my foot. Here's her blood.'

'Where is this girl? What was done with her?'

Someone spoke up from the back of the crowd. 'We was going to bury her along of the thieves.'

'She's here, Gatta. It's his girl all right.' The men made way as a stout woman bursting out of her pink gown, her dyed hair twisted with black veiling, and a quantity of gold chains round her neck, pushed forward, followed by another skinny one in garish purple. They carried between them a hurdle. On it lay a shape under a dirty cloth. 'Used to go in and out of the camp to his tent all hours. Taking away our living.' She put down her end of the hurdle and stood arms akimbo, copying Michelotto in defiance. 'That's all she got for it.' She bent and jerked the cloth back.

They had washed her and tidied her up, but someone with a slit throat is never going to look appealing, even to soldiers used to the sight. There was a murmur, and Gatta wheeled his horse closer, bending from the saddle to stare.

'I know this girl.' He looked across at Michelotto. 'You brought her to me at the palace. She said Donato Landucci put the gloves in the box.'

'That's what she told me.' Michelotto's voice was unconcerned.

285

'That's what she was told to tell.' Sigismondo, pulling off hat and hood, his bare head instantly recognisable, came out of the crowd. 'Michelotto wanted suspicion to fall on Landucci.'

Gatta's horse responded to an involuntary jerk on its mouth by backing and sidling.

'*You*!' Gatta stared at Sigismondo, disbelieving in so solid and imperturbable a ghost, disbelieving in his power to escape from the prison. 'How did you get here?'

Michelotto stood completely still, eyes wide.

'Hey, there was a window, there was a wall. It was that or the keyhole.' Sigismondo made a ring of thumb and forefinger and peered through at Gatta, who laughed abruptly.

'What I can see is that you're a man hard to make sure of. Why did Michelotto want suspicion thrown on Landucci?'

Sigismondo made a derisory sound between a hum and a laugh. 'Why should he do any of these things? Why try to kill the Prince, why try to kill the Prince's son? Because they were standing in your way.'

'*In my way*?'

Sigismondo shrugged, flung out a hand towards Michelotto. 'Your loyal captain, Gatta. He was going to make you Prince of Viverra.'

Gatta turned in the saddle to fix his gaze on Michelotto. His voice was soft. 'Is this true?'

Michelotto paused for only a second. Then with a flourish he bowed.

'You *are* Prince, Gatta. Viverra waits for you. Your army waits for you. Venice is for you.' He nodded across at the young prince, listening intently a few paces off. 'What was not done at dinner can be done at supper.'

He swooped and retrieved his dagger from the ground, and tossed and caught it, his meaning clear: if Gatta gave open consent, Prince Francesco could be murdered now and Viverra taken within the next hour.

Gatta's tone was reflective. 'You have done all they say?'

'It was done for you, Gatta.' He was triumphant, without regret, excuse, remorse; a voice that expected reward.

'For me.' Gatta considered it, the great sword cradled across one arm. Then he turned and pointed. 'Bring that rogue here.'

The guards holding Fracassa hauled him forward.

'You're Landucci's man. A traitor's man, eh? What would you do with Michelotto?'

Fracassa tossed back the greasy mane and spat, quite accurately, at Michelotto's feet. 'I would kill him. He raped and killed my mother and my sister. Kill him!'

Gatta smiled. With a brusque movement he signalled to Fracassa's guards to free him, and tossed him the sword. Fracassa, though startled, was swift. He caught the hilt and used the sword's own weight to give impetus to the swing and, as Michelotto stepped back, a hand held out in protest, he struck down at the join of neck and shoulder. A jet of blood hit the horse Gatta rode and it reared, trampling on its hind feet and neighing.

Benno fell on all fours and vomited on the ground. Michelotto was bad enough in one piece: divided, he was terrible. All round, the stunned silence broke in uproar.

'A wedding gift, Highness! Your revenge.' Gatta brought his horse, stamping, snorting and bespattered with blood to Francesco, who was still unable to take his eyes from the butchered body. Fracassa had not stopped at one blow, and was now swirling the sword in exultation, and prancing, while Aldo hoarsely cheered and the whole camp shouted. Dazed, Francesco realised that the shouts were for Gatta. Literally at a blow, the camp had lost the man responsible for all the unpopular measures that enabled it to be well run. Also, justice had been done, and Michelotto's dreadful punishment was designed to satisfy the prince as well as the army. If this man was to be his father-in-law, he must take this as the first instalment of Caterina's dowry. He smiled into those yellow eyes.

'My father will rejoice at another enemy's death.'

41. WHAT MORE COULD HE DESIRE?

'Have mercy, Prince! My son is innocent. Don't take him from me too.'

Countess Landucci was on her knees before the dais. Strands of hair had come loose from their silken net and straggled over her clasped hands. Prince Scipione, working his own hands on the carved arms of his chair, uneasily regarded her. His black eye gave him, to Countess Landucci who saw him through a veil of tears, a threatening look. She turned in despair to the Princess, so beautiful, so remote, in her chair by the Prince; she held out her hands.

'You too have an only son. I beg you to have mercy, as you hope for mercy before the Judgement seat . . .' She broke down, overcome by her weeping. The Princess turned her head towards her husband. She felt the strength of this plea after so nearly losing Francesco, nor could she bring herself to believe that Donato had meant to poison either her or the Prince. That lovelorn lad's intention had been quite otherwise.

Before she could speak or the Countess find her voice again, the curtains at the far end of the audience hall were pulled aside, and all heads turned, court and council alike, as Gatta, ever impatient of ceremony, ushered in Prince Francesco himself. The Princess controlled her desire to rise and go to welcome her son, whom she had last seen storming out when Gatta had gone. This appearance offered a hope that their only protector had not been alienated for ever despite her own personal efforts to attach him to their cause. Gatta's face was not readable; his expression might as well be a snarl as a smile. He spoke as he came to the foot of the dais, hardly giving Francesco time to kiss his father's hand.

'Highness. I have news for you. Your enemy, the one who sought to poison you, is discovered and is dead by my order.' He stood, planting his feet apart, ignoring in his jubilation the kneeling woman who, checking her sobs, turned her head to stare up at him.

'My enemy?' Prince Scipione's perplexity was understandable. He had recently lost two: Landucci in a fight, Carlotti in an explosion. Whom had he got left? Could it be that Gatta had summarily executed young Donato? He avoided looking at Lady Landucci. It really would be very awkward. She evidently had the same thought, for she sank back on her heels and covered her mouth with both hands.

'Your secret enemy, Highness, and mine. My captain, Michelotto della Casa. It was he that arranged for the poisoned gloves to be laid out in your room, and so killed my poor Ginevra—' Gatta had to pause, and grimaced as if to force back a tear. He went on, 'Only in this very hour he attempted your son's life.'

'Francesco!' The Princess after all started to her feet. She met her son's smiling eyes and, reassured that he would hardly be before her now if the attempt had succeeded, she collected herself and sat.

Gatta was now quite definitely grinning. 'Your Highness! Your son is safe, and Michelotto dead, a traitor to my honour and to you. We must look to the future, to a wedding, not a funeral.'

The Prince had been primed for this: during Gatta's absence the most furious councils had taken place. Although at the word *wedding*, tense and anxious faces all down the room recalled the dismay the Princess Dowager had created, the Prince, inwardly contemplating the awful complications of extricating Francesco from the Scioggia negotiations – the return of gifts, the cost of appeasement – summoned a benevolent smile. Gatta was Viverra's safety.

'My lord Ridolfi! We are in accord! Bring your daughter to the palace so that we may welcome her; she shall be betrothed to my son in the chapel here as soon as you wish, and the marriage contract be drawn up tomorrow.'

The Princess leant forward graciously. 'Viverra shall see a wedding of magnificence in the cathedral.'

It was as if the whole company breathed a corporate sigh of relief. Linked by marriage to the family, and with the status it would give him, Gatta would protect their interests as his own. The Princess Dowager, whose passionate attack on Gatta's presumption had put everything at hazard so short a time ago, now sulked in her apartments, unable to turn for consolation even to Brother Ambrogio, that castigator of worldly values.

'Highness!' Lady Landucci had been forgotten in all this talk of weddings. Her thoughts were still on executions. 'My son . . . You have heard that he's innocent. He never sought to poison you. He has suffered.' She rose to her feet. 'He will swear allegiance to you now his father is dead, and you can trust his word; on my soul you can.'

'I believe that is true.' Sigismondo, tall and grave, drew all eyes as he stepped forward to stand before the Prince. 'Question the men who tried time after time to rescue him, and you will hear that Donato Landucci keeps his word.'

He turned with a gesture. Aldo and Fracassa, brought from the camp at Sigismondo's behest, were pushed forward by their guards, Fracassa's clothes stiff with Michelotto's blood, and thrust down on their knees before the Prince. Sigismondo quietly took up their interrogation.

'Did you seek to take Donato Landucci back from Viverra to his father?'

'It was to me.' Lady Landucci put out a hand as if to protect the kneeling men. 'It was to me. I sent them. I knew my husband designed some stroke against your Highness and

I feared for my son's life when it came.' She choked again at the thought of how right she had been.

Prince Scipione began to speak, but realised he could not well blame a woman for failing to betray her husband, particularly a husband prepared to risk the life of his hostage son.

Sigismondo's question to her came quietly, asking information without any suggestion of threat. 'Did Count Landucci tell you, when we came for him, that his escape was planned?'

'He was angry; called me a fool for weeping; he said Michelotto had told him to arrange a rescue—'

Gatta seized Sigismondo by the arm. 'Michelotto told me *you* arranged the rescue. I meant you to die for that; and for killing Landucci. He died to cover a conspiracy, but it must have been Michelotto's, not yours.'

Lady Landucci sobbed again.

'My man saw Michelotto kill Count Landucci.'

'That devil lied and lied to me. He had too good a death.'

Sigismondo pointed to Fracassa. 'He did his best . . . He and his friend here tried more than once to rescue Count Donato. Let them tell us why they failed.'

'*Because he wouldn't come!*' Aldo, indignant, glared at Sigismondo as if he personally had dissuaded Donato. 'We were going to have to take him away by force. He told us he'd given his word!'

'His *word*!' Fracassa spat out in echo through his hair.

Sigismondo turned to the Prince and spread his hands. 'Your Highness may see. The young man's word can be trusted if he swears allegiance to you as Count Landucci.'

'Trust him, Father. I'm sure Sir Sigismondo speaks the truth.' Francesco urged it with conviction. Neither he nor his mother were ever going to mention any other reason Donato might have for wanting to stay. 'He was my friend and I hope he will be my friend again.' He put a hand on his father's. 'Landucci and Viverra to live in harmony? Let him be freed, sir, so that he may come to my wedding.'

292

'Free him, Highness.' Gatta, genial at the reminder that he was soon to see his beloved daughter so superbly married, grasped the kneeling men, Aldo by his collar, Fracassa by his tempting mane, and dragged them upright to a sharp yell from Fracassa. 'Free these men too. They were loyal to their lady and I've been taught a lesson in loyalty today. Besides—' He seized Fracassa's ear by guesswork through the shaggy mass of his ringlets. 'I owe this man an executioner's fee. He shall have gold.'

Fracassa's squeal was silenced. The Prince rose, the Princess with him, authority in action.

'Lady Landucci, your request is granted. Your son shall be pardoned on condition that he take oath as Count Landucci to Us and to Our state. These men shall be at the disposal of Lord Ridolfi, Count of Mascia.'

As the Prince descended the steps he crooked a finger at Sigismondo, who approached him with a bow. Around them rose the hum of courtiers supplied with gossip for days, of councillors supplied with argument for months, of voices greeting Gatta by his new title. The Prince must be in excellent mood: his enemies, even those he hadn't known he had, were dead; a likeable young man was pardoned and accepted as vassal; the young prince on the brink of a marriage that would secure Viverra from attack – what more could he desire?

He beckoned Sigismondo closer and spoke in a fierce whisper.

'Find Doctor Virgilio. He must be brought back. I need gold more than ever.'

42. Out of Orpiment

'I thought Doctor Virgilio was blown up.' Benno, trudging over cobbles in the hot autumn sunlight, was of the opinion that his master was called upon far too often to go in search of missing persons. Sigismondo, however, neither complained nor showed any signs of fatigue.

'So everyone thinks except Prince Scipione. Mmmm. He may know best. He told me he saw the laboratory that night, not long before the explosion, and it was deserted. Everything taken except a few books belonging to the Prince and, of course, some of the ingredients that helped to make the place vanish later.'

'But why'd the doctor go? The Prince was giving him money.'

'You need gold to make gold, yes.'

'Then why'd he clear out?'

Sigismondo stopped to cup his hands under a spout of water falling from a carved lion's head at the street corner. He drank and shook the drops off his face. 'Have you forgotten Brother Ambrogio?'

For a moment, Benno had. 'The Doctor didn't mind Brother Columba, though. Sent him packing.'

'Not the same thing at all. Would you care to stand up to Brother Ambrogio? Sooner or later he would do what Brother Columba had failed to do. I believe he went to the laboratory that day and put the fear of God and, more immediately, of the Viverra mob into Doctor Virgilio. Hey, quite *suddenly* it seemed very sensible to look for the Philosopher's Stone in a totally different and distant place.'

'So why are we looking for him here?'

Sigismondo had stopped outside a shop Benno recognised. There was the smell of new bread, the sign of the Silver Pestle hung overhead. The awning next door was up and in its shade the street barber was shaving a large man who had evidently been saving his beard for more than a week.

'Questions, Benno, do I hear more questions?' Sigismondo disappeared into the apothecary's dark doorway. Benno followed, and Biondello, scuttering after, just avoided a bowlful of water flung by the barber.

Inside the shop stood a man Benno knew. Leone Leconti, in a doublet of violet velvet, was buying pigments. The short-sighted Master Buselli had his spectacles firmly fixed on his nose, and repeated the items the artist was requiring to a wizened gnome of a man who went promptly to a drawer or a jar and got out what was wanted for Master Buselli to weigh and package. Something about this assistant teased Benno's memory. He had seen the little man recently, and in trouble, but he couldn't think where.

'Orpiment, Master Buselli, orpiment. I'm quite out of orpiment. My rascal of an assistant must be selling my colours on the sly. That's why I have come myself, in person, today. Now if I'd lost any of the Prince's lapis lazuli I could never find gold enough to replace it, so I suppose the villain knew better than to take that.' He looked round and, seeing Sigismondo, acknowledged him with a bend of the head. 'Master Sigismondo? I never forget such a face. If you've the leisure, I'd be interested to take your likeness. I've only a sketch or two in my book.'

He did not amplify that he had plans for using Sigismondo's face, with judicious supplement of horns, pointed ears and malignancy, as the Devil in a commissioned picture of the Last Judgement. People were apt to take such things amiss, and the man might not appreciate that it was the quality of brooding power in his face that Leconti saw as suitable for the Prince of Hell.

'It's leisure I lack, Master Leconti, or I would certainly sit for you. I'm here to buy information.'

The apothecary had seemed to shrink into his shabby gown like a tortoise into its shell as Sigismondo emerged from the shadows. Clearly he knew again the man who had so disturbed his confidence a few days ago. As clearly, he was afraid of worse questions to come. The assistant, perched once more on a stool behind him, was in a patch of reflected light; it was to him that Sigismondo spoke.

'You worked for Doctor Virgilio.'

Now it was the gnome's turn to be apprehensive, but Sigismondo's tone was peaceful, almost unconcerned. 'The Prince desires to know where he has gone, so that he may employ him again. Do you know?' A broad hand put a piece of gold on the marble slab of the counter and the gnome approached eagerly.

'He didn't tell me. One of the others, though, the younger ones that were going with him, said it would likely be Germany. There's a Margrave there who's been angling after him for quite some time, letters and letters.'

'Do you know what route he took?'

The gnome, watching the gold piece, his hand going out to it and withdrawing, shook his head. 'They didn't know and I dare say he'd not told them. Brother Ambrogio said he'd be burnt as a heretic if he stayed in Viverra and he didn't want anyone coming after him to fetch him back.' His gnarled hand, scarred like the Prince's with burns of fire and acid, closed on the coin as Sigismondo pushed it towards him.

'Brother Ambrogio had best look out.' Leconti was collecting his packages in a cloth, helped by the apothecary. 'Viverra's had more than enough of him. Now that wretched Brother Columba has disappeared, thanks be to God, and Brother Ambrogio himself is ill, we may get peace at last.'

'Brother Ambrogio is ill?'

It occurred to Benno that he had not seen Brother

Ambrogio about for some time.

'He was praying in the palace chapel, and the Devil caught him by the left arm and he fell on the floor in convulsions.' Leconti laughed. He had not forgotten the sight of his painting propped up to be burnt. 'Perhaps God spoke in his right ear about charity.' He tied the corners of the cloth and picked up his package. 'That will stop him from wandering about the palace poking his nose into everything. He's been telling me how to paint, and the Prince's doctor how to restore his Highness's constitution after the accident. No doubt he's been telling the chamberlain how to run the palace. Let him go and advise the angels how to stop their wings moulting.'

He paid Master Buselli, and with a salute to Sigismondo left the shop.

Outside the apothecary's, Sigismondo demonstrated that he had not been quite truthful when he disclaimed leisure; he patronised the barber. Benno refused the offers of the barber's assistant to bleed him, wash his head or trim his beard, and crouched on his heels watching the extensive operation performed on his master. Biondello amused himself by growling at a cat that peered elegantly from a balcony.

The barber deftly skimmed the razor over Sigismondo's scalp, and was happy to discuss recent events in the city.

'That Brother Columba! There's some say he was taken up to heaven in a chariot of fire but my opinion is that he fell in the river preaching to the fish to give up silver on their scales. Good riddance.'

In token of the innocent luxuries Brother Columba would have denied, he unstoppered a flask of aromatic oil and presented it under Sigismondo's nose. It was approved, and he took some on his hands and set to work massaging Sigismondo's head from nape to noble crown to jaw.

'And as for Brother Ambrogio . . . Hasn't had much luck with his prophecy, has he? Our Prince is as well as he's ever been, and smart as paint, getting his son married to

Gatta's daughter. There'll be high old jinks at that wedding, fountains'll run wine I shouldn't wonder. Now, Gatta, there's a man—'

Sigismondo abruptly snatched the towel from his neck and was on his feet, wiping his head and paying the man. Benno found himself returning to the palace faster than his legs enjoyed. If time could be spared for a shave, what was the hurry now?

'The Prince is going to be sorry about Doctor Virgilio,' he panted, avoiding a vast man who had been forced to step aside for Sigismondo but saw no reason to make way for the halfwit at his heels. Sigismondo's reply came over his shoulder.

'If we don't get there soon, the Prince may well be dead.'

43. It Is a Miracle

Sigismondo was now known as the Prince's agent, and no one held up his progress through the palace. Benno, with his dog safe under one arm, came close behind him.

Sigismondo entered the Prince's chamber before the startled page could prevent him. The Prince was closeted with Brother Ambrogio who, at the moment, was ministering not to his soul but to his body. Both men turned their faces towards the door in a tableau of surprise. Brother Ambrogio stood bending towards the seated Prince, holding a spoon towards his mouth, which was open to receive it like a child being fed.

'Are you trying to make your prophecy come true, Father?'

Brother Ambrogio did not move for a long moment. Then he grimaced, a hideous spasm. His back arched. He cast the spoon away in a glittering parabola and his right hand gripped his left arm. The flask cracked on the floor and released a viscous fluid that spread reluctantly on the grey marble. Brother Ambrogio toppled and fell, struggled for a moment and was still.

'What – what is it?' The Prince rose to his feet.

Sigismondo had reached the friar as his brief struggle ceased, knelt by him and pressed fingers to the hollow between jaw and neck. 'Had you taken what he was offering?'

'Alas, no. And it's all spilt.' The Prince cast a regretful

glance at the golden liquid creeping towards his feet. 'Has he had another of his attacks?' He stooped to take hold of the friar's shoulder and turn him on his back, and as he rolled over they all saw the face relax from its paroxysm and resume the expression of sweetness that characterised it. The eyes were open, fixed, and the lips parted. The Prince crossed himself, Sigismondo's and Benno's hands following suit. 'God have mercy!'

Benno went on one knee, and put Biondello down to press his hands together in prayer. The little dog extended an inquisitive nose to the spilt liquid, and Sigismondo reached out a long arm, picked him up and flung him back to Benno.

'Keep him from that. It's poison.'

'Poison!' The Prince, straightening up, looked at Sigismondo in amazement. 'No no, it is *theriaca antidotos*, the true triacle of the ancients. It was to have done me so much good. It clears the system of all poisons. It's from Venice, the very best. Brother Ambrogio was giving it to me for my stomach pains. He carries it with him against snake bite on his travels . . .'

The Prince's voice died away as he took in Sigismondo's expression.

'When had your Highness these pains first?'

'Yesterday. The good Brother gave me some of the triacle in the morning to strengthen me, for I have been so stricken by events: my son . . . the Doctor and the laboratory. . . the effect of the fumes . . .'

'Was the dose before or after the pains, Highness?'

'Why, when I rose in the morning. The pains were towards noon . . .' He looked down at the dead man; Sigismondo was holding the eyes closed.

The Prince reached suddenly for the arm of his chair, found it, and sat down. He whispered, 'Why did he want to kill me? How could he? He is a holy man.'

Sigismondo rose to his feet. 'For the greater good, perhaps. You were turning again to what he believed to be the Devil's works, Highness, in searching for Doctor Virgilio.

Viverra itself is turning away from him, to what he believed to be the ways of sin – it is hard to live a life of perfection in the world. He had proclaimed that you would die. If you did so, Viverra would surely be brought to see that he was the mouth of God's word, as he felt himself to be; the city would turn back to penitence.'

Suddenly, unexpectedly, the Prince laughed. 'You are saying that he was about to kill me from the best of motives. Every day, it seems, brings me enemies I never dreamt of.' He paused, and looked down again at Brother Ambrogio. 'My mother will be distressed, but who else? Only last week Viverra thought him a saint. Now I think they will be glad to have him gone.'

'If I may suggest to your Highness?' There was an undercurrent of amusement in the deep voice. 'Brother Ambrogio wished well to your city and might still serve it. Suppose your Highness were to represent to his Order how faithfully he carried out his preaching duties here and beg their permission to bury him in your new chapel? Viverra would be glad to welcome him as a future saint. Indeed I would advise your Highness to have a watch kept over the body before burial; sharp knives procure good relics.'

Prince Scipione's laughter verged on the hysterical. 'It shall be done. The Holy Father shall know I have a saintly man to protect Viverra, as well as a condotta.'

He stopped abruptly and put a hand to his throat, stammering,

'The poison – I took it yesterday. Will I die?'

'Highness, you would be dead by now. You ate many sweetmeats accidentally poisoned by Donato Landucci – ate them slowly here and there over a period of time, and this gave you, steadily, a resistance. There was arsenic in the sugar that covered them, and arsenic in the pigment that Brother Ambrogio stole from Leconti to put in his mixture.' Sigismondo bent his head towards the still-spreading pool with its smell of honey. 'It could be said that the Princess Isotta saved your Highness's life by inspiring love in Donato Landucci.'

The Prince was still pale from the fright. He slightly shook his head, unable to appreciate these subtleties yet. 'It is a miracle I am alive; and I owe it to you. It shall not be forgotten. When I heard of you, and sent men to look for you, I did not think that I should come to owe my life to you.'

Sigismondo bowed over the Prince's hand. Benno thought, he doesn't even know my master fixed his son's marriage too.'

The Prince's attention, drifting from the newly shaven scalp before him, came to rest vaguely on Biondello in Benno's arms.

'What a nice little dog. How did he lose his ear?'

44. With the Blessing

Benno thought it a pity he had not been able to think up a good story to account for Biondello's ear. It had been missing when they met. He thought the probable explanation was not very nice: that the ear had most likely been lost in the thwarted effort, in the starving village where Biondello was born, to turn him into puppy pie.

'Do you think the Prince will be all right now?'

Sigismondo tipped the last of the jug of wine Rosaria had brought them into both their cups. It had been a long day and Benno had dined voraciously on the best food in the inn: two bowls of pumpkin soup, grilled duck, rabbit roasted with rosemary; now he was eating wonderful ripe plums, the juice running stickily down into his beard.

Under the table Biondello lapped noisily at a bowl of water into which Benno had splashed wine. Biondello, too, should celebrate. He had been saved from a horrible death by poison.

'The Prince should do well, I think. Gatta will protect him from further enemies now they are united by family ties, and his health will certainly be better.' Sigismondo smiled widely. 'I wonder what he'll be looking for now that the Philosopher's Stone has moved to Germany?'

'Pity Doctor Virgilio never found any gold.'

'The Prince thought he had.'

'*What*? And did he?'

'Doctor Virgilio certainly showed him a lump he said he had made. Just after the sermon warning the Prince to get rid of him.'

'Oh! You mean . . .'

'It's possible the Doctor had the gold waiting until just such a moment to be shown. So I told the Prince.'

'Did he believe you?'

'He didn't want to– but in the end . . .' Sigismondo shrugged. 'He won't need gold so much, now Gatta has a stronger reason than ever for serving him and will certainly show off with a fabulous dowry for Caterina. Mmmm – I *wonder* about young Francesco. Riding alone into Gatta's camp was either a shrewd and courageous move or it was foolhardy. I think, with Caterina as his wife, Donato Landucci as his friend and ally, and Gatta behind him, he'll make a good Prince of Viverra when the day comes. Meanwhile, without the search for the Philosopher's Stone, Prince Scipione'll be at a loss how to spend his time.'

'Perhaps he'll spend it with the Princess. She was really pleased with that Book of Hours he gave her, wasn't she?' Benno drained his cup and looked sly. 'D'you reckon she's—' he rounded thumb and finger, 'with Gatta? Don't suppose the Prince would notice.'

Sigismondo was sampling a dish of candied peel and almonds that Rosaria had dumped beside him, with a full jug of wine, on her passage through the room supervising the service. 'Mmmm. If she did, and I don't suppose she will continue if her son is to marry his daughter, then I believe she may have thought it would keep Gatta on her husband's side; and perhaps at a crucial time it did. I don't doubt her real loyalty to Prince Scipione.'

'Funny thing, loyalty.' Benno reached out a grubby and sticky hand into the dish of almonds. 'That Michelotto was loyal to Gatta in a way, right? Doesn't seem fair what happened to him. I mean he was doing it all, trying to poison the Prince and get his son killed and conspiring with Landucci, just to make Gatta Prince of Viverra.'

'Hey, Benno, don't ever try to do good to people *your* way. Michelotto thought Gatta's loyalty to Prince Scipione was weakness – thought he should be helped to get where he ought to be. But such men as Gatta don't like having things done for their good behind their backs. It offends their pride. Look where it got Michelotto.'

Benno's inward eye looked where it had got Michelotto, he gagged on an almond and was saved from choking by Sigismondo's slap between the shoulders. Recovering, he said, 'And there's Brother Ambrogio. *He* meant well too.'

'It may be the shock of seeing what he was really doing that killed him.'

'Didn't he have a lovely funeral Mass, though? Wasn't it lucky the Bishop was well enough to hold it in the cathedral?' The Bishop had conducted the Mass for Brother Ambrogio with great solemnity, but people had remarked on his strange appearance of enjoyment; the charitable put down his recent apoplexy as the reason for his small, lopsided smile. 'Pity we couldn't stay for the wedding.' Benno consoled himself with another handful of almonds while Sigismondo poured him more wine.

'Too many people *wanting* us to stay. I like to move on.'

'I expect you made a bit of an error at Mascia when you gave Scala a head start on everybody.' Benno roared with laughter at his joke, and Rosaria came over, thrusting her bulk between tables with blithe disregard for customers' elbows. She stood, fists on hips, looking at Sigismondo.

'Don't think I haven't heard what you've been up to, lover. People who come to my inn tell me all that goes on in the city. You're supposed to have saved the Prince, bedded the Princess, been blessed by Brother Ambrogio, God rest his soul, as he died; Gatta loves you like a brother and you're not staying for the wedding because you're off to Germany to bring back the Philosopher's Stone for the Prince and if you come back with it you're to have the hand of the little Princess Emilia—'

307

'But isn't she about eight?' Benno asked.

Rosaria traced the scar across Sigismondo's brow with her finger. 'Did the Princess give you that lovebite?' She glanced at Benno as she stroked Sigismondo's head. 'Do you think patience isn't one of your master's virtues? But he won't wait for a princess if I know him. There's more fun to be got here and now.' She turned and clapped her hands, dominating the din of dishes, wine-jars, and talk. 'Who's got a drum or a tabor?'

A sharp little man in red and blue proved to have a pipe, and Rosaria's strong man reached behind a door and bashfully produced a small drum. The long table, at Rosaria's command, was taken down to make a space in the middle of the room and, while the drinkers banged their cups and stamped their feet, Rosaria took Sigismondo's hand and advanced majestically into the space. She called to the piper with the name of a tune and he nodded and started up a brisk tootle, while the drum, all but effaced under the strong man's hand, gave a slow firm double beat under the melody and it was to this they moved, Rosaria's feet carrying her weight lightly and with precision, Sigismondo matching her. First to her side, then to his, they stepped, hands linked, arms held upward– they slowly circled to the thud of the drum, both faces intent and absorbed, the intricate movements of their feet seeming to have no effect on the carriage of their bodies. Benno watched with mouth ajar; this was a side of his master new to him.

The end of the dance, a flourish of the drum accompanied by a similar piece of bravado with the feet, brought a roar of applause from the drinkers, Benno stamping with the rest. Refusing any encore, Rosaria went off to supervise the drawing of wine, and Sigismondo, with gleaming scalp, smiling, came to sit again and take the wine Benno had poured for him.

'Michelotto.'

A strange figure lurched forward to confront them, hands splayed on the table, head lowered, the eyes having difficulty in focusing. It was Pio.

Sigismondo spoke quietly and confidently. 'He is dead. Michelotto is dead.'

Pio shook his head to clear it, tried again to find Sigismondo with his eyes and, failing, wandered off among the tables. There were more dancers in the middle of the room and Rosaria, emerging from the back, fielded Pio from blundering among them and passed him to the large man who had drummed.

'Take no notice, lover,' she called. 'His wits have gone. Came out of the river a few days back, like a walking water rat. I let him stay and wash dishes.'

Benno wondered if Sigismondo's words had conveyed anything to Pio's concussed brain, and if he would ever find his friends again or get back to Landucci. He had a vision of Pio making his way home, staggering along, headbutting all obstacles in his path, from walls to robbers. In his way Pio had something of the indestructability of Sigismondo.

'Where're we going, then? Is it Germany?'

Sigismondo had picked up Biondello and was feeding him a sliver of duck left in his bowl with a scraping of sauce. He raised his eyebrows.

'Germany? Why Germany? The blessing of Brother Ambrogio will travel with us wherever we go.'